Return to the Garden

Reclaiming the Garden of Eden

Jeff Shakespeare, PhD

with Barb Bouse

WESTBOW
PRESS®
A DIVISION OF THOMAS NELSON
& ZONDERVAN

WestBow Press books may be ordered through booksellers or by contacting:

WestBow Press
A Division of Thomas Nelson & Zondervan
1663 Liberty Drive
Bloomington, IN 47403
www.westbowpress.com
844-714-3454

Scripture quotations marked KJV are taken from the King James Version.

ISBN: 979-8-3850-2210-6 (sc)
ISBN: 979-8-3850-2030-0 (e)

Library of Congress Control Number: 2024906379

Print information available on the last page.

WestBow Press rev. date: 04/16/2024

Part I

The Garden of Eden

We are stardust
Billion-year-old carbon
We are golden
Caught in the devil's bargain
And we've got to get ourselves

Back to the garden - Joni Mitchell

Introduction

Ramallah, West Bank, late 2020's

Fourteen-year-old Aashif is walking the two miles to the water distribution station in Ramallah. Drought is ravaging the Middle East and it is his responsibility to carry the two containers each morning and get the daily ration of fresh water for the family. Aashif is too young to fight and too old to be cared for like a child, but he feels a responsibility to do all he can to help his family. As he walks along, he is joined by other men and women, all diligently intent on getting their share of the precious water to make it through the day. The street is crowded and the sun is blazing even this early in the morning. Many of the shops have been closed for months and the atmosphere is one of quiet desperation.

He thinks of his sister Saabiya and her new baby. Timing couldn't have been worse. Although there is enough fresh water at the hospital, medical care is expensive and only the wealthy can afford it. Saabiya, like other women in her neighborhood, had her baby at home under the watchful care of the local midwife and her mother. Their father died years ago in the Israeli-Palestinian conflict, leaving Aashif as the only man in the little family.

Things had been getting progressively more hopeless in the last few years. Although the technology exists to make fresh water using desalination plants, the West Bank and Gaza areas still rely on the rains and surface water. Wells are dried up. The Jordan River is now just a trickle and there is not enough water to drink, let alone for farming, sanitation and washing. Several months ago, in an effort to reduce cholera, the Water

Authority converted all the mains to filtered salt water from the Dead Sea. It was acceptable for sewage and sanitation, even showers and personal hygiene, but not for gardening or farming. With each passing month, the water ration per family had been reduced until there was barely enough to drink. Some desperate souls had taken to drinking the salt water, they were so terribly thirsty. They died shortly after, since the urge to satisfy thirst is one of the strongest in life. Desperation led to violence and the daily demonstrations and riots had been getting much more intense in recent weeks.

Aashif is very worried about his sister and her new baby. He overheard her telling their mother that she did not feel her breasts were full and that the child fussed when nursing. His little mouth was dry and the urine was a deep brown color indicating dehydration. She has no way of knowing if the child is ok, and the yellowish tinge of the child's skin fills her with dread.

No one in the family is healthy. Saabiya herself is getting cramps, has dark urine and is often confused during the day. She has had hallucinations and has more and more skip beats of her heart. She is terrified that if anything happens to her, there will be no one to take care of the baby.

Their mother is worried too and despite Aashif's daily trips across town to carry the water home, she feels they are not getting their fair share. What she doesn't know is that the water line is not a safe place to be. Once people's lives are threatened, violence quickly follows. The lack of sufficient protein in Aashif's diet resulted in stunted growth and full-grown men would often roughly cut in line, making the usual two hour wait even longer. The air at this hour of the day is stifling and Aashif sometimes feels that by the time he gets the water, he has lost almost as much from sweat just standing in line. The terrible feeling of thirst haunts him always. The Palestinian Authority posts armed guards around the distribution centers, but Aashif suspects they are often bribed to look the other way. More than once he was accosted and beat up as he left the distribution center, losing the precious, life-giving water to the thieves. Now, he keeps a bottle of mace in his pocket and is not afraid to use it.

Aashif daydreamed as he walked along, hoping to see a young girl named Bariah who comes to the water station around the same time each day. The Water Authority established rationing sectors and there were times assigned for each sector to keep the crowds under control. Bariah lived just a few blocks away and is about Aashif's own age. She always has a shy smile for Aashif, and her family is struggling like everyone else. Bariah confided in Aashif that she drank only a small cup of the daily ration, saving it for her mother who was very ill from cholera. The few minutes that they walk together are like a holiday for them. Aashif prayed to Allah that one day the rains would return and he might find work, make a life for the two of them, and live happily.

Chapter 1

Michael's razor-sharp intellect, combined with the socially awkward personality, made him a bit shy in high school and college. He was an African American PhD candidate at the Massachusetts Institute of Technology with a novel thesis about how the pyramids in Egypt were built using water. His classmates, undergraduate students and even professors had great respect for him, and he felt comfortable in the academic environment. Technically, he was very knowledgeable and was hoping that someday he would start a venture and become independently wealthy. Today was the culmination of six years of exhausting work. He would defend his dissertation about using water to build the Great Pyramids in front of the best science professors in his field.

Michael spent some of his early years overseas with his white, middle class adopted parents and vividly remembers seeing the Great Pyramid while they were stationed in Egypt. Something about seeing the pyramids triggered his curiosity and his analytical mind sought to understand how they were built.

Now, he just needed to show up this morning and deliver his theory in a clear, concise, confident presentation. He mentally rehearsed his opening statement again as he showered and dressed. Michael drank some juice, had a bagel for his breakfast and checked his watch a dozen times. He planned to arrive at the MIT campus early to give himself plenty of time to set up before the faculty arrived.

It was a short walk down Massachusetts Avenue to Pierce Lab, the home of the Civil Engineering Department at MIT. The walk got his blood pumping and his brain engaged. On this particular morning his prayer was a bit more fervent than usual, and rather than being only about thanksgiving, he also asked for the strength, courage, wisdom and ability to pass his defense. Inwardly, Michael was very religious, although not associated with any particular denomination, he was a strong Christian who believed in the Golden Rule and tried to live his life in a way that helped as many people as possible. Thanks to his adopted grandmother, he knew all the Bible stories by heart and found it interesting to see how much those lessons could impact his day-to-day life, even now in the modern world.

Michael was still a few blocks away from Pierce Lab when he saw a group of three black female students walking and chatting on the other side of the street. Just then, a beat-up old car with four white men pulled up alongside of the students and they began shouting racial slurs. The women ignored them, but then the car stopped and two of the men got out heading for the students. Other students looked on but no one came to their defense. Without really thinking, Michael dropped his backpack and ran across the street toward the two men. "Move on guys," said Michael. "There's nothing for you here."

"Stay out of this, boy, if you know what's good for you." Said one of the men, and with that he pulled out a gun and began waving it around. They had obviously been drinking, giving them a serious disadvantage in reflexes. Of all the martial arts kicks that Michael knew, he made an assessment to approach the gun wielding suspect from the side and deliver the strongest 'roadhouse' kick he'd ever used. His opponent's knees buckled and he hit the pavement with a solid thud, dropping the gun and yelling profanities. A crowd had gathered and someone called the campus police while the gunman wretched on the pavement holding his stomach. Michael picked up the gun, cocked it and pointed it at the gunman's knee. Fortunately, he heard a voice inside his head *How oft shall I forgive my brother, seven times? Jesus said seventy times seven.* So, Michael put down the gun just as the campus police arrived.

"What's going on here," said one of the officers.

"That guy pulled a gun on us," said a student. "But then he came along and helped us," she continued pointing at Michael. "Thank you so much."

"Ok, we're going to need a statement from you." Said the officer. "Are you a student here?"

"Well, actually officer, I am just heading to my doctoral thesis defense, in fact I'm late already. Can I give my statement later today?" asked Michael.

The campus police were much more sympathetic to academic life than the city police. "That will be fine. Just come by the campus police station and we'll get your statement. Good luck on your thesis."

Relieved, Michael went back across the street, picked up his backpack and hustled to his thesis defense. *Interesting,* Michael thought, *the students stood by their friend in spite of the danger and the drunken coward ran off.* Two of the young women were crying, but the other looked Michael directly in the eye and smiled as he crossed the street. He often wondered why life was so difficult for people with dark skin like his. *Was that God's plan? How could it be?*

The committee members and several of Michael's colleagues began filing in on schedule and Michael was relieved as they finally all were seated and ready to begin. The room was a small auditorium sized classroom with tall windows along one wall. Committee members sat around a long table and the audience of about twenty or so, mostly students, sat in the back of the room. The environment was very familiar to Michael from all his days of teaching there as a graduate student.

"Today we have Michael Walters presenting his dissertation for the degree of Doctor of Philosophy in the Department of Civil Engineering." Michael's major professor, Professor Levit, began. "His dissertation is on the building of the pyramids in Egypt, particularly The Great Pyramid of Cheops. Mister Walters, the floor is yours."

"I want to start by thanking the members of my committee for their time today. I've been interested in large civil engineering projects since I was very young. As I mentioned in my proposal defense, The Great Pyramid is certainly one of the oldest and most mysterious of the ancient wonders of the world. There are many theories as to how this feat of engineering was accomplished. Today I will show you how it could have been done with minimal labor and machinery as a result of previous climate conditions and some astonishingly clever engineering."

Michael could feel the attention in the room as he delivered this opening statement. He noticed that his hands and voice were shaking as a result of the incident outside. He was feeling a bit stronger, now that the beginning was over, but his major professor gave him a curious look as if to say, *what's wrong?*

"The Great Pyramid of Cheops is constructed of over 2½ million blocks of stone each weighing nearly 20 tons. The structure is oriented true north/south to within less than 1 degree and covers an area of over 13 acres that is dead level to within a quarter of an inch."

Michael was looking around the room and although there had been some rustling of papers and murmuring initially, the room got quiet and all eyes were on Michael. He went on to explain, occasionally stumbling on his words, it had been suggested that these blocks of stone could have been quarried, dragged by ropes and pulled into position by Israelite slaves over the course of many decades or perhaps even centuries to complete this project. What had not been satisfactorily explained is how the blocks got up the slope to the higher levels without the use of steel to hold pulleys and make cables. Some suggested that the blocks could have been hauled up ramps, but as the top is approached, the ramps would have been narrower, meaning that the workers would have been in each other's way. Some suggested that the stones could have been pulled on top of an enormous pile of sand and the whole thing built from the top down.

"Clearly these suggestions did not come from civil engineers," said Michael. Some chuckling from the audience, which made him feel a bit better, but his heart was still racing with excitement and the quivering of his voice threatened his confidence.

Michael continued while moving through a slide deck with his points and some very interesting, sometimes comical pictures. He told them that another controversial question is the age of the most imposing pyramids, including the Cheops one. "Most archeologists believe that the structures were built around the time of the Israelite enslavement, some 4400 to 4600 years ago. However, several new pieces of data, including rainfall erosion and star charts, suggest that they are much older, of order 8,000 to 10,000 or perhaps even 20,000 years ago."

"Question, has this data been published?" Professor Kowalski, who spoke with a thick Eastern European accent, was very discriminating when it came to data.

"I do have several references in my bibliography," said Michael. "But this data is in no way commonly accepted by the archeological community. If you will bear with me for a few minutes I will try to tie this all together."

"Thank you, continue," said Kowalski.

"There are many other theories about pyramid construction, including that they were built by some advanced extra-terrestrial visitors. In fact, a Caliph of Baghdad named Al-Ma'mun chopped his way into the Cheops pyramid in around 800 CE. He reported finding glass that could be bent but would not break and shiny metal that didn't rust. Other items such as tiny intricate machines, extremely large jewels and optical glass lenses were said to have been found inside the pyramid." More chuckling from some in the room. "I could spend much more time discussing each of these, but with your permission, I would like to get to the core of my thesis and introduce some new concepts." Michael dove right in.

Michael explained that for as long as mankind has been moving heavy loads, it is by water that the heaviest things have been transported long distances. The Phoenicians and the Romans both had thriving trade routes in the Mediterranean using ships with tons of cargo on board. That is why, even up until present day, the largest cities are on the water, on rivers, lakes or the sea. In Europe, rivers were extended to inland areas by a complex system of canals. This allowed grain, ore, wood, coal and many other heavy things to be moved to where they were needed.

Michael was watching his audience closely as he got into the details of his thesis. He told them that the Egyptians were blessed with one of the largest and deepest rivers in the world. In addition to being deep for most of the year, the spring rains in central Africa that fed the Nile caused annual flooding that deposited silt in the river basin and made the area very productive for farming. Michael was warming to his subject now, but struggled a bit to rebalance his breathing while delivering his defense.

He continued with the presentation and told them that climate records of rainfall in central Africa are now just beginning to be reconstructed based on corings and tree ring data. It is becoming clear that the Nile floods were once much higher than anything that has been experienced in the last several thousand years, especially just after the last glacial maximum around 18,000 years ago. The changing weather patterns, as the earth began to warm and glaciers receded, could be thought of as climate change on a scale that dwarfs the current concerns about global warming.

"How high did the river get?" Professor Levit, Michael's advisor, asked in an effort to clarify Michael's focus on the details of the climate in ancient Egypt.

"We don't really know, but if it spilled over the banks and rose by a hundred meters or so, it would allow the stones to be placed on each level as the Nile rose and fell.

"Did you say a hundred meters?" Kowalski with the thick accent now sounded incredulous. He scowled and raised his eyebrows, looking around the room.

"Yes sir," said Michael. "One other thing to look at." Michael showed a topo map of the area.

"Do you see how the Giza Plateau is sort of unique on the topo map? It sits right at a narrowing of the river bed between elevated regions on either side. This suggests that as the Nile flooded, it would cause the water to be dammed up and to rise possibly several hundred meters right at the point where the pyramids were built. So, Giza is an ideal spot, assuming that the stones were placed by boats during the Nile flood." Michael was downright enthusiastic at this point. He was looking each professor, and occasionally the audience, directly in the eye to make his point. You could hear a pin drop in the room, and people near the back were leaning forward to get a better look at the slides.

"Now, let's talk about the engineering aspects of placing the stones." Michael showed a slide of an Egyptian boat with a large stone on it from a Harvard lecture on Egyptian archeology.

The picture showed that the boat was constructed with high bow and stern, and had what looked like a series of logs beneath the stone which would allow it to be floated into position at the construction site. "This is not to say that there wasn't an enormous effort to quarry each stone and float it along canals carved in the rock quarry to the waiting ship. But the hydraulics of getting the stone out of the ground and onto the ship are very similar to the hydraulic principles used in our heavy machinery today."

When the boat arrived with each stone, it could have been flooded and the stone floated off the deck. The workers could then push it around in the water to place it in exactly the right spot on the structure. It would have involved lots of labor, but nowhere near as much as dragging the stones up a ramp. It would have also taken lots of time and a good understanding of the Nile flooding, but it was possible.

"So far, no one has come up with a theory that is even possible, let alone probable." Michael was beaming as he saw the open mouths and interested stares of the room. He had them.

"Well, alright, this is very interesting, but are you going to fill in the details, such as how long it took to complete each pyramid and the purpose of some of the internal structures?" The professor from industry was very interested.

"I think this whole idea preposterous" said Professor Kowalski. "If the Nile got that high the whole country would have been under water"

"How do you know it wasn't under water?" chimed in Levit.

"Well, where is the evidence?" Kowalski was like a bulldog once he saw a slight crack in the wall of a thesis.

"Ok, ok" said Michael, "but we don't have evidence that it was not under water either."

"Lack of data does not prove anything." Kowalski retorted. "I suggest you study your maps and support your theory with more information," said Kowalski, whose secret racial bias occasionally surfaced, despite his professed support for equal opportunity.

"Now hold on Peter," said Professor Levit. "This is a theory on how the pyramids might have been built from an engineering standpoint, not another theory on global warming 10,000 years ago. What do we care about meteorology? You got a better idea on how they were built?"

Another member of the committee spoke up saying "This is certainly a novel and well thought out concept from an engineering point of view. Climate is the question. I agree with Professor Kowalski that we need more information on the height of the Nile at this time, but I am very interested and would like to learn more. How was the structure oriented due North and South?"

"Yes, thank you for asking," said Michael, feeling his pulse quicken a bit more with another member of his committee questioning his work. He explained that there are two major chambers or rooms commonly known as the Queen's Chamber below and the King's Chamber above. This is from early archeological theories on the purposes of the pyramid. It was thought that the structure was a monumental tomb for the pharaohs. However, some believe these chambers could have been observatories. What is even more interesting are the passages leading to the chambers. A passage that is three feet, five inches wide by three feet, eleven and one-half inches high descends into the bedrock at a reported angle of 26.5 degrees. It is not clear how accurate this angle measurement actually is. This passage is oriented due north and south and ends in a rough-cut pit in the bedrock.

Michael flashed up a side view of the Great Pyramid showing the shaft in the bedrock. It also showed a direct sightline along the shaft to the North Star.

"What is fascinating to me about this is that the latitude of the site is 29.98 degrees. This means that within a tolerable error, the passage, because of its great depth, would have allowed viewing the North Star and only the North Star at any time of the day or night.

"Actually, Polaris was not the North Star at that time, it was Thuban since the Earth's axis does wobble a bit. But this descending passage could have acted like a surveyor's transit or theodolite for managing the angles and orientation of the pyramid structure on the site. No such instruments existed at that time."

"So, your idea is that the building was sited by the North Star?" Professor Levit was now actively trying to support Michael and Michael knew it. He could feel the droplets of sweat forming on his forehead. *Really,* he thought, *I'm actually failing my dissertation defense.* "Ok, how about the site leveling? How was that accomplished without modern instruments?"

Michael suggested that although the site base is dead level to within a quarter of an inch, the foundation of bedrock on which the pyramid is built is not planar. But the perimeter of the pyramid forms a plane which is very precisely level. The fact that the Giza plateau was flooded each year allowed the pyramid builders to cut a trench in the bedrock to hold water. The water is, of course, perfectly level and could have been used to carve the bedrock around the perimeter so that it too is level. When limestone is submerged in water, it remains soft and easy to shape. Stones could have been underwater while being cut then put aside, for years perhaps, until the pyramid building progressed. Michael had given this issue much thought over the last 5 years.

Professor Kowalski spoke up "Is there anything else you can say about the engineering and architecture of the pyramid? I feel that your thesis is woefully underdeveloped."

Professor Kowalski was becoming more and more restless as the defense wore on. "This is all very interesting, but could we get back to the thesis? We have discussed archeology, meteorology, horology, and I think other 'ologies,' but not so much civil engineering. I have a class to prepare for and would like to wrap this up, unless you have some more quantitative analysis for your theories."

The defensive aspects of Michael's personality now started to leak out and he said, "Civil engineering? I just told you how the most incredible civil engineering project ever accomplished was done. What more do you want?" Fire flew from Michael's eyes with this last statement, and several of the committee members were startled by this outburst.

"Do you even know whether the boat will float with the heavy stones on board?" fired Professor Kowalski.

"Yes, and what about the rest of Egypt with the water level that high? Have you looked at the burial sites to see if they were under water?" asked the member from industry. Committees can be like sharks. When they smell blood, there is a tendency for a feeding frenzy.

Michael stood, inwardly seething, and willing his inner strength to help manage the intense indignation that was overcoming him. His one simple goal at that moment was to abstain from yelling. He knew that if anger takes over from intellect in a disagreement or defense, the argument is lost.

Professor Levit spoke up with a bitter tone in his voice, "Are there any further questions for Michael?" University politics can be treacherous no matter how well prepared a student is.

"Just one," the woman committee member asked, "how did you find all this information? Certainly, it is not in refereed journals," the implication being that it was very anecdotal and not worthy of a scientific study.

Michael said, "I have been interested in these massive engineering projects since I was in high school. In fact, I hope to someday be able to be a part of one of them. The information is out there, but it takes patience and diligence to find it."

"Well, I want to thank you for an interesting presentation today." The industry member looked over at Levit and began to clap. The others followed, a few looking down at the table. Kowalski just scowled but clapped briefly.

"Ok, Michael, we will need a few minutes to confer. Please wait outside. Everyone else is excused. Thank you very much for attending."

Michael and the rest of the audience filed out into the hall. Michael's officemate, Steve Williams, had been sitting in the last row and now slapped him on the back as Michael left the room.

"Good work!" said Steve.

"Nice job Michael," said another of his fellow grad students, "I had no idea about the pyramid. And I really like what you said about the power of water to lift and carry things. I gotta keep that in mind for my projects."

"Thanks," Michael was wondering how the rest of the audience felt about his defense. Based on some of them clapping lightly and looking down, he wasn't so optimistic. *Maybe I should have done a lot more meteorological research. Maybe I should have shown more calculations. I wonder why Kowalski is so stubborn?* thought Michael. As he stood there lost in thought, Michael began to wonder what the other consequences of a higher Nile could be, especially in the spring with much more rain in Central Africa. *Actually, I have been concentrating on the Nile River, but not any of the surrounding areas, especially to the west and further upstream,* thought Michael. He was then left to his thoughts as the committee decided his fate. Unfortunately, a feeling of doom mixed with his lingering anger. But he had done the best he could and his decision to help the black students was the right one, regardless of the outcome.

Michael said a quick prayer of supplication, but he could see the look on Professor Levit's face as he approached from the conference room. His heart sank as Levit said "Michael, we have some problems. The committee is not quite ready to sign off on your dissertation. I am so sorry. I have been at odds with Professor Kowalski for nearly twenty years, but he has a lot of influence in the department and some of the younger faculty are afraid to go against him. He feels there are two areas that need more work. You need to show the water level in the Nile could have been that high. And also, you need to calculate the weight of the stones and resulting displacement of the boats. I just want to tell you that you did a fine job on this dissertation and on today's presentation. As you know, these things are often more political than technical." Michael was looking his professor directly in the eyes as he tried to process these words, as if the deep stare could pry into his professor's brain and find the truth behind the explanation.

"Thank you so much Professor," said Michael as his face fell and his indignation briefly surfaced. "I have to tell you that I very much appreciate all of your help and support on this project. All of this is a labor of love for me. I'm sorry this work didn't measure up. What do I do now?"

Levit was somewhat embarrassed, but tried to be as encouraging as possible. "Well, as you know, the grant for this work runs out at the end of this semester. You can always finance further work yourself, but the school has limited funds. Look, you've got a great education from a top-notch school. You won't have any trouble getting a great job. I will help you as much as I can. I do have contacts and I'll give you a strong recommendation."

"Thank you, Professor," said Michael. They shook hands and Michael walked out the door, down the steps and back toward his apartment, ready for the next challenge of the day, telling his girlfriend, Ariana, and his mom and dad. He thought, *I work my tail off for six years in this place and all I get is "sorry."*

As he walked back toward his apartment, he suddenly remembered he promised the campus police a statement about the morning's confrontational incident. He turned right and headed to the campus police station.

"Hi, I'm Michael Walters," said Michael as he approached the desk. "I was told to report here and give a statement about the incident this morning."

"That was you!" said the officer on duty. Apparently, the incident had been reported in the on-line Campus News for the day and the whole community was buzzing about it. "Thank you for having the courage to intervene."

"I guess I did it before I really thought about it. I'm just glad no one got hurt."

"We spoke to a number of the bystanders and they told us what happened. No need for anything else, unless you have something you want to add."

"Nope, thanks. Have a great day." Michael turned and walked out a bit more positive about the day than when he came in.

But his disappointment turned into outright fury as he approached his apartment. *I just didn't feel right,* thought Michael. *Maybe I just should've kept going and not gotten involved outside with those students,* he thought. *There were lots of other people around, couldn't they help? Not exactly the good Samaritan way of thinking, Michael old buddy.* As he looked back on this day in years to come, Michael would examine his faith again and again, reaffirming he made the right choice. *I can't just sit idly by while someone is in trouble. If I do, I'm no better than those cowards that caused all the trouble to begin with.*

Chapter 2

Back at his apartment near campus, Michael sat on his couch, in shock and denial about his unsuccessful thesis presentation. The news on the TV was just background noise. The last thing Michael needed was a TV news show with all the depressing events of the day, but watching the news was a bad habit, like occasional drinking, for him. He certainly wasn't going to do or think about anything else right now. His indignation, anger, and disgust for Kowalski were making their way through his rationalizing mind. His girlfriend, Ariana was hosting a business luncheon on the other side of town and promised to meet him at his apartment when it was over. He had been planning on celebrating, but now.... Still, he wasn't going to cancel.

Today, the latest crisis was in the Middle East ..., again; only this time it was climate change and the resulting drought. *First the wildfires in California, then the shrinking of Lake Mead and the Mississippi River, drought, floods, rising sea level, disappearing glaciers, and now this. Wow, and I thought I had problems.* But many Middle Eastern cities had rioting in the streets with bricks and Molotov cocktails, standing in lines waiting for the daily ration of precious water, while the Ethiopians struggled with the worst flooding ever recorded in that country. The scenes kept intruding on his thoughts and dragging his eyes to the TV set. *Why is the veneer of civilization so thin,* thought Michael. *Whenever there's a hurricane, a flood, a fire, or some political issue, people just start rioting and looting. Incredible.*

Just as he was about to turn it off, the newscaster said "The Israeli Government announced today that a prize of $100,000,000 is being offered to anyone who can resolve the water crisis in Israel." That got Michael's attention, *wow, that's a lot of money,* he thought.

His phone rang. "Well, how did it go?" It was Michael's mom and dad, the call he'd been expecting. *No doubt Dad had a few drinks and is calling to offer some fatherly advice, mostly on things he knows nothing about,* thought Michael. He loved his dad and was very grateful for everything his adopted mom and dad had done for him in his life. But right now, with all the swirling emotions, this call was the last thing he wanted.

"Ah… well to be honest, they said I needed more work. I didn't pass."

Greg Walters was anything but subtle. A life in the State Department had given him the gift of persistence. "That's exactly what I was afraid of. Now maybe you'll get a real job."

"Dad, please, can I call you back? I will explain it all," Michael was thinking *Yeah, and I didn't say when I'll call you back.*

"Sure, no problem." Greg and Sofia hung up the phone.

Almost every minute in Michael's days had been filled, for the last six years. Watching the news and hearing about Israel's offer of $100,000,000 to solve the Middle East water crisis caught his attention and briefly provided a break from thinking about his defense. But now, having given his mom and dad the brush off, the initial disbelief about his dissertation turned to guilt about how he had just dismissed his parents phone call. Thought Michael, *I gotta remember to call them back.* The all too familiar anger abruptly returned, and Michael knew it as the curse of being an only child with an overbearing father who could take the idea of social drinking to the limit.

The difference between the stipend for a graduate student vs. the salary of a venture capitalist, like Ariana, was clearly visible in the look of Michael's apartment. Bare floors, a rickety side table for a TV stand, a few old pictures on the wall and a threadbare couch were the décor for Michael's place. Ariana greeted him warmly with a bottle of champagne and a knowing smile. She thought that the probability of Michael failing his dissertation defense was about as remote as a snowstorm in July. But when she saw his face, her attitude fled.

"I failed," Michael said, with a shrug.

Ariana was stunned. The blood drained from her face and she blurted out, "What happened?"

Michael said angrily, "You know, all went pretty well and there were some good questions, but that Kowalski guy was the problem. I knew he was going to be tough. He was the same way at my general exam. I just don't think he gets it. I mean, why ask questions about the weather and how the water level could get that high? That wasn't the point. The point of this whole study was to show that *if* the water level was high enough, then they could have built the Great Pyramid using clever but not necessarily unbelievable technology available at that time. And, by the way, we don't even know what's going to happen next year, let alone 5,000 or 10,000 years ago. I have to tell you; I was afraid his comments would carry the rest of the committee and they did. He derailed the whole thing."

"And your major professor let that happen?" Ariana raised her eyebrows.

"I guess I was hoping he wouldn't, but you never know. The comment about how the whole country would have been flooded if the water got that high has me thinking though. I should have studied the topo maps a bit more, especially for the area west of the Nile." Michael seemed lost in thought as he said this last sentence. "There's something else," said Michael as he searched for how to explain the incident with the drunken guys and university students. "Just as I was getting to the building this morning, there was an incident with some guys from town. I mean, I know there have been muggings in the area, but usually they're at night. And this was more about racial hatred than money."

"What happened?" Ariana was now staring into Michael's eyes searching for the real issue.

"Well, it started with them yelling the N word at some black female students, then two of them got out of the car and approached one of the girls. One looked like he was drinking or on drugs. I wasn't thinking, I just dropped my backpack and ran over there. I kicked the guy with the gun, knocked him down and his buddy ran away. But then I picked up the gun and ..."

"Oh no! Tell me you did not shoot the guy."

"No, but I was going to. Some students called the campus cops and I guess I came to my senses just in time. I just lose my temper when things like that happen. Anyway, when I got to my defense, I was shaking all over and must have had some kind of PTSD. Even my voice was shaking."

"They could not postpone the defense?"

"I really didn't want to, but then when I started getting so many questions, I kind of lost it and yelled at the committee." Michael looked back on it and now he realized he should have rescheduled the defense.

"Ok, what now?" Ariana, always the pragmatist.

"Not sure," said Michael. "But I think I need some time to think about it. Maybe you should go back to your apartment for a while. I'm not much company."

Michael's experiences growing up overseas made him somewhat of an army brat. And the fact that he is an only child, adopted after his single mom was killed in a drive by shooting, exacerbated the problem. As a result, Michael always had a bit of a brittle personality when it came to confrontational interaction. He repeatedly admonished himself not to say anything at all if he can only find negative things to say, but when someone attacks him, either physically or emotionally, he can lose his temper very easily. Later he often regrets this behavior.

"You are throwing me out?" said Ariana. "The first time there is a rough patch you want to get rid of me!"

"It's not like that," said Michael. "I just need time to think."

"Yes, but why alone?"

"Go!" Michael had tipped over the edge and now the disappointment exploded out of his mouth.

"Don't you ever treat me like that again. I am going home. Talk to me when you are not obnoxious." Ariana grabbed her bottle of champagne and walked out the door, slamming it loudly behind her.

Well, that worked out well, thought Michael. *Might as well make it a hat trick; parents, school, girlfriend.*

Chapter 3

When he first came to MIT six years ago, Michael was fortunate enough to find, on campus, a small but passionate group of students from many countries, each bringing the strong traditions of their home religions, to an organization dedicated to finding this common ground of faith among all mankind.

The organization was called The Temple of World Faith and was, in many ways, an ecumenical social as well as religious group with parties, prayer meetings, dances, readings and lectures to share traditions among the members and promulgate tolerance, acceptance and cooperation. Of course, there was no actual Temple building; in these times of social media, even the Temple was sometimes virtual or sometimes in academic conference rooms on campus. There were Muslims, Jews, Christians of many denominations, Hindus, Buddhists, Mormons, Confucianists, Native Americans, as well as lesser-known indigenous faiths and scientists of every discipline, since science itself is a form of faith. There were even those who sought to revive old and abandoned traditions such as the Celtic Paganism and Norse Gods of Odin and Tyr. When Michael first learned of the TWF, he was surprised and delighted to hear that the organization believed violence is acceptable for defense only, resolving one of his most troublesome philosophical issues.

Michael joined the Temple of World Faith organization soon after coming to MIT and took to its tenets right away. He especially liked that everyone, no matter their beliefs, was included in the organization. One of the best ways to learn a subject is to teach it to others. Michael volunteered to share the Bible stories at the weekly prayer meetings and learned every detail from the questions asked by Hindus, Muslims, Buddhists and others in the group.

The organization had, as one of its goals, proving to the modern world that the tenets of most religions were based on the need to live together in peace and harmony. Although logic and modern science played a role, the ideas of faith and belief in the unseen were central to the organization. Michael thought that where many of the ancient belief systems went off the rails was when the natural human tendency to compete for alpha status resulted in behaviors of the leaders that were harmful to other human beings, including their own followers. The fact that, for many centuries, there was little control over the canonized texts, also led to things being added to these documents, for political purposes, that were far from the message that the Deity and prophets sought to convey. Even the Torah, which was carefully controlled by the rabbis, was not free of error or editorial, as evidenced by the Dead Sea scrolls. So, the various canonized texts had to be shared in a way that separated the Deity's message from the message of the human copiers to the best of the believer's ability. The Golden Rule was used as the guidepost in this communication.

There was a group in TWF from Palestine that came to MIT to learn civil engineering, hoping to improve the water situation on the West Bank and Gaza. Now with climate change and severe drought, Michael established a relationship with these students and offered to help them in any way he could, especially in planning their engineering projects back home. One of the Palestinians that Michael liked very much was named Abdul. He was an undergraduate and Michael, as a teaching assistant, taught him sophomore level civil engineering courses. They would chat after class and attend the TWF meetings. Michael learned much about the plight of the Palestinians and the two of them became very close friends.

One of the things that Michael enjoyed the most about the TWF meetings was the opportunity to engage in challenging debate. Abdul was a favorite opponent in these discussions, primarily since his perspective was from the oppressed point of view.

One day as they were finishing a TWF meeting, Abdul said, "You know I am so worried about my niece Bariah in Ramallah. She is struggling just to find enough water and food to stay alive. Her mother is sick and her father, my uncle, was killed in the fighting. She is a strong young lady, but I just wish I could do more to help her."

"Isn't that what we're here for?" asked Michael. "What do you have in mind?"

"Well, if I had some money, I would send it to her to help with her mom's medical bills. But I'm on scholarship myself."

"Could we just send her some food and water? It's cheap here." Michael always had ideas.

"I just don't think it would ever make it to her. You don't know what it's like over there. Thieves are everywhere, even in the postal delivery service. Let me think about it." That was where they left it. Wanting to help people is one thing; figuring out how to do it is something else again.

The TWF was founded on the basis of shared worldwide beliefs. One of the most profound of these overarching principals is **tolerance**, which was illuminated one day by a Hindu member who told the ancient story of the blind men and the elephant.

"This story has many possible origins but is generally associated with Eastern thought." Said Ravi. "The story goes something like this, although there are many forms and endings. A group of blind men touch an elephant to understand what it is like. Each one touches a different part and then they come together to compare their experiences. The one touching the trunk says that an elephant is like a tree branch, while the one at the tail says it is like a rope, the blind man at the leg thinks an elephant is like a pillar, the one at the side claims it is a wall while the one at the ear thinks it is like a fan. They are all in complete disagreement and begin fighting amongst themselves, because, obviously, if an elephant is like a rope, it cannot also be like a wall. Clearly someone is wrong and someone else is right. In some versions this degenerates into a war. Then a wise man appears and tells them that they are all right, but just experiencing a different part of the elephant. The point of the story is that it is possible for them *all* to be right and only touching different aspects of the same thing. In this way the conflict is resolved and each man gains an appreciation for the beliefs of others, while maintaining a sense of appreciation for the veracity of his own beliefs."

"So, the point is", added Michael, "it's not necessary for someone who disagrees with you in matters of faith to be wrong in order for you to be right. I guess it's best to keep an open mind toward other views and faiths, to be tolerant. To paraphrase the great Roman orator, Cicero, Tolerance is the Soul of Enlightenment." Michael felt very strongly about this and it was one of the reasons he fit in so well with the TWF. *What if there could be one world shared religion? The traditions of all the local religions could be preserved, but the common elements of faith would be shared,* thought Michael.

One Wednesday night at the weekly meeting, it was Michael's turn to read the Creation Story from the first chapter of Genesis in the Bible. As he came to the part about the river that divided into four heads, a young lady raised her hand and asked, "Do you think the Garden of Eden really existed?"

Michael responded without hesitation, "I do. And I think we still have the river Euphrates today in Mesopotamia. That's where most Biblical scholars believe the Garden of Eden actually was located."

"What about the other rivers?" The young lady pressed. "Where are they?"

"Good questions," said Michael. "I think most archeologists are happy with just having one river as a clue. Except for the evangelicals who take the Bible literally, most Christians and Jews think the stories are allegorical." But her questions started Michael thinking about the crossroads between archeology, anthropology and the Bible.

Chapter 4

Ariana awoke at 6:00am the next morning feeling angry and betrayed. She had her coffee and a piece of fruit, showered and decided to go back to Michael's and try to mend fences.

"Sorry about yesterday," said Michael. "I don't do well with rejection, especially when things aren't going well. And, you know, I put six years into this thing. I can't believe I got nothing out of it."

"Obviously. But not so fast. You learned a ton during this program and now you really can do great things, big projects. Why don't you take a shower and I will make some coffee. We have work to do today. You need to stop feeling sorry for yourself and actually do something; prove to these people that they do not know everything. Oh, and also, I am very proud of you for coming to the rescue of those students. You are my knight in shining armor. Even though it was the most important day of your life, you were the Good Samaritan."

"Thanks. But you know I keep thinking about what Professor Kowalski said yesterday at my defense. I just wonder what does happen in Egypt when the water level in the Nile gets that high. I'm going to spend some time this week and figure that out. And you know what? Who cares about a PhD. Both Steve Jobs and Bill Gates dropped out of college to start billion-dollar companies."

Michael had one of those epiphany moments as he went to take a shower. As is so often the case, a supportive friend can change a person's life outlook in ways that are unexpected. *She's right*, thought Michael, *I have to get out there and prove that these professors don't know everything. Maybe it's time to grab hold of something and just do it. I've been lost in the past with the pyramids and ancient Egypt. Time to stop feeling sorry for myself and look to the future.*

Ariana spent the next hour catching up on work emails in between thoughts about her possible future with Michael. They had been dating a few months and Michael's passion for new ideas combined with his brilliant grasp of innovative technologies continually surprised her. Their early dates often lasted hours as they discussed the latest scientific discoveries, and Michael was the first relationship where she felt an intellectual connection along with a romantic one. Ariana's work title at Whitelock Partners, 'Venture Capital Analyst,' was a perfect fit. She had always been passionate about finding new start-up businesses, very articulate and multilingual, with an MBA from Harvard.

Michael showered, dressed and thought about how he would "figure that out."

When Michael came back into the living room, he seemed calmer and Ariana held her breath, waiting to see if he was still lost in depression or thinking about moving forward in a positive way. He surprised her by saying "I was thinking, we now have pretty good topo maps from the satellites. I wonder if there are topo maps of the desert west of the Nile River that I haven't studied. I think that's the place to start."

"Here's some coffee" Ariana was right there with him in his quest and once again she felt thrilled to share new ideas with this man who she was falling in love with.

Michael headed for his computer. It took him all of about five minutes to locate the topo images of Egypt from the satellites. He called Ariana to come have a look.

"Is it my imagination or does it look to you that there was once a much larger river delta here? I've studied these maps for years but I am seeing something today that is new to me."

"Yes, I see it too." Ariana's interest was piqued. "And look at the area far west almost to the border with Libya. That area is really low, almost like Death Valley here in the U.S. I wonder if that could have been filled with water at some point?"

"Yeah, or maybe at multiple times depending on the climate? You know it was interesting to hear my mom's dream about a flood in Egypt after the river had been dried up for so long. And there's that article in Science News about the dried-up lake beds on the Arabian Peninsula. Depending on the climate, they were either occupied or not." Michael was beginning to feel some missing pieces come together.

"But how did the water get in there?" Ariana was still not sure about all of this. "It could have been millions of years ago, not thousands."

"Yeah, I can't really see the various elevations. This map is just not detailed enough. Let me do some more digging. I want to spend the next few days studying the maps and topography. And I somehow need to reconnect with my parents because I didn't handle my dad's criticism very well last night on the phone. Any chance you might want to go sailing today? We had tentative plans to go sailing today, kind of a celebration day for me getting my PhD. I guess the celebration will have to wait. I have to explain it all to them sometime, might as well be today. Can you go with us?"

Ariana had been hoping to meet Michael's parents for the past month, now that she was starting to fall in love with him. He had talked about his adopted parents with both pride and anger, alternately loving them and being angry at them, depending on his mood. Ariana wanted to know more about this dynamic before losing her heart completely. Today would be the perfect 'experiment' to observe this unique family.

As they walked toward the boat slip, Michael explained that he and his dad both loved boats and he had learned to sail on a Comet, a sixteen-foot sailboat, as a kid. But because his dad worked overseas so much, they usually only sailed on vacations until the past year or so.

"How big is your dad's boat?" As Ariana asked, they were arriving at a sleek sailboat named Sofia's Choice.

"This is it," said Michael and his mom and dad waved as they walked out onto the dock.

"Come aboard," said Greg. "Hi my name's Greg and this is Michael's mom Sofia." Michael helped Ariana up the step to the cockpit and felt her warm hand grasp his arm, ready to steady her if she lost her balance.

The boat was a 56-foot Beneteau with a center cockpit and fore and aft staterooms decorated with a blue and white theme. The galley was fully appointed with glass top cooking surface, an oven, a refrigerator and even a microwave. A small washer and dryer and a head with shower completed the space. Ariana imagined that this craft could easily sail to Europe or Hawaii.

Michael loved sailing and despite the acrimony and disagreements between Michael and his dad on almost everything, sailing was the one thing they had in common and usually enjoyed together.

"Ariana, would you like some coffee?" Sofia and Greg were very gracious hosts and the perfect weather had everyone in an upbeat mood.

"Oh, I am fine, but thanks so much anyway."

"What d'ya say we get underway? It's a beautiful sailing day." Greg started the engine and the smell of diesel mixed with the salt air evoked all the deep-sea fishing trips, sailing adventures and family vacations on the water that their family had experienced. Michael forgot all about the pyramids of Egypt, and felt thankful to be on the water with the sparkling sun and possibly an exciting new girlfriend.

They reversed out of the slip and turned to move into the main harbor, a slight chop giving the boat life and sway. Sofia and Michael went onto the foredeck to hoist the main sail. They were heading east, directly into the wind and the sail began to snap and flutter as the breeze took it. Ariana saw how smoothly all this activity was taking place while Greg gave the captain's commands with words that she didn't know, such as jib, main sail and halyard. As the wind filled the sails, the bow drove hard into the morning chop and spray came over the starboard gunnel. After motoring for a few minutes, Greg shut off the auxiliary engine and the only noise was the flapping of the sails and sound of the waves on the bow.

"It is so quiet" Ariana whispered with almost reverence. This was the time that gives every sailor, no matter how young or old, the thrill of being part of an ancient, venerated tradition. During this brief time on the water, Ariana and Sofia had time to share life experiences and bond. They learned much from each other that day.

A few days later, Michael invited Ariana to his apartment to continue their discussions about the history of the Nile and how the ancient civilizations grew along that ever-changing river. The disappointment about his unsuccessful thesis was still raw and no matter how many times he read the Psalms Scriptures from the Bible, he could not find the peace and fortitude to move forward. His mind was accepting but his heart was aching. Sailing with Ariana and being with his parents the other day was a distraction but today he feared facing his future alone. Where did this fear come from? He reluctantly called Ariana, knowing that her beautiful smile could brighten his day and they worked together so amazingly well when they shared their ideas.

Ariana was happy to hear from Michael, she knew he was almost at the edge of a deep depression and the only thing she knew to do was spend time with him talking about his ideas. She knew that dealing with feelings would be too much for him today and she looked forward to finding out if he had any more theories about the Nile River. When she arrived at Michael's, there were more maps on the walls and floor of his apartment. Was he a mad scientist?

Michael hugged her and seemed almost like his old self, not as broken as a few days ago.

"Let's have coffee and I can't wait to show you some new maps!" he said.

Michael pointed to a more detailed map of Egypt and parts of the Middle East. Not the time to talk about how he was feeling; Ariana followed his conversation to the maps and he pointed excitedly and said, "Ok, so the climate was different 10,000 years ago; maybe this low area west of the Nile had other rivers and lakes. There could have been trees, grasses, all kinds of animals and maybe people living in this area. The Sahara wasn't always a desert," said Michael.

"Yes, so do you think that recently, like 5,000 to 10,000 years ago, ancient people could have lived there. I wonder how far back it goes?" Ariana's mind was racing ahead.

Michael said, "You know your question at the Harvard lecture? Ok, so the same way the carvings and murals are really just engineering drawings, maybe the religious books like the Bible, the Gita and the Quran are really just history books." Michael first met Ariana at a lecture on Egyptian art and archeology at Harvard. After that lecture, they spent the rest of the evening debating whether ancient Egyptian art was a record of the engineering from ancient history.

"You mean like the creation story in the Bible?" said Ariana.

Michael was surprised that Ariana mentioned the Bible, she was from Iran and never wanted to talk about her private beliefs. For the few months that they'd known each other, she had been a fun party girl who also enjoyed hearing about his engineering theories. Michael realized that he didn't know the real Ariana at all. And yet their minds seemed to fit together in the most extraordinary ways.

They stood there staring at the topo map while the wheels turned in their brains and at almost the same instant said "What if the Garden of Eden is actually in Egypt and not in Mesopotamia like everyone thinks?"

"How much do you know about the Garden of Eden? Aren't you Muslim? There's no Garden of Eden in the Quran." Michael was puzzled.

"You do not know everything about me, Michael," said Ariana. "And you know there are Bible passages that describe the area. Do you have a Bible?" Ariana asked.

"Yeah, it's on the bookshelf in the bedroom." Ariana went and got the Bible which was a King James Version and quickly found the relevant passages:

Genesis 2:8-15

8 And the LORD God planted a garden eastward in Eden; and there he put the man whom he had formed.

9 And out of the ground made the LORD God to grow every tree that is pleasant to the sight, and good for food; the tree of life also in the midst of the garden, and the tree of knowledge of good and evil.

10 And a river went out of Eden to water the garden; and from thence it was parted, and became into four heads.

11 The name of the first is Pison: that is it which compasseth the whole land of Havilah, where there is gold;

12 And the gold of that land is good: there is bdellium and the onyx stone.

13 And the name of the second river is Gihon: the same is it that compasseth the whole land of Ethiopia.

14 And the name of the third river is Hiddekel: that is it which goeth toward the east of Assyria. And the fourth river is Euphrates.

15 And the LORD God took the man, and put him into the garden of Eden to dress it and to keep it.

"Ok, ok," said Michael. "So where are these rivers? The maps have the river Euphrates in the Fertile Crescent, in the ancient Mesopotamia area. But I have a thought – you know, when people move, they sometimes carry the old names with them for new places. There is a Bethlehem in the Middle East, but there is also a Bethlehem in Pennsylvania. The settlers in Pennsylvania named their town Bethlehem, hoping to create a religious community. So maybe if people migrated from Egypt to what is currently Turkey, Syria or Iraq, maybe they named rivers in their new place after the rivers they knew back in Egypt. Maybe way back when, they called one of the rivers in Egypt the Euphrates. Then they migrated out of Egypt to Iraq or Syria and called the new river Euphrates." Michael had the uncanny ability to see through the most difficult technical issues.

"Hmmm... that would mean, maybe that the biggest river is named Euphrates, if indeed we are right. Maybe there was an original Euphrates River in Egypt, before the one we currently have in the Middle East?" Ariana's analytical mind was processing all this at a fast pace. "So, let's put the Euphrates River at the deep canyon or riverbed west of the Nile in Egypt, here." She pointed to the spot where a major valley branched from the Nile.

"Sold!" said Michael. "It says the river Gihon goes down toward Ethiopia. Well, there's no Ethiopia in Mesopotamia. Based on this map, it looks like that is the river we call the Nile today." Ariana Googled the Nile River. "It says here that in the first century CE, the great Romano-Jewish historian Flavius Josephus wrote in his *History of the Jews* that the Gihon River is also known as the Nile River." She was becoming more animated by the minute.

"That is two of them." Said Ariana.

"The river Pison, it says, encompasses the land of Havilah, where there is gold. The only place I see for that is this smaller branch of the Nile here." Michael pointed to a ravine that branches off the Nile just south of the Giza Plateau.

Ariana put the name 'Havilah' in her phone to look up its meaning and found that it was a Biblical name that meant 'stretch of sand'.

"What about this low river valley in the northwest corner?" Ariana was not yet convinced. "Couldn't that be the river, Pison?"

"Ok, but then how do you explain the statement in the Bible that the Pison encompasses the land of Havilah? There's no record of people living there and certainly there is no gold there that we know of," Michael said.

"I see your point, but the ancient Egyptians did use a lot of gold in their jewelry and art. Did you know that?" said Ariana. "And we are going on the assumption that each of these ravines or valleys was full of water at that time. What if the climate favored the Nile and most of the rain was in Central Africa in the area of the Blue Nile? Maybe the area to the north was dry as a bone at that time?"

"Good point," Michael was really getting into it.

"There is something else," said Ariana. I remember a passage in the Bible that a mist came up and watered the earth. Let me try to find it."

"Wow, you really know your Bible." Michael just stared at her.

"I remember that too. Standard Garden of Eden stuff," said Michael. Ariana searched and finally found the right passages.

"Here it is!" Ariana read the passage aloud.

Genesis 2:5-6

> 5 And every plant of the field before it was in the earth, and every herb of the field before it grew: for the LORD God had not caused it to rain upon the earth, and there was not a man to till the ground.
> 6 But there went up a mist from the earth, and watered the whole face of the ground.

"That would be just what would happen if the Garden of Eden was in a desert with no rain," said Michael. "I was in California on the northwest coast and every morning there was a mist that watered everything near the ocean. As you got further away from the coast, the land got drier and browner. And that would mean, maybe at that time, the ravine or river bed to the northwest was empty 'cause that area was a desert." Michael was putting more pieces together.

"Ok, we have got three of them." Said Ariana. The last one, called 'Hiddekel' is supposed to go to the east toward Assyria. The only one I see for that is the one at the top with that small lake." Ariana pointed to the ravine at the top right of the map.

"This is what we have so far." Said Michael, showing the marked-up topo map.

"Oh, wow," said Ariana. "This is going to be the biggest archeological breakthrough in history!"

"I think you're right," said Michael. "And what's more, the so-called Garden of Eden was really a region around a lake, let's call it 'Lake Eden,' and that would mean my mom's dreams make a lot of sense." Michael's mom, Sofia, was born and grew up in Egypt and often had vivid dreams. She told them of her dreams of an ancient lake with many different types of people there, including aquatic people, who lived in and around the water. "That lake would've dried up as soon as the level of the Nile fell below the connections to the tributaries. North Africa has been drying out for thousands of years and it's still drying out today. There are only a few oases left."

"Where are the oases?" asked Ariana.

"Let me check." Said Michael. Michael googled oases in Egypt and a map popped up.

"Look, look, the oases are all along the ancient Euphrates riverbed! There's Kharga, Siwa, Farafra, Dakhla and Bahariya. So maybe that's what's left of the river. There must be underground aquifers all along that area. I wonder if they could be drilled and used for crop irrigation like's done in the American Southwest?" Michael was getting more excited too.

Ariana looked at Michael as if she were seeing him for the first time. His excited face and energetic gestures were overpowering, in a good way. She had never met anyone who had such quick ideas and connected information the way Michael's mind seemed to operate. Ariana's mind could relate to Michael's ideas, but she was more intuitive and less scientifically focused.

"Doesn't it make you start thinking about why there aren't more water projects in the Middle East? Water is even more precious there than it is in the American West." Michael was very pleased with himself for suggesting this idea.

"Well, it is not so simple." Said Ariana. "A lot of these countries, like Egypt, are very poor. They don't have money for things like water projects when their people are starving. Israel is a different story, but they do have amazing water projects. And now Saudi Arabia is investing a lot." Michael suspected that Ariana knew much more than she was willing to tell, for proprietary reasons, at her venture company, Whitelock Partners. Proprietary information is the life blood of venture capitalists.

"Hmmf… I am thinking of the 'Promised Land' and a passage when Moses was leading the Israelites out of Egypt that detailed what land was promised to them by God. I need to find it." Ariana began leafing through the Bible trying to find the part about the Promised Land. "Oh, here it is. It goes," She read it aloud to Michael and they both took a few moments to let it sink in.

Genesis 15:17-18

> [17] **And it came to pass, when the sun went down and it was dark, that behold, there appeared a smoking oven and a burning torch that passed between those pieces.**
> [18] **On the same day the LORD made a covenant with Abram, saying: "To your descendants I have given this land, from the river of Egypt to the great river, the River Euphrates—**

"Ok, but then…" Michael was astonished at the implications of what they had just discovered. "It would mean that the so called 'Promised Land' is really just the area west of the Nile to where we think the original River Euphrates actually was!" Michael drew a big red circle around the new Promised Land.

"Are you saying that the rabbis are wrong now too, just like Einstein? Wow, you are arrogant!" Ariana was smiling as she chided Michael. He had been telling her that Einstein didn't have the whole story about the speed of light, that the speed of light was dependent on gravity and not just a universal constant since the only place it had been measured was here on earth. She was very skeptical, especially since Michael was not a physicist.

"C'mon, I think that the interpretation of the Bible passages is just naïve. How do they know what God's plan is? Maybe we could pump enough water out of the underground aquifer to make the whole area a lush tropical paradise. Not only that, but the Promised Land we currently think of as east to the current river Euphrates is nothing but desert. Who wants to live there? Nothing but salty lakes like the Dead Sea and sand. If the region of the original river Euphrates can be pumped and greened up, it could be a tropical paradise with fruit trees, grain, recreational lakes and who knows? Now that's a Promised Land."

"I think you are exaggerating," said Ariana. "But I will give you that the new Promised Land has lots of promise" Ariana was smiling broadly and winked at Michael. He just stared at her. "Ok, what do we do now?" said Ariana.

"Well, we have to document all this, but I'm not quite ready to write an article for the American Journal of Archeology just yet." Michael's graduate work began to kick into high gear. "I wanna share this with someone, but not with anybody who'll ridicule us."

"Yes, this is just too exciting!" said Ariana. "What about your mom and dad?"

"No way. I just don't want to hear a lot of nonsense. I've taken enough from my dad, especially after this dissertation fiasco. I wish we could just tell Mom, 'specially since my mom shared with us her dreams and it may well be that ancient Egypt is where those dreams actually took place. She grew up in Cairo." Michael was beginning to get back a few shreds of his self-esteem, thanks in large part to Ariana.

Michael set about printing out the maps and marking them up to show what they now believed was the real Garden of Eden. At the center was a large lake he marked "Lake Eden." He began to study the topo maps more carefully in order to show where there were larger lakes and wider sections of the river corresponding to higher levels of the Nile in ancient times. Ariana started reviewing the Bible passages in more detail. The more she read, the more the pieces began to fit together.

"Oh, here is something, look." Ariana read the passage of being thrown out of the Garden of Eden.

Genesis 3:24

²⁴ **So He drove out the man; and He placed at the east of the garden of Eden Cherubim, and a flaming sword which turned every way, to keep the way of the tree of life.**

"Isn't that 'flaming sword' really just the desert? And if the Garden was in Mesopotamia, wouldn't the flaming sword be in the west? said Ariana. "And look at this."

Genesis 3:18

¹⁸ **Thorns also and thistles shall it bring forth to thee; and thou shalt eat the herb of the field;**

"So, nothing but scrub brush and briars grow there once the lake dries out and becomes salty. No wonder people had to leave. They would be starving."

Genesis 4:16

¹⁶ **And Cain went out from the presence of the Lord, and dwelt in the land of Nod, on the east of Eden.**

Based on the finding that the Garden of Eden was to the west of the Nile River, apparently the land of Nod was along the Nile, thought Michael. *That seemed to fit in with Mom's dream narrative of flight from the desiccated Lake Eden and then dwelling along what is currently the Nile River today. It also makes sense from a climate change point of view. The Sahara has been drying for at least the last 5,000 to 10,000 years since the last glacial maximum.*

Chapter 5

It was now the next morning and Ariana was wondering how Michael was doing with his maps and documentation.

"I think I have everything drawn up," said Michael. "You know, looking at those topo maps in more detail, I do believe there was a lake that was there after the feeding rivers dried up. It's in the northwest corner of Egypt, like you said."

"That fits in with your mom's dreams and the idea of a Dead Sea or Great Salt Lake kind of a place. I am starting to think that her dreams are more than just imagination," said Ariana.

"And speaking of salt, remember the passage about Lot's wife during the destruction of Sodom and Gomorrah? Here it is." Ariana showed Michael the passage.

Genesis 19:26

26 **But his wife looked back from behind him, and she became a pillar of salt.**

"I think that is a reference to the drying of the area and the salt lakes. And it is still happening today."

"Yeah, and look at this," said Michael. "It really doesn't seem like too much pumping would be needed to get that underground aquifer to yield. Looks like some pretty fertile areas could be in the vicinity of the low spots on what we think is the Old River Euphrates. I'm thinking that there was an enormous amount of silt washed down there over the millennia." Once Michael got an idea, he was like a bulldog, just like his dad.

"Yes, it could be some of the best land in the country once you get away from the Nile riverbed." Ariana was impressed. "Hey, wait a minute, why couldn't we just refill the lake by diverting water from the Nile River? We could win the Israeli Water Challenge prize and be rich! Then you could make a donation to MIT and they would name a building after you. Talk about turning the tables on them!"

"Are you kidding?" said Michael. "There's no way... I don't think... Well maybe... but it would be the most unbelievably large civil engineering project ever!" Michael thought the idea ridiculous. He also had the techy plague of "Not Invented Here," meaning that he didn't think of it first, so it couldn't be a good idea.

"Hon, there's something else." Michael's voice took on a serious tone. "If there were really people or even other hominins living along the Lake Eden shoreline, there should be some archeological evidence. I mean all this time they could have been 'digging in the wrong place' as it were." Michael smiled broadly. "It makes me wonder what kind of things we could find there."

"Hmmf... Not only that, but it seems like if the water began to dry up after the Nile River level dropped, we might be able to excavate the shoreline progressively and see a sort of stratification of artifacts as the lake receded." Ariana was right there with him.

"We could use the topo maps to see where the original shoreline might have been and start digging there. Thing is... that's a lot of shoreline. It's almost the size of the whole country of Egypt. How do we figure out where to start?" Michael was trying to process all the possibilities.

Ariana said "One thing we could do is talk to some anthropologists and try to get an idea of the best spots where people could live. Also, didn't I read somewhere that there is a sort of subsurface acoustic scanning technology just developed. They use it to find archeological sites, buried walls and everything. Do you think your father knows anyone in Egypt that has that kind of technology?"

"What're you talking about? We're at MIT. We have the most advanced subsurface sonar in the world. Let me talk to some of the professors and get the latest. I just don't want to take the chance of letting on what we've discovered."

"Relax," said Ariana. "With all these archeologists, anthropologists and Bible historians, don't you think they would have thought of this? We are probably full of it."

"I once had a professor at MIT who taught a course in invention and innovation," said Michael. "He started his first lecture with a story about a man named Charles H. Duell, who was Commissioner of Patents for the U.S.A. back in 1898. He famously said 'Everything that can be invented has been invented' in his letter of resignation from the patent office. Ha ha. The point was that so many times when someone has a good idea, it seems so obvious that the response from people is 'they already have that.'"

"I get it," said Ariana. "But you know I still cannot get past the idea of refilling Lake Eden."

When he experienced push back, Michael would suddenly sometimes snap and lash out at the person. It was one of his character issues, and he would almost always regret it, but couldn't stop himself either, especially if he was under stress. "That's because you don't understand engineering. The technology simply doesn't exist. Plus, even if it did exist, the cost would be astronomical!"

"Technology…, I have made hundreds of millions of dollars on new technology for Whitelock. So far, you have made and done nothing!" Ariana was furious. She wasn't used to being yelled at. "Technology is invented to fulfill a need, not the other way around. I cannot believe you could be so closed minded after your lecture about Duell or whatever his name is." She was now in full heat of the argument.

"Ok," said Michael, "let's consider the facts. Number one, a dam on the Nile big enough to refill Lake Eden would have to be miles long based on these topo maps. Number two, we would flood the Aswan Dam. Number three, we would be stealing water from the cities like Luxor and Cairo along the Nile downstream. Number four, we would inundate some very important antiquities. But most important, how do you get the money?"

"I should not be telling you this; I could get fired, but Whitelock has been looking for a solution to the Water Challenge since it was first announced. They have nothing," said Ariana. "I think this is much better than nothing and I am betting we can get them on board."

"Even Whitelock doesn't have that kind of money, and what about Egypt? Don't you think they would have something to say about this?" said Michael.

"Whitelock has contacts. And now I've said enough." Michael never liked the idea of having a secret kept from him. They continued arguing the pros and cons of building a dam through a take-out dinner and late into the night. Ariana twice threatened to go home and Michael couldn't help himself from shouting. The stress from the previous day had him emotionally unstable. They finally agreed to sleep on these ideas and reconsider everything in the morning.

That night, as Michael slept, he had a dream. It was one of those where everything seemed familiar even though he knew he had never been there before. He was in a large, modern city with gleaming tall buildings, yacht harbors, miles of fruit and date trees, broad rivers and lakes. A voice spoke to him in the dream. "I have chosen you as the architect of the Crystal City. Believe in me and you will have your reward."

The next morning, Ariana noticed that Michael seemed like a different person. He was calmer and did not bring up their disagreements of the previous evening. Instead, he hugged her tightly and said that it's all going to work out and Ariana hoped he was right.

Chapter 6

Cairo, Egypt

Professor Ahmed Morsi of the Al-Azhar University in Cairo was one of the most notable archeologists in the Middle East. He made a name for himself by discovering a cache of mummies near the ancient pyramid of Saqqara. Morsi was one of those 'out of box' thinkers who could imagine what things must have been like in the times of prehistory 5,000 to 10,000 years ago. When Michael's adopted father, Greg Walters, was stationed in Cairo twenty years ago, it was Morsi who took him under his wing and showed him some of the most ancient archeological finds in all of Egypt. During that time, the United States had a Student Exchange/ Study Abroad program sponsored by the State Department and Morsi was one of the preceptors in Cairo. Morsi never missed an opportunity to talk about the ancient world and his beliefs about how civilization actually started in Egypt. He had a profound knowledge of not only the history and archeology of Egypt, but also of the many historical characters of Europe who discovered and looted so many of Egypt's most important treasures. In fact, Morsi specifically cultivated relationships with people like Greg Walters so that this type of plundering never happened again in Egypt.

Morsi, like Michael Walters, in Boston, had also given a lot of thought to topography in and around the Nile River, although not in the far western desert. His latest archeological excavation was in an area of the Qarun Lake, just southwest of Cairo. The lake had once been freshwater fed by the Nile River and, in ancient times, had been much larger than it is today. Over the years as the level of the Nile River continued to drop in accord with the drying of North Africa, the lake shrank and became a saltwater body similar to the Dead Sea. Morsi reasoned that if the lake was much larger in antiquity, then people must have lived on and around its shoreline. The shoreline could be estimated based on topography maps and the known levels of the Nile River over time. His thesis was that the archeological time periods could be mapped as the shore of the lake receded, similar to depth stratigraphy in modern archeology. Most of his colleagues thought he was grasping at straws. So many archeological treasures were yet to be explored in and around the Valley of the Kings.

Morsi was in the middle of excavation of one of the sites that showed artifacts corroborating the shoreline dating technique he was pioneering. Archeological sites were typically sectioned off with lines and divided into dig areas. To one side, there were tents and some scientific instruments and, in each sector, groups of archeologists and their students were on their knees with small trowels, sieves and brushes to find even the smallest bone or artifact from the site. Very strict records were kept of the depths at each dig sector so that the time period could be accurately gauged.

Morsi and his students had discovered what they believed was a race of humans with elongated heads as was shown in the carvings and murals on ancient building walls in Egypt.

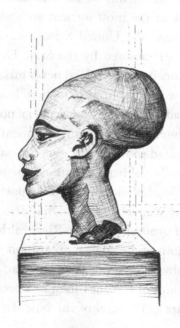

He carefully explained to his students that climate change was anything but straight forward.

"Greenland is covered with ice, or at least it has been in recent memory. So why is it called Greenland instead of Whiteland? Can anyone tell me?"

Silence from the group of students gathered around.

"It's because when Greenland was discovered by the Vikings in about 1000 CE, it actually was green and covered with grass. This was a period of time on the earth known as the Medieval Warming Period. The Vikings founded colonies there on Greenland and they did very well for a few hundred years until the so-called Little Ice Age came along in about 1300 CE. The glaciers returned to Greenland and the Viking colonies there failed. Against an angry indigenous people, they had to be abandoned. It was a bloodbath. This doesn't correlate with any natural earth axis wobble, so it had to be the sun and some type of solar cycle. Bottom line is, we don't know as much as we think we do.

"And that brings up another important point," said Morsi. "The pyramids are very controversial, not only as to how they were built, but also when they were built. Could these pygmy people with the elongated skulls be a smarter species than our own and could they have been the architects of these magnificent structures? If in fact the pyramids were actually built over 10,000 years ago, then the chronology we see here all seems to fit and make sense."

"Professor, couldn't the elongated heads be from head binding?" His favorite student, Aya, asked the best questions.

"That's a very good question, Aya." Said Morsi. "But have a look here." Morsi pointed to the sutures where the parts of the skull come together. "If the elongated skulls were from head binding these fontanelles would be much larger, expanded. These are not, indicating that the skull developed normally. Clearly these were not produced by head binding."

Chapter 7

Kharga Oasis, Egypt

The Kharga oasis is the largest and most strategic of the oases in the Western Desert of Egypt. Throughout the millennia, it served as a strategic outpost for the caravan routes connecting Thebes with Nubia to the south and the Mediterranean Sea to the north. In Roman times, the Kharga oasis was a military outpost for the Roman Empire. Remains of the Roman fortresses adapted from ancient Egyptian temples can still be seen on the hilltops of the city. It is believed that during the 27th Dynasty, there was a migration from Thebes to this desert city, one of the very few places west of the Nile to obtain water during a long caravan journey.

Ancient ruins such as the Temple of Hibis on a hill near the town are evidence of how long this area had been inhabited. The location of this oasis makes sense with respect to the original location of the Garden of Eden and Lake Eden, fed by the original or old River Euphrates. When the level of the Nile dropped and the Euphrates was no longer fed by Nile waters, the Western Desert dried out, except for those parts of the Euphrates that were low enough to allow the underground aquifer beneath the riverbed to reach the surface. These were the famous oases of the desert and the town of Kharga was the largest and closest to the Nile, just west of Luxor (ancient Thebes) by about 130 miles as the crow flies.

It is probable that when the river dried up and Lake Eden turned salty, some of the people who fled made it to Kharga and have remained there for thousands of years.

Even today, tourists can be seen climbing on the pillars of salt that have been deposited in Kharga at the old River Euphrates, similar to what is seen in the Dead Sea and other desiccated places in the Middle East. The story of Lot and the destruction of Sodom and Gomorrah, where Lot's wife is admonished not to look back or she will turn to a pillar of salt, may be an allegorical story of the drying of the region since the last glacial maximum and formation of pillars of salt. Anyone who has second thoughts about fleeing these desert areas will be nothing more than a bit of dust or salt like these pillars.

Genesis 19

> **¹³ For we will destroy this place, because the cry of them is waxen great before the face of the Lord; and the Lord hath sent us to destroy it.**
> **²⁶ But his wife looked back from behind him, and she became a pillar of salt.**

Few archeological digs have been done in Kharga, but since the way of life integrated Egyptian, Roman, Greek and Byzantine cultures, there are many impressive temples and art objects that have been discovered and studied in this unique city. Some archeologists believe that there is a treasure trove of undiscovered ancient finds beneath this city dating back perhaps as far as 7,000 years ago. The people of Kharga have always been rebellious even in ancient and Roman times.

The family and ancestors of Hanbal Aziz have lived in the Kharga Oasis for as long as anyone in the city can remember. It is possible that Hanbal's family was part of the original migration from the desiccated Lake Eden that happened as the weather patterns changed when the Earth began to warm after the Last Glacial Maximum.

Hanbal had a very difficult life, especially since his father had been killed in the Arab Spring demonstrations years ago.

At the age of 18, Hanbal went to study the Quran in Syria where he found a group of young men with very similar dysfunctional family histories. The men developed very close bonds and Hanbal now considered them more of a family than the one back in Kharga.

Shortly after Hanbal started at the school, he met a young man named Mohammed Hussein who was also new to the school.

"My family is so hard to live with," said Hanbal. "I'm very happy to be here in this place."

Hanbal attended a meeting held by Mohammed's father who was a local political leader, "Friends we have a camp some miles east of here where we train to fight. There are many great fighters there. If any of you would like to join us, please come with me tomorrow. We will meet here at sunrise after morning prayers and head to the camp."

"I'm coming" said Hanbal to Mohammed. "I feel like the men in this room are like me, like brothers. And I agree, we have to fight these ones who destroy our society and kill our women and children. It is our duty to Allah."

"Thank you, my friend. You will meet many more like family there." When the talk was over, Mohammed introduced Hanbal to his father.

"We are very glad to have you join us," he said. "We have many brave fighters with us and we will prevail."

The next morning Hanbal met Mohammed at his father's house and several trucks were filled with young men just like him. They drove an hour east to a deserted area many miles from any paved road. When Hanbal arrived, he saw a number of tents and a shooting range where others were already taking target practice.

The rest of the morning was spent on the firing range getting used to the gun and delivering better groupings with each succeeding target he put up.

Up until that moment, this was the most power Hanbal had ever felt in his life. The huge grin on his face told the story of his reaction to this new found thrill.

"I really like this Mr. Hussein" said Hanbal. "Thank you for bringing me here. I want to be a part of your army."

"And you will be my young friend. Come let's see to our noon prayers."

Hanbal's uncle had two daughters, one of whom, Lapis, was a few years younger than Hanbal. When Lapis was 14, her father arranged for her to be married to his adopted son, Hanbal, over his mother's objections. But women had no say in decisions either financial or social, so the uncle's arrangement stood. When Hanbal turned 18, the marriage took place and both Hanbal and Lapis felt trapped and unable to cope with the new life they had been pushed into.

The marriage got off to a rocky start. Hanbal's resentment of his adoptive father, combined with the abuse of his mother, left him bitter and angry with the whole world. Hanbal's anger came out in his treatment of his new wife, Lapis.

Hanbal left for Syria and Lapis continued to live with her father, glad that Hanbal was away. As Hanbal became more radicalized and militant, Lapis became more unhappy with her situation and wished she could escape. The problem was, there was nowhere to go and no way for someone like her to make a living if she did run away.

A small group of women in Kharga would meet in each other's homes when the men were away and talk about their lives. It wasn't really possible to keep them away from the TV, smart phones and computers completely and it wasn't long before they saw how the women of the West were able to live, driving cars, working in offices, dressing fashionably and enjoying status similar to the men. Many desperately wished they could enjoy life in that way too.

Chapter 8

Ramallah, West Bank

Things were getting continuously worse for Aashif and Bariah. With industry ground to a standstill, food production and distribution were slowed and the supply lines for everyday necessities were stretched to the breaking point. Not only did the two young people struggle for the daily water ration, but they were hungry nearly all the time. Civil order had broken down almost entirely in Ramallah and thieves were everywhere.

One day, as they walked together to the water distribution center, Aashif said, "We have to do something. We're going to die here. The only people getting enough food and water are rich people and thieves."

Bariah just looked down at the ground. "Every day when I get up, I have terrible pains in my stomach and I can hardly get out of bed. But I know I have to. Seeing you is the only time of the day I look forward to." Aashif was deeply touched and knew in his heart that this girl was the love of his life. In that moment, something changed in his young mind and he thought *I'm done with the law, nobody obeys it anyway. It's everyone for themselves.* He resolved to take action and improve the situation for both his family and Bariah's. The way of Islam was just not working. Afterall, the Imams were not starving or thirsty. *Ok, time to act*, he thought. *Maybe I should trade my pepper spray bottle for a gun? But where to find one? Hey, wait a minute. The thieves have guns. I'll just take one of theirs.* A plot began to form in Aashif's mind as to how to attack one of the thieves that had robbed both him and Bariah several times before. The relentless thirst and now, gnawing hunger was enough to overcome his fear and put his clever mind at work. Most of the thieves hung out within a few blocks of the water distribution center. They tended to prey on the weak and stole both their water ration and their money. The weak rarely, if ever, fought back. Aashif would be doing them a favor.

Next day he told Bariah about his plan. "If you get caught, they will put you in prison and then what will happen to your mother and sister?" she said.

"What's the difference? If I do nothing, they'll die anyway." Most violence is born of desperation and fear. "If they don't see me, they won't know who did it."

"How can I help you?" Although traditional in her culture, Bariah was not unaware of the movement to free women from their second-class status in society, even in a place like Palestine.

Aashif carefully explained his plan the next day on the way to the water station. He would make a hood of old cloth and wait behind a door in the place where they had been robbed before. When the thief appeared and demanded the water from some thirsty soul, he would give him a spray of pepper gas, take his water, money and gun, then slip away. The money could be used to buy more water and food on the black market. When it ran out, he would do it again. "What you can do is just observe and see when a lone thief attacks. I think most people are just glad it's not them, so they look the other way. And the guards are at the water station."

"Ok, tomorrow, after we get our ration." Bariah and Aashif decided to split up after getting the water and take separate paths home.

As it turned out, the next day there was no need for Bariah to observe the thieves. Aashif was accosted near the same area as before by two men, one with a gun, demanding the precious water ration.

"Hello my young friend. It is time to pay us once again," said the taller one, holding up the gun. At that moment, something snapped in Aashif's mind and as he handed over both water jugs, he sprayed the one holding the gun with pepper and quickly turned to get the other one, with a perfect aim at a distance of almost 8 feet. They both grabbed their faces and the gun dropped to the ground.

"Not this time," shouted Aashif. Then he took the water, money and gun and ran.

* * *

Ariana is one of those people who gets very excited about an idea, especially if it's hers. Her coping strategy is to dive into her work. So, a few days after Michael failed his dissertation, she went to work early and began research in earnest on the Israeli Water Challenge. The situation was actually much more difficult than she imagined. Israel was in real trouble and there were long lines of people outside the desalination plants waiting for the daily water ration. Industry had slowed to a crawl and food was being horded, not just by the poor, but by the wealthy as well. Many who had come to Israel after the Holocaust were making plans to go to South America, the U.S. or Canada.

As was the case for any investment pitch, a firm foundation of need had to be established before the partners would consider an investment. This was Ariana's sweet spot. Over the course of a morning, she put together a compelling pitch for investing in a megadam project across the Nile River that would turn part of the largest desert in the world into a lush paradise. *Now...* she thought, *all I need to do is convince Michael to figure out how to do it. We'll all be rich and we will save so many lives.*

Easier said than done. What Ariana didn't realize was that the megadam would have to be over 23km long and 300 meters high to do what she was suggesting. Not only that, but the plan involved moving both Israelis and Palestinians to Egypt, an even bigger challenge than building the megadam. As she got more deeply into the research on the project, it became clear that the megadam was not the only way to provide more fresh water to the region. It turned out that the water flowing into the Black Sea was another alternative. As the last Ice Age was drawing to a close around 5,000 to 7,000 years ago, sea levels were rising tremendously and many coastal areas were flooded. One of the most important events was the flooding of the Bosporus Straight in Turkey. Robert Ballard had shown years earlier that the rising Aegean Sea allowed salt water to pour into the Black Sea, trapping quasi-freshwater above it and cutting off oxygen supply to the depths, hence the name Black Sea. Everything on the bottom was black. His brilliant research using deep water submersibles showed whole cities near the coast were inundated. Some believe that was the basis for the story of Noah and the great flood in the Bible.

Genesis 6:17

17 And, behold, I, even I, do bring a flood of waters upon the earth, to destroy all flesh, wherein is the breath of life, from under heaven; and every thing that is in the earth shall die.

As a result, the huge quantity of fresh water flowing into the Black Sea from the Danube River was contaminated with salt water. But if the water could be diverted before reaching the sea, it could potentially be piped to the Middle East and relieve the water crisis there. The problem with that solution, aside from the politics, was that it required building a quarter mile diameter pipeline or canal over 1200 miles long. *That's more difficult than the megadam*, thought Ariana. *Maybe I overestimated what humans could actually do*, she thought.

"When in doubt, communicate" was Ariana's motto since joining Whitelock. She needed to talk to her boss as well as some of the partners and get some feedback on the plans. As she pondered the alternatives, her mind raced ahead.

Fortunately, Whitelock had been pursuing huge projects with the Saudis for over ten years and had helped finance some amazing things, such as the 100-mile-long linear city. It turned out, the key to success in this line of work was substituting profit for politics. *The megadam project is no exception*, thought Ariana. *The key is the technology and the profit.*

Ariana's previous successes at Whitelock relied on using sound scientific data and her persistent personality.

This time, things were much more difficult. Ariana had worked her way around the junior partners, presenting to them, but in the end, in each case, there was skepticism as to whether the megadam could be built at all. Now, she needed the most senior partner, Henry Pitt, to support the project and the others would almost certainly fall into line. The night before her meeting with Henry, her sleep was restless and troubled. As Deborah in the Bible had a vision from God, Ariana heard in the dream, God's voice "Awake, awake, Ariana. This was God telling her to do whatever was necessary to save the people of Israel.

Judges 5:12

[12] Awake, awake, Deborah: awake, awake, utter a song: arise, Barak, and lead thy captivity captive, thou son of Abinoam.

When Ariana awoke, the first thing on her mind was the meeting with Henry.

"Ok," said Henry, the senior partner, "explain to me the whole plan." They were sitting in the bar at The Langham, a magnificent 5-star restaurant in downtown Boston a week later. Henry was a middle-aged man with greying hair, tall, square jawed with piercing eyes who rarely, if ever, smiled.

"In a nutshell, we build a huge dam across the Nile River and cause water to flow into an old tributary of the Nile that's been dried up for 5,000 years. The water flows into a basin called the Qattara Depression in the Western Desert of Egypt and the gigantic freshwater lake becomes a major new city development in Egypt. Then we move the Israelis to the new land which they purchase from the development company, owned by the Saudis, Egyptians and Israelis. Palestinians and other Middle Easterners could buy places there too, in fact, the whole world could. Water crisis solved and we win $100 million."

"Sounds simple," said Henry. "Just a few minor points I want to clarify. How big is the dam again?"

"Well... it's about 15 miles long and 1000 feet high, I think."

"You're joking, right? Has anything even close to that big been built anywhere in the world by anyone?"

"No, but that doesn't mean it can't be done."

"Fair enough, but listen here, we are not going to invest in something that can't be done. So, figure it out and then come see me again. Oh, and how are you going to get the Israelis to agree to move from their Promised Land over to Egypt?"

"Well, wouldn't you rather move than die of thirst?"

"Ok, good point. But there has to be more money in it for us than $100 million. That's pocket change. We finance multi-billion-dollar projects."

"There is over 100 billion dollars of development potential around the lake, plus the $100 billion annual revenue from the ongoing taxes to Egypt and all the stakeholder countries along the Nile. That is more than Egypt's current annual budget now.

"As for the technology, I have some engineers from MIT who believe they have some new breakthroughs that can do it. I believe in them, and is that not what a venture capital firm is all about? At least let them present to you." The tried and true "fake it 'til you make it" startup mantra of Thomas Edison was top of mind for Ariana in this exchange. She knew they didn't actually know how to build the megadam yet. But she believed they would figure it out.

"Hmmm," said Henry. "There may be another angle to this. Let me think about it.

Chapter 9

Boston, Three Days after Thesis Defense

Michael woke up and remembered his vision of a beautiful new city, especially the voice saying that he was chosen as the Crystal City architect. *It's not my nature to shy away from a challenge*, thought Michael. *Just because I don't know how to build a megadam doesn't mean that it can't be done.*

Michael was very introspective and could be called a deep thinker. When he was 12 years old, his dad gave him a complete copy of Sherlock Holmes and Michael read it cover to cover, adopting many of Holmes' methods and interests, for technical problem solving rather than criminal mysteries. The result of this was that Michael had many deep thoughts and philosophies that did not play well with his colleagues and friends.

This same type of critical thinking also applied to technical challenges. Michael would often wake up around 4:00 in the morning turning over technical roadblocks and various solutions until he hit on something that might work. When he got up in the morning, he made it a habit to immediately research and document his solution. Most of his brilliant ideas happened this way. The megadam was no exception and it dawned on Michael that since the megadam was so long and high, the only way to get it done in reasonable time had to be automation. He resolved to talk to his officemate Steve as soon as possible that morning.

Pierce Lab was located on the main quad at MIT and was a large structure in the imposing Greek style. Michael's office was located on the first floor. When he arrived at his office, his officemate, Steve Williams, was already there.

"Hey Michael, how's it feel to be a doctor from MIT? Did you and Ariana have fun celebrating?"

"Well, actually I... I didn't pass."

"What? Oh no, what happened?" Steve searched Michael's eyes and raised his eyebrows.

"How much time do you have?" Michael had decided to share his thoughts with Steve, and see if his friend had any ideas, especially about the megadam. Michael explained what Professor Levit had said and how Kowalski had belittled him. "So, now, I have to prove that the water level could have been that high, that is *if* I go on with all this. And there's something else making me rethink everything. I started looking at the Topo maps for western Egypt. Ariana and I saw something that could be a major find. We think we found the original site of the Garden of Eden."

"Hmmmf," said Steve. "Where is it?"

"It's in the western desert of Egypt, west of the Nile. And that's not the only thing. We found the four rivers from the Bible and what looks like an ancient lake in the northwest corner of the country."

"I thought it was all just sand."

"Yeah, but it wasn't always. So, listen to this. Ariana wants to build a gigantic dam on the Nile River and refill the lake at the Garden of Eden. We're calling it Lake Eden. I just don't see any way to actually do it."

"So, basically she wants to build a huge dam across the Nile and you wimped out?"

"Well, obviously you can't build a 15-mile-long dam that's 1000 feet high. The Hoover dam is a little over 700 feet high and only 1200 feet long. You're as unrealistic as Ariana!" Michael shouted. The past few days pushed him over the edge. Fire flew from Michael's eyes.

"Not so fast," said Steve, who was used to a rough and tumble environment, having grown up in New York City. "Don't get so upset."

Steve was another one who, given a challenge, would turn over the possibilities in his head, like Sherlock Holmes, until a solution suggested itself. "Lemee think about it. Actually, no, I don't needa think about it. This is what I've been working on and just waiting for. So...How much time do *you* have?"

"All day…, I'm on break from this place. I do have an idea I wanna run by you. But, what dya have in mind?" Michael replied.

"Obviously, the in-situ calcination is a perfect match, assuming there is limestone in the Nile basin," said Steve.

"Yeah, I think there is," said Michael

"Tell me more about the in-situ calcination," said Steve.

Michael explained, "The problem with building a concrete dam like the Hoover Dam is that the concrete overheats and doesn't fully cure. That's why they had to put in pipes all through the thing with cooling water from a refrigerant plant. The concrete is still curing today. But if we build an earthen or rock dam, we can mix concrete in with the rocks. The concrete comes from a lime kiln on site next to the conveyors loading the rock to make the dam. Then when the dam fills, the water cures the cement 'in-situ' and cools it and the whole thing is stuck together."

"Brilliant!"

"So…," said Michael, "what we need is an ***automated*** way to blast rock from the bedrock along the dam path and then convey it to the site, pile it up to 1000 feet high, and bond it together with in-situ cement. An earthen rock dam is the only way I can see to do it. Let's think about how to automate the blasting and conveying. Otherwise, it'll take forever to build the dam."

"Ok, don't you know a guy from Caterpillar who might be able to help us?" said Steve.

When Michael was in high school, his family took him to see the Hoover Dam and this was another life-changing event, similar to seeing the Great Pyramids as a child. That experience catapulted him into the technology and engineering life and set him on a course to seek out and accomplish the largest civil engineering project of all time. When he began his graduate work in Civil Engineering at MIT, he looked for the most significant civil engineering project in history, as a dissertation topic, in order to study how it was accomplished. He settled on the Great Pyramid of Cheops and spent the next six years delving into the possible ways the ancients could have accomplished this feat, as well as why they did it.

"The key to this whole thing," said Steve, "is to scale up the machinery so that the blasting, conveying, crushing and calcination are all automated and run 24/7. What we need to do is to get with someone from Caterpillar or Komatsu and put a design together."

The issues for this kind of project were how to scale up the machinery like conveyors and crushers, where to get the energy to run the motors and the lime kilns, and how to design the control systems and transport structure so the whole thing could move as the dam was being built. Steve would take the lead in this activity, working closely with Michael's contact at Caterpillar to develop the capability.

In the minutes before waking at four in the morning, Michael's dreamlife had always been very active and scary. The dreams tended to be mixed replays of the day's events in combination with old memories and insecurities. He often had dreams of school with all the attendant experiences, such as being late for an examination, forgetting he is taking a course, getting lost in the engineering building or the classic "phone won't work" dream. At times old girlfriends would show up, especially ones for whom the breakup was rocky. A very unsettling recurring nightmare had him at the bottom of a well and his mother standing at the top looking down. This dream happened at least once a week and left Michael trembling and sweaty. But the most important aspect of Michael's dreaming had been the occasional prescient dreams. He had these maybe several times a month and when the incredibly unlikely event from his dream actually happened, it seemed to overwhelm him, continuously challenging the left brain understanding of the world. The most intriguing aspect of these prescient dreams was that, although the dreams seemed to actually happen in real life, they almost never forewarned a significant life event. Michael simply could not understand why that is.

On the night following his meeting with Steve, Michael had a dream about the machinery needed to build the dam. In the dream there were many explosions, loud sounds like crushing rock and shouts of someone falling…, falling…. When he woke up, he was beginning to have some ideas as to how to automate the building of the earthen, or really, rock megadam. It would take many months to flesh out those concepts and have something viable.

Chapter 10

Boston, a few days later

By midafternoon Michael was ready to reconnect with Ariana so he texted her *"I talked to Steve, and he was nowhere near as pessimistic about the megadam as I was."*

Ariana texted back. *"Well, I did some investigation and you know we have been working with the Saudis for years doing all kinds of huge projects. So, no matter which way we go, I think my firm, Whitelock, is the way to approach the financing."*

"Dinner tonight?" As soon as the text left his fingers the uneasiness did as well.

"What time?"

"As soon as you can get here."

Ariana left work early with the excuse that she was pursuing an investment lead. Michael was home doing research on the megadam when she arrived. He had already looked at the lithographic maps for the Nile Basin and found a solid site for the megadam. He also did a more thorough investigation of the four major oases in the Old Euphrates River valley. *If we refill Lake Eden and the dried up river valley,* thought Michael, *we will inundate the oases, especially the Kharga oasis. That's an issue beyond just being able to build such a large dam.*

"I'm so sorry," Michael said. "I can be really pigheaded at times."

"Me too," said Ariana. "I don't know as much as I think I do."

"I spoke to Steve and he is up for the dam project. He thinks that the in-situ calcination is a perfect match for this project."

"Really? I am not sure what that is, but… great!" said Ariana.

Ariana said, "I did some research as well. You know Whitelock has some major contacts in Saudi Arabia, including the Crown Prince. From a political standpoint, we might be able to move things forward using plain, old-fashioned greed."

"One other thing," said Michael. "I had a dream after our argument, about being in a 'crystal city.' I heard a voice saying I was chosen as the architect of that city. I'm curious as to what that's all about, but I don't think we can build a crystal city unless we build the megadam." What Michael didn't say, but thought, was, *throughout history, God talks to his prophets through dreams and visions. Was that God talking to me?*

Ariana said, "Between my contacts at Whitelock and your engineering, I am a believer."

"You know, my mom always said, 'You can never go back, Michael.' But this time it's something special, something from God. This time, we can go back. We can all go back, back to the Garden. Let's do this," said Michael. "You work the politics and financing angle. Steve and I will find a way to engineer this thing. I'm a believer too, let's build the megadam."

In his heart of hearts, Michael was hoping to do a monumental civil engineering project since he first saw the Hoover Dam in high school. His struggle with the technical challenges and defensive personality plus a touch of "Not Invented Here" were all that kept him from going all in on the project when Ariana first suggested it. As is the case with many who attain greatness in life, Michael had to hit bottom before rising to fulfill his destiny. It was a perspective, an attitude of believing in oneself, regardless of the mistakes and failures of the past. *Nowhere to go but up from here*, thought Michael.

Michael was definitely moving out of depression now. Finally, he was relating to the Biblical scriptures as messages that seemed to speak to him in very practical ways. All he needed was the right challenge to rise to, although he was not quite convinced about building the megadam. The breadth of his interests allowed him to relate to nearly anyone and he wanted to become a better leader. His structured approach, in the method of Sherlock Holmes, to problem solving gave him vast latitude as to what he could tilt at.

One of the things that happens to children of alcoholics is that they are continually seeking validation from the alcoholic parent. Michael's case was no exception, so when he and Ariana made the commitment to each other to build the megadam, Michael wanted to tell his dad and get some approval. He desperately hoped it would, in some way, make up for his failure to pass the dissertation defense.

Michael called his mom and told her he needed to talk to them, and was invited for dinner the next evening. He and Ariana arrived at his parents' apartment, a luxurious condo on the 40th floor overlooking the Boston Harbor, at just before 6pm. The condo was a corner unit and had magnificent floor to ceiling windows on the two sides facing the harbor.

Once Michael decided to pursue a project, he was like a bulldog and never gave up. That's what it takes to create the largest dam in the world. The issue for Michael was actually deciding to pursue a project. He could be decisive, when in the midst of a project, but the initial decision to engage was elusive for him. At least some of this indecisive behavior came from his domineering father, who always seemed to have something negative to say about essentially anything Michael wanted to do. Whereas Michael's thought process was basically data driven, his father's thinking was mostly emotional/political. Choosing a course of action for Michael's dad was much like choosing a sports team to root for. This fundamental conflict between Michael and his dad led to arguments, anger over decisions and regular confrontation when Michael was around his dad.

When Michael's mom opened the door, she gave them each a hug and graciously invited them to come in and sit down. Sofia had a concerned look on her face as Michael and Ariana came inside. Greg was sitting in his favorite chair staring out the window.

"Michael, Ariana, so great to see you" said Greg as he stood up and gave them each a hug. Michael could feel his hands starting to sweat as he realized how much of an emotional minefield he was in.

"Hi Dad," said Michael. "Hope we aren't disturbing you." Michael was thinking, *oh no, how do we get out of this?*

"Not a bit, what's on your mind?"

Well, I might as well dive in and tell him, then get out of here as soon as possible after dinner, thought Michael.

"Remember when we told you about discovering the Garden of Eden?"

"Yes, I'm so proud of both of you," said Greg.

"Well, the Israelis are offering a hundred million dollars to anyone who can solve the drought crisis."

"I heard that," said Greg.

"We think we have a solution," Michael was watching Greg's face closely as he said this last.

Greg glanced out the window at the harbor and then said, "I'm listening."

"Ariana and I want to build the largest dam in the world and refill the Garden of Eden lake."

"How?" Greg's eyes bored a hole in Michael's face.

"My buddy Steve has some great ideas."

"Yeah… you know that these kinds of projects are done by huge engineering firms like Bechtel?"

This was exactly what Michael was afraid of, instant withering criticism before he even had a chance to explain. "I know that, but we feel if we can get Ariana's firm to finance it, we can do it."

"There is no way!" shouted Greg.

"Greg, that's enough," said Sofia. She was frustrated and trying to find a way to deal with Greg.

"Ok, how big is the dam?" asked Greg.

"It has to be 15 miles long and 1000 feet high. But listen, don't worry about that. Steve and I have a way to do it. My question is, what about the Israelis? Do you think they will go for it if we show them how it can be done?"

"I think you must be joking," he said.

Sofia put her hand to her mouth and burst out crying as she ran from the room.

"Thanks so much for your support," said Michael. "Come on Ariana, we're leaving." *So much for family,* thought Michael.

The two of them jumped up and left while Sofia was still in the bedroom.

The next day, Greg decided to call his acquaintance Professor Ahmed Morsi in Cairo.

"Ahmed, Greg Walters," Greg was calling the first person on his list of "trustworthy" academicians in Cairo. It was midafternoon for Greg.

"Greg! Long time, no hear from," Morsi was very pleasantly surprised to hear from his old friend. "How are you, what's new?"

"Great to hear your voice, Ahmed. Things are very well here. I am in Boston and enjoying my retirement.

"Sofia is great and Michael is still fooling around with his PhD in Civil Engineering from MIT."

"Wonderful news, so what's next for him?"

"He's trying to work that out. He and his new girlfriend, Ariana, love it in Boston and I can tell you, they are always busy with something."

"Oh yes, my oldest son Ali is off galivanting around the planet for the United Nations, helping some of the poorer countries with agriculture and water management. We have to beg him just to call us once in a while let alone move back to Cairo. Our daughter Marwa is still in school at Baylor in the U.S. working on her Master's in Public Health, and thank you so much for helping her get in to a good school there."

"It was my pleasure, Ahmed, but you know she did it all by herself with her grades and smarts."

"So, Greg my friend, what can I do for you?"

"Without being too much the proud papa, and just between us, I think my son Michael has discovered something very interesting and important both scientifically and politically." The day before, Michael had an intuition to not tell his dad about the real reason to build the megadam, which was to recreate a new Garden of Eden. Michael knew his dad was prone to indiscretions, but he and Ariana had to tell someone and both thought it would not do any harm, so they had gone ahead. At the time, Michael thought, *if you can't even keep a secret in the Foreign Service, what good are you?*

"Sounds interesting, Greg. In fact, I would be pleased to tell you our latest, as yet unpublished, finds from the Qarun Lake excavation. I think you will be astonished and impressed with what we've found. It will be like old times."

"Michael believes he found the true location of the Biblical Garden of Eden." Greg wanted to strike while the iron was hot and just blurted it out. He was itching to be the one to break the news to a prominent archeologist. He had no intention of telling Michael or Ariana about his discussion with Morsi.

Morsi just laughed, "Yes, Michael and everyone else. For hundreds of years scholars had been talking about the location of the Garden, if there ever really was such a thing."

Part II

The Age of Aquarius

When the moon is in the Seventh House
And Jupiter aligns with Mars
Then peace will guide the planets
And love will steer the stars
This is the dawning of the age of Aquarius
Age of Aquarius
Aquarius
Aquarius

The Fifth Dimension

Chapter 11

Tel Aviv, Israel Two Weeks Later

"Shabbat shalom," said Larry Lipman. It was Shabbat and Larry was visiting his brother-in-law, Adam Levy, at his house in Tel Aviv. The women were preparing the Friday night meal and it was nearly sundown. The ancient ritual was a most important one, and although Larry and his family were of the Reformed sect of Judaism, he wanted to be sure his children would have the reverence and respect to carry on the traditions that had held the Jewish people together for so many generations. Early that day, Adam Levy, who was the CEO of the National Water Carrier in Israel, went to the water distribution center like everyone else to bring home the life-giving water. Adam strongly believed he had to set the example for everyone in this time of crisis.

Adam's family had aligned with the Orthodox tradition when they moved to Israel, so there were some more complicated practices in the Talmud that were not so familiar to his brother-in-law, Larry and family.

Candles were lit, hymns were sung, Kiddush was recited over the wine, ritual handwashing was done for bread or challah. Shabbat prayers were said and tonight, a special prayer thanking God for the life-giving water was recited as had been done since the parting of the Red Sea during the time of the Exodus.

"Blessed are You, L-rd our G-d, King of the universe, by Whose word all things came to be." In this time of water emergency, Adam added, "We humbly beseech you, L-rd our G-d, to bring back the rains and fill our wells with water." The room was still with everyone's eyes closed, thirsty and silently praying for water. At each place setting there was a glass of water ¾ full, emphasizing how precious the daily water ration had become.

Adam's youngest son, Caleb, was a bit ADHD and was always running, climbing, throwing things and playing. He was a handful. Today was no exception, and Caleb was squirming in his seat, arms and legs flailing about while he shouted and laughed. Business as usual, but this day, with Larry and family visiting, Caleb managed to stand up on his chair, pulling the tablecloth slightly and spilling his water, a scene repeated in millions of households all over the world. When Adam's wife, Eva, saw the precious water spilled on the tablecloth, she burst into tears and ran from the room. Adam patiently told Caleb to sit back down and behave, then he went to comfort his wife. "I have to go talk to Eva," said Adam, excusing himself from the table.

"Water is more expensive than wine," she cried. "We just can't go on like this."

"The L-rd will provide for us," said Adam. "He has a plan."

The families began to eat the Shabbat meal. The usual dinner conversation proceeded with small talk about the weather and local events. Of course, the elephant in the room was the current water crisis.

Adam spoke up, "When I moved here twenty years ago, I never in my wildest dreams thought there would be such a severe drought. No matter what we do or how fairly the water distribution is organized, people resent us, well… me, and think they are being cheated out of their rightful share. Every day the violence gets worse. People, children are dying and there's nothing I can do about it. There's more of a distribution system on the black market than from the government. Not only that, but I have been getting death threats several times a week."

"You never told me that," said Adam's wife.

"I didn't want to scare you," said Adam. "I can deal with threats on my own life, but not my family. I've hired armed guards to keep an eye on us, 24/7." Silence for nearly a minute at the table.

"Well, maybe you could buy water from Egypt? They seem to be getting more with global warming and the increasing rainfall in Central Africa," said Larry.

"Brilliant! All we have to do is build a 300-meter diameter pipeline from the Nile to Jerusalem and then arrange for the Egyptians, who dislike us by the way, to sell us all the Nile River water."

"You don't have to get nasty; I'm just trying to keep an open mind and think outside the box." said Larry.

"Sorry, Larry, but you know how long I've been struggling with this issue. And my friends in the Knesset just want to pretend we, or really, I, can have it all under control so they can focus on their parochial issues, like settlements and rocket attacks. I'm starting to wear out. I've had it."

"You're not thinking of moving back home, are you?" They had just heard what Adam's wife said.

"No, this is our home now. I'm just at wit's end. There must be a solution somehow." Adam's sincerity and struggle touched Larry deeply. But he was no better equipped to think of solutions than anyone else.

It was a week later. Larry and family were still at Adam's house in Tel Aviv. Adam was just home from work when a large angry crowd of Palestinians gathered outside his residence. They were shouting threats and throwing rocks at the house. Eva was scared and said, "What are we going to do?"

"We're going to call the police," said Adam. "Eva, take everyone to the basement and lock the door."

"You may not have time for that," said Larry. "They're threatening to burn the house down."

"Yeah, I hear 'em." Adam was frustrated, exhausted and angry. The two security guards stood by the doorway to push back any attempt to break into the house. Although some of his neighbors installed security bars on the windows, Adam resisted being a prisoner in his own home while the real criminals had total freedom. In a moment of anger and panic, Adam grabbed his AR-15 and went out the front door. As he did, a man in the crowd threw a Molotov cocktail through the front plate glass window and the living room erupted in flames. Larry ran for the fire extinguisher and began spraying out the flames.

Adam saw the man do it and watched as another man readied to throw a second one.

It was another five minutes before the police showed up. Arrests were made but the damage was done.

Meanwhile, Larry was getting the flames under control. Adam went back inside and helped douse the furniture and curtains that were still smoldering. Larry's hands were shaking. He looked at Adam and said, "Maybe we should think about heading home."

"Good call," said Adam. "This place is not safe, obviously. I have to think about what to do to get my family out of here. Just don't know where to go."

"Are you alright?" said Larry.

"Yeah…." Adam just hung his head.

Chapter 12

Boston, Two Weeks Later

Michael was now in his element since he was focusing on building the largest dam in the world. Although the discoveries of the past few days were intoxicating, for both Michael and Ariana, what Michael wanted his whole life was an opportunity to plan a civil engineering project so massive and grand that it would go down in history as one of the wonders of the modern world. He finally had that chance, as long as the politics and finances of the modern world didn't derail the whole idea.

Ariana was just as excited as Michael and was often now at his apartment. She spoke to her cousins and simply told them that this affair was a once in a lifetime. She loved Michael, trusted him and was thrilled to be a part of their megadam project. She told them she hoped they would not tell her family.

The first thing, of course, was to scope out the project. How high does the dam have to be and what is the resulting area of the rivers and Lake Eden. If Michael was right about the location, and that was far from confirmed, then how long would the dam have to be? The engineering calculations would follow for water pressures at the base of the dam and how big the bypass channels would have to be to dry out the river bed of the Nile (*the Nile River, are you kidding?*) so the dam could be constructed. All of these questions would bear on the practical engineering and the financing for the project.

Michael sat down to get started and began by examining the Nile River in the area that looked best for the dam.

The problem with the site originally suggested by Ariana was that, although there are mountains on both sides of suitable height to contain the water, the length of the dam would have to be over 50km in this area. *It's like I'm trying to build the Great Wall of China*, thought Michael, *we have enough trouble building it high enough, let alone making it that long. What am I thinking?*

He ended up thinking that another site just a few miles south would be better. This area had the same high cliffs on either side, but it required a length of only 23km. *Only*, thought Michael. *Ha… whoever heard of such a thing. I need to do some more research and thinking before I go off proposing something like this. They'll laugh me out of the profession.*

He decided to spend some time in the library doing background research on the various types of dams and what each technology was best suited for. Although the journals could mostly be accessed online, the books and maps were best viewed in the library building itself. So, he drove over and found a quiet study cube back in his favorite corner. Based on the topo maps, in order to refill Lake Eden, the megadam would have to be over 900 feet high. *That's basically the height of the Empire State Building*, thought Michael, *and it has to be 23km long at that height.*

Engineering the megadam involved finding out the flow of the Nile so as to design the bypass tunnels, determining the height of the dam to cause the Nile waters to flow into the Old Euphrates riverbed, estimating how long it would take to blast out enough rock for the dam structure, and figuring out a way to build and operate automated machinery along with the in-situ calcination facilities.

Michael next decided to talk to his high school friend's father, Walt Jay, who was a VP at Caterpillar. Steve Williams, Michael and Ariana got on a Zoom call with Walt Jay.

The ideas and specs were discussed for the dam building equipment. Michael's goal in this introductory meeting was to gauge the feasibility of making automated equipment that would build the dam. Michael was careful to mention that they would be competing for the Water Challenge offered by the Israeli Government, so expense to develop this huge version of equipment was not an issue.

"This is the goal of the project," said Steve. "A dam across the Nile River large enough to fill the main river of the delta and refill the lake that used to exist at the Qattara Depression."

"Ambitious project," said Walt with a touch of incredulity in his voice. "Ok, just so I understand, we need a number of major projects to be done to start work on the dam."

"Let me talk to my team and we'll get back with you in a couple of weeks or so with some concept sketches."

Walt's boss at Caterpillar, the CTO, was a man who reached this lofty position by politics, not by exceptional technical skills or ability to innovate. As often happens, nepotism trumps performance. George Jeffries took a dim view of anything new. He loved the status quo as well as his lofty salary and was not afraid to demote or fire people who disagreed with him. New proposals rarely got more than a glance. He got away with this attitude primarily due to political momentum. George had the unfortunate affliction of a severe facial tic. It would sneak up on him and make a sort of right eye winking spasm and then, as if in answer, winky George would wink the left eye on purpose, just so it didn't look too out of control. His direct reports had endless fun winking whenever they referred to him.

"George, I have something I want to show you," said Walt the day after the conference call. "Some folks from MIT want to automate the building of a huge dam to solve the drought crisis in the Mideast."

"What's in it for us?" said George, cynically.

"Could be substantial profit as well as a piece of the action." Walt was prepared for pushback.

"We're an equipment company, not a venture capitalist. We don't take risks with a client." Once again, George was close-minded and uninterested. "We're swamped with new equipment designs, can't spare the engineering time."

"This project could save millions of lives. At least let them present to us." Walt persevered.

"Well... one hour, that's it," said George. "And don't make any commitments without my approval."

"Thank you, sir." Walt was convinced that if Michael could present a compelling story, George might relent and go for it. Walt maintained his position in the company by not going against his boss. This time would be no exception.

The day of the presentation, Walt had his team, George Jeffries and Mort Cohen, the CEO of Caterpillar, in the conference room for the presentation. George was a few minutes late and Walt's team was busy winking at each other prior to George's arrival. Mort was the last one to arrive.

"Mort, what are you doing here?" said Jeffries.

"I heard there was something interesting going on," said Cohen. Jeffries just looked at Walt with a disapproving stare followed by a series of winks. He suspected Walt went around him and invited Cohen behind his back and was furious. Walt bit his tongue hard to keep from laughing, but his direct reports were not so well behaved.

"I'd like to introduce Michael Walters and Steve Williams from MIT who will present a proposal for a new automated dam building technology to address the drought crisis in the Mideast." Walt began the meeting.

This was Steve's presentation and he began by explaining the 30,000-foot view of the project. "I'd like to show you what we have in mind for accomplishing the building of the megadam in the minimum possible time. As you know there is life and death urgency to getting this project accomplished." Slides showed the various pieces of machinery mounted on rails along with construction offices and sleeping quarters that moved with the crushers, in-situ calcination equipment and conveyors as the dam was built.

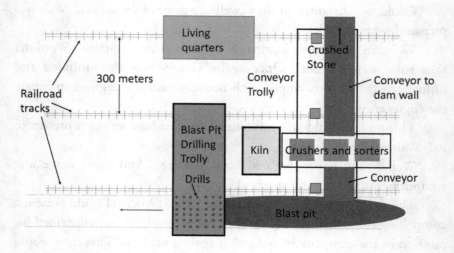

Earthen Dam Construction Equipment

"Question, how big is this dam?" Jeffries was playing like he didn't know the answer. The size of the dam was mentioned by Steve at the outset.

"It is to be 15 miles long and nearly 1000 feet high."

"Is that all?" Jeffries laughed, but no one else did.

"Sir, if you look at these calculations, we think that automation is the key to …"

Jeffries turned to talk to Cohen, interrupting Steve, and then made some coughing and snorting sounds as he said, "I didn't know they have a drug problem at MIT."

"I've heard enough. We have real work to do. This meeting is over," said Jeffries.

Michael and Steve just looked at each other, crestfallen, and then at Walt. Cohen said nothing but did not look pleased. The executives as well as most of Walt's team just got up and started to walk out. There were some members of Walt's team that were cronies of Jeffries and didn't want to offend their boss's boss.

Michael could never understand why so many people reject his ideas and inventions. Deep down inside he felt that he was way ahead of the crowd in his thinking and that the only reason people rejected his bold new concepts was because of their pride, hubris and unwillingness to admit that someone else may have a better understanding of the problem. This way of thought led to a general mistrust of other technologists. Exceptions to this are those few gifted individuals who Michael considers personal heroes. In dealing with his heroes, Michael defers to them a bit more than is prudent, mostly due to their proven record of accomplishment.

When it was just Steve, Michael and Walt, Michael said, "Ok, what now?"

Walt was furious and said, "You did a great job with this presentation. I've been dealing with this guy for 15 years. But I learned from my mentor years ago that the best way to deal with this is with a skunkworks effort. What he doesn't know won't hurt him, and it won't hurt me either. Give me a month or so to pull a team together and I'll get back to you." This was not the first such world changing skunkworks project in a large corporation. The UNIX operating system had been developed at Bell Labs as a skunkworks, under the radar, development begun with lunchtime sketches on the back of a napkin some fifty years earlier.

Michael and Steve left the building having learned Politics 101 for corporations, large and small.

Another fallout of Michael's way of thinking is that he has no tolerance for mediocrity. Although he does his best to keep his expectations of everything and everybody as low as possible to prevent being disappointed, deep inside he resents people who don't demand excellence from themselves and others. This is another aspect of personality that has led to few close friendships for Michael and much more infatuation-based relationships with women than deep and abiding bonds.

True to his word, a month later there was a conference call with Michael and Steve. Walt showed a sketch of the layout of the equipment that illustrated what new machines would have to be developed.

"Ok, let me just go over the general concept of operation and the specifics of the new or modified equipment we are expecting to design," said Walt.

"The basic idea is to build an earthen dam much larger than anything that has ever been done before. We will build the dam from both sides simultaneously, so we will have the construction equipment shown in this figure on both sides." Walt showed a drawing of the equipment they were planning to develop.

"We have the development of this new equipment under the capable hands of Bill Wong, our Director of R&D. Bill, why don't you take them through your plans."

Somehow, Jeffries found out about the skunkworks project and meeting, as it is very hard to quash watercooler conversation and his cronies were like spies in the organization.

"I specifically told you we are not working on this!" shouted Jeffries at the staff meeting next morning.

"Not so fast, George." Cohen had been aware of the project and paying close attention. "I think there's great potential for automated water management equipment, especially now with all this climate change. Tell you what guys, I have a special kitty for new projects that aren't part of our usual business model. Walt, why don't you take a few of your best guys and treat this as a sort of research project. See what you can come up with." Michael and Steve heard this whole story from Walt several days later, that Cohen had family in Israel and they were struggling along with everyone else. He was anxious to help them.

Chapter 13

Boston, Two Months Later

Ariana, with Henry intrigued, was confident enough to bring the megadam concept to Whitelock now that the engineering, concrete and equipment plans had started to materialize. As customary, she scheduled a meeting with the partners and now the day had arrived for the presentation.

"Good morning, everyone and thank you for coming. Today we are pleased to have Michael Walters and Steve Williams from MIT who will discuss their bold new plan to address the water crisis in the Middle East. Full disclosure, Michael and I have been seeing each other for several months now, but I assure you, this idea is very novel and world class, just the kind of venture that Whitelock has built its reputation on."

There were smiles and glances exchanged during this last disclosure, but Whitelock was a very profit-oriented firm, and conflict of interest was the least of their concerns.

"Are you suggesting that this concept might actually compete for the Water Challenge?" Henry Pitt, Ariana's boss, asked, looking to lead the rest in the right direction and glancing briefly at Ariana.

"Well, yes, but the $100,000,000 is chump change compared to the potential for this project. I believe you will be pleasantly surprised. So, without further introduction, Michael and Steve, the floor is yours."

Michael began the presentation. "With climate change raging in the Middle East, there are essentially three sources of water to deal with the severe drought conditions; ground water from the aquifer which was stored there thousands of years ago, water from the Danube River before it becomes contaminated with saltwater after draining into the Black Sea, and the Nile River."

He went on to explain that the underground aquifer could be tapped, but, as in Saudi Arabia, it gets depleted; so that is not a long-term strategy. There is an enormous amount of water in the Danube River, and it is essentially wasted by flowing into the Black Sea which is salt water. However, a pipeline or canal over 2000 feet in diameter and 1000 miles long would be required to bring that water to Israel. Even with current civil engineering technology, that is far-fetched. There were knowing smiles around the room.

"Why couldn't we repurpose the oil tankers and just haul the water from the Black Sea to Haifa?" One of the junior partners was trying to make an impression.

"That is a great question," said Ariana. "It could be done, but there is no way to guarantee that the price would not skyrocket once Israel becomes dependent on Danube water." Henry had a hint of a smile at Ariana's well thought out response.

"That leaves the Nile," said Michael. "Recently Ariana and I discovered what we believe is the vestige of a major tributary of the Nile that ends in what was once a large freshwater inland lake. Four major oases still exist along this ancient waterway, which was fed by the Nile during the period of time when the Sahara Desert was green. These oases are replenished by the aquifer extending west from the Nile along the now dried up riverbed."

"The Sahara has been drying out since the time of the last glacial maximum, 18,000 years ago," said Ariana. "Our proposal is to refill this lake and create a lush tropical garden area as it was so long ago. Such a project would allow fruits and vegetables to be grown over a vast area similar to the agricultural areas in southern California, which are partially fed by water from the Colorado River and the Hoover Dam.

"I'll turn the meeting over to Steve Williams to explain how we propose to do this."

"Thank you, Ariana." Steve began to explain how the water level in the Nile was once much higher, especially during the annual floods and that was how the pyramids were constructed, according to Michael's recent dissertation.

Steve continued, "Here is a satellite topo map of the region showing the ancient riverbed, the Giza Plateau and the Qattara Depression, an area that is below sea level similar to Death Valley in the American West. We believe that this depression was once a large inland freshwater lake, fed by four Nile tributaries as suggested in the Book of Genesis from the Judeo/Christian Bible." Steve pointed to the Euphrates, Pison, Hiddekel and Gihon/Nile. He flashed the next picture on the screen which showed a closeup of the area of the proposed megadam.

"Our proposal," chimed in Michael, "is to build a dam high enough and long enough to cause the Nile waters to flow into the ancient 'Old Euphrates' riverbed and refill the Qattara Depression, which we are calling 'Lake Eden' after the Biblical Garden of Eden." Michael pointed to the megadam site and the area where the Nile connected to the Old Euphrates River.

"How long would such a dam have to be?" Henry Pitt again. "And how high would it have to be?"

"We figure the dam would have to be 23km or about 15 miles long and 300 meters or 1000 feet high." The room erupted in laughter.

"Is that all?" another partner laughed.

Ariana was a bit flustered, although ready for the questions. "If you'll just give Michael and Steve a chance to explain, I'm sure you will understand." There was a sharpness in her tone that gave away her ire at being laughed at.

For his part, Michael was not at all flustered, he was angry. The experience with his dissertation defense made him determined not to back down again, no matter how influential his audience might be. *Not this time!* He thought.

"I'd just like to point out," said Michael, "that the Great Pyramid of Cheops is constructed of two and a half million blocks of stone each weighing over twenty tons. Compared to this structure, what we are proposing is trivial, and yet there it stands from 10,000 years ago when none of our modern technology was available." The room got quiet and all eyes were on Michael and Steve.

Michael and Steve proceeded to explain their technology and plan for building the megadam. They were peppered with questions from the room.

"What is this 'in-situ calcination' and how does that help?" said one of the junior partners.

"That's a great question," said Steve. "Does anyone know who invented cement?"

Silence from the room. "The answer is it was discovered, not invented. The Romans found this rock-hard ash from the Mount Vesuvius eruption when Pompeii and Herculaneum were destroyed. It was at the seashore and only formed where the ash was in contact with the sea water. It turned out that some of the ash was limestone sedimentary rock that was blasted out when the volcano erupted. The heat calcined the limestone and made cement. The Romans then learned to build limekilns to do the same thing with limestone from quarries. And that is what we do today. My patent is to take some of the rock blasted out of the path of the dam face and put it into a kiln in real time as the rest of the rock is forming the dam rock wall. Then when the water rises behind the dam, it will glue the rocks together. This allows the entire process to be automated and avoids the cooling pipes required at the Hoover Dam."

"Brilliant," said Henry.

"Ok, so you automate the blasting, calcining and conveying process to build an earthen dam of rock. What type of rock is there at this dam site?"

"Good question." Michael was ready. "As you might imagine, this area was once flooded when the Nile was much higher and wider. So, the lithographic maps show sedimentary rock, mostly limestone, which is perfect for the in-situ calcination technology."

"Isn't there a dam already there at Aswan?" Henry Pitt again with leading questions.

"Yes, sir, but it is nowhere near high enough or strong enough to raise to the height needed. And... there's one other thing." This was the part that Michael was trying to get to.

"Go on."

"The Russians built the Aswan Dam over a period of ten years in the 1950's, displacing more than 50,000 people to create Lake Nasser. When the dam was originally planned, the technology was not as sophisticated as today. But there are problems."

"How so?"

"Well sir, the Aswan Dam is sited on a major fault line, one of the few active fault lines in the region." Michael was measured in his response since he expected the reaction.

"Preposterous, even the Russians aren't that clueless." The tall partner sitting near the front of the table was incredulous and his body language said it all.

Steve spoke up. "As many of you know, the region around the Nile River and the Red Sea is known as the Afar Triangle. It is where the Arabian, African and Indian tectonic plates come together. This region is a very active seismic site and has been for many millennia. In fact, some believe the great plagues at the time of Moses and the Exodus were the result of volcanic eruptions there."

Exodus 7:17

[17] Thus saith the LORD, In this thou shalt know that I am the LORD: behold, I will smite with the rod that is in mine hand upon the waters which are in the river, and they shall be turned to blood.

"A tsunami accompanying an earthquake could have actually parted the Red Sea enabling the Israelites to escape."

Exodus 14:21

[21] And Moses stretched out his hand over the sea; and the LORD caused the sea to go back by a strong east wind all that night, and made the sea dry land, and the waters were divided.

"Hmmf..." Heads around the room turned to each other. They were clearly impressed with the research that had been done and now were listening closely.

Michael said, "We think that the Aswan Dam may have been damaged by the earthquakes in the region. In April of 2021 a magnitude 3.1 quake hit Aswan itself. And in November of 1995 there was a magnitude 7.2 quake at Nuweibaa in Saudi Arabia that was felt throughout the region."

Ariana added, "We believe that at some point the Aswan Dam could give way, flooding the area and killing millions. It will have to be rebuilt and strengthened anyway. In fact, very recently there was a major deluge that hit Libya and several dams in the region broke, killing over 10,000 people. So, it can happen."

"Interesting…This is a huge project. How do we know that, with the climate change initiatives, the whole problem won't just go away?" The tall partner sitting in front was hoping to do an end run around the Water Challenge. "I've read that with the initiatives already underway, this whole thing might be reversible."

Michael said, "Why, when the area is covered with white snow and ice, is it called Greenland?"

Silence from the room. He had them. "In around 900 CE, there was a climate change known as the Medieval Warming Period. The snow and glaciers disappeared from the island and when the Vikings discovered it, they were able to colonize and farm the area. This lasted until about 1300 CE when a period known as the Little Ice Age happened, restoring the glaciers on Greenland and forcing the Vikings to abandon their colonies there. When the Little Ice Age ended in around 1850, the higher temperatures at the end of the growing season allowed a potato fungus to cover Ireland resulting in the Great Famine."

Steve added, "We have made some good observations on climate change here on earth, but we know very little about the sun and its atmosphere. Some believe the sun is responsible for these climate blips, but we don't have enough science yet to predict them."

Ariana, "Of course we are still coming out of the last ice age, so although the greenhouse gases are contributing, they are not the only cause of global warming. So no, we do not believe mankind can reverse these trends."

There was a lot of head nodding around the room. Ariana said, "Are there any further questions?" Silence. Everyone turned to look at Henry.

"Thank you for this proposal," said Henry Pitt. "I think you may just have something here." It was abundantly clear that Henry, who had just the hint of a smile, had something in the back of his mind but wasn't ready to discuss it yet.

"We would like to thank everyone for your attention and time today," said Ariana. The meeting ended and everyone filed out. Ariana would catch up with each of them throughout the day. Michael and Steve headed back to campus, completely unaware that the success of the meeting had turned on Ariana's compelling discussion with Henry.

Chapter 14

Cairo, Egypt

Although Morsi laughed at Greg's assertion that Michael had found the Biblical Garden of Eden, he was determined to explore the area. In a few weeks after Greg's call with Morsi, he had all the equipment and personnel arranged for the roughly 250-mile trip to the archeological site at the Qattara Depression.

By the end of the following week, a dig had been established at locations found by Morsi's student Aya. The excavation began in earnest and soon some unexpected discoveries were made that immediately rocked the scientific world.

Australopithecines had been found in East Africa near fault lines that exposed much older layers, but never in the desert of North Africa and never in layers cohabited with Cro-Magnon modern humans. *Could these creatures have been enslaved by the inhabitants of the Lake Eden region?* thought Morsi.

They were digging in site 4C when this find was made, which was even more shocking since it would have been more logical to find these skeletal remains in the much older 4A and 4B locations when the lake was much larger. *So, what are we going to find there?* He thought. *Maybe we will go back to the site that is presumably the oldest, when the lake was largest.*

It was on day five of the excavation of site 4A. About 6 feet of overburden sand had been removed and the students were just beginning to see evidence of some rock formations that could have been made by humans or hominids of some sort.

"Professor, look over here!" Aya shouted with her usual enthusiasm, and Morsi came running over. "It looks like some sort of cave or something."

A vertical opening in the bedrock was visible partially filled with sand. The students were carefully digging out the sand and sifting it for artifacts. As more sand was removed, it became clear that this was the opening to an underground cave. It was not clear whether the cave had been excavated by the inhabitants of the area, but it appeared to go back into the bedrock for some distance.

"Aya, would you like to be the first inside since it is your discovery?" Morsi was the consummate university professor, always aware of the need to encourage his students and to give credit where it was due.

Aya took the light Morsi handed to her and ducked into the cave entrance. "Professor, it goes way back and down deep."

Morsi followed her into the cave entrance and was awestruck by the size of the cavern visible inside.

"This may be the most important thing we've found yet," said Morsi. "Looks to me like this was formed by the water of the ancient lake seeping through the limestone. "Let me have a line so we don't get lost in here like Tom Sawyer and Injun Joe," a reference to the famous book by Mark Twain about life on the Mississippi River. Morsi began walking down the sloped passage at the other end of the giant cavern. The passage was tight but Aya followed along staring at the rock formations and shinning the light all over the cave walls. The passage led to a cliff; a steeply sloped wall that didn't seem to have a bottom anywhere visible. Into the side of the wall there were foot holds carved. It almost looked like a path on the cliff wall, but much too steep to walk down. Morsi worried that they couldn't see the bottom and could easily fall to their deaths. "Aya, be careful. Don't go down there."

But she was young and adventurous. Aya began to climb down, shining the light into the darkness. As she took her first step, her foot slipped from the foot hold and she began to slide uncontrollably down the steep wall, wet with condensation. The path was actually a sort of sliding board carved into the cliff wall. It was extremely slippery and she helplessly tried to grab onto the footholds with no success as she slid further and further into the darkness, winding around a large limestone rock formation that appeared to be a giant stalactite. After sliding for what seemed like minutes, she shot out onto the damp cave floor.

Above her from the ledge Morsi was shouting, "Aya, are you alright?"

"It's a sliding board and there's water down here." She shouted. As she got up and started to walk along the path, each step created a flash of light, bioluminescence from algae on the rock formation. A few steps further led to a large pool of groundwater. "Who would believe it," said Aya. "A swimming pool in the middle of the biggest desert on the continent!"

The water was absolutely crystal clear and perfectly still. As she shown the light into the water, she saw the bottom of the pool, only a few feet deep. *What in the world is that?* She thought. On the bottom of the pool there was a webbed foot print, quite large, in the silt. The print showed the heel and toes, human like, but there was webbing between the toes and the toes were very long and thin. She snapped some pictures and then it began to dawn on her that she was in a cave at the bottom of a steep cliff with no way to climb out. "Professor, how do I get out of here?" she shouted.

No response. Morsi had gone back out to get some help and a rope to get her out of there. The panic began to set in, but still curious and buoyed by her discovery of the webbed footprint, she walked a bit further. The passageway led around the pool to a small opening giving onto another large cavern. Aya was snapping pictures furiously.

As Aya shown the light around the cavern walls she saw something that made her heart skip a beat. "Allahu Akbar," she said. "Is it even possible?"

The rock wall was covered with hand prints, and not just any typical Cro-Magnon hand prints like the cave at El Castillo, Spain. These were webbed like the footprint she just saw.

"Professor, I found something." said Aya. "Let me have a closer look." She walked up to the wall and shone the light directly onto the stenciled prints.

These are webbed hand prints here. Incredible! Most of them are left hands, thought Aya. *I guess that's what you would expect if the subject is right-handed. I do actually see one or two right hand prints, so they must have had a small percentage of lefties, just like us.* She took many pictures and then the full gut-wrenching panic set in. She decided she needed to find her way back out.

"Professor?" she shouted.

"Aya, where are you?" she heard Morsi's voice but because of the many passages and caverns, the sound was uncannily bouncing around the walls. She couldn't tell where it was coming from. At first, she ran in one direction, then another as the sound seemed to be getting further away. *Now, I can't even find my way back to the cliff*, she thought. Making matters worse, the light she was carrying was beginning to dim out. The batteries were draining. In the darkness, she cried.

"Aya, come here, I'll pull you up." She could hear Morsi calling, but couldn't find her way back, especially now with the dim light from the lantern.

The idea of trying to climb back up the slippery cliff was out of the question anyway, even with a rope. Her pulse quickened as she realized *I could be trapped down here.* She almost ran down the passageway, ducking into tunnel offshoots and finding them dead ends. After what seemed like an hour but was probably only fifteen minutes, she realized she wasn't going to be able to get back to the cliff wall at all. *Ok, ok* she thought. *Got to get more methodical. The only passage that seems to go anywhere is the one I'm in.* The tunnel sloped down making her believe she was going deeper into the earth. But on the walls, she saw drawings of fish and crabs in the dim light. *I'm not the only person who's ever been here*, she thought. *Just keep going*, her mind told her. As she walked 50 yards or so further, her heart racing and mouth dry, the passage seemed to level out and take a sharp right turn. She saw a tiny glimmer of light ahead just as the last of the lantern light went out. Another 30 feet and she saw rocks partially covering an opening to the outside. She pushed the rocks away and poked her head out.

"Hey everyone, I'm down here." She said as she felt a flood of relief. The students standing fully 150 feet above her near the top of the depression looked over and waved. "Professor, she's down there," one shouted to Morsi pointing down the hill.

Morsi looked at the pictures with the rest of the students huddled around the monitor. The palm part of the hand in every case was quite large and the fingers were correspondingly short. "I've never seen anything like this," said Morsi. "These prints do not look human, certainly not Cro-Magnon."

"It's almost like there's something between the fingers," echoed Aya. Her young and quick mind had made the leap in just a few seconds down in the cave. "Could it be webbing?"

"Mermaids?" said Morsi. "Preposterous!"

"No, you know the book by Elaine Morgan 'The Aquatic Ape Hypothesis' where she makes the argument that the reason we walk upright was not to see over the grass when we came down from the trees, but to get our noses up out of the water. If that's true, then maybe some species of aquatic hominids would have webbing on fingers and toes. But would they be living out here in the desert?" Aya was very skeptical.

"It wasn't a desert then," said Morsi. "But they might have been trapped in this lake surrounded by desert that they couldn't get through. This could be the last place on earth that this species actually lived. We need to look for skeletal remains, here in this cave and maybe in the dwelling places above."

"I saw cave drawings down there," said Aya. "We need to do much more exploring."

The aquatic form of primate, as opposed to chimps and gorillas, evolved many characteristics associated with water. Most aquatic mammals have lost their hair, can hold their breath and have some method of closing off their breathing hole, like dolphins and whales. If human ancestors were aquatic, it would explain the love of water, walking on two legs, loss of hair, the down turned nose to prevent water rushing into the lungs when diving, the ability to control breathing which then led to language and singing, and even crying is thought by some to be a way of ridding the body of extra salt when feeding on fish in salt water. Leboyer birth, where the child is born underwater and immediately swims, holding breath is another part of the Aquatic Ape Theory. Although rare, cases of webbing on fingers and toes are reported in humans but not on other primates. Chimps and gorillas hate the water, but humans will pay hundreds of thousands of dollars more for a house with a water view.

"Ahmed, Greg Walters." Another clandestine call to Morsi.

"Greg, how are you?" said Morsi. "Great to hear from you!"

Morsi practically shouted on the phone "Greg, I must tell you that your son, Michael, is a genius. We found places to dig in the vicinity of the ancient lake at the Qattara Depression, the one he is calling Lake Eden and we have made a most momentous discovery."

"Really? I must confess, I was a bit skeptical of finding anything at all. The site is so big, it's really just a guess. What did you find?" Greg was now very curious.

"We are still evaluating the age of the items, but it appears we have found evidence of an ancient aquatic hominin that lived near the lake. We found hand prints with webbed fingers and a footprint with webbed toes, just as the Aquatic Ape Theory predicts." Morsi explained that they had found a cave system similar to the Gara Cave at the Bahariya Oasis. It appeared that the cave actually connected to the lake providing an underwater route to the deeper part of the lake. Morsi's team also found an almost intact hominin skeleton that could be one of the aquatic species. The hands and feet had very long, thin bones as though to support the webbing seen in the hand prints on the cave wall. Some scientists believe this species could have mated with the Cro-Magnon species and is responsible for some of the differences in form between humans and chimpanzees. "This is the most exciting thing that's ever happened to me. And I owe it all to your son, Michael."

"So glad to hear it," said Greg. "And so will Michael."

Chapter 15

Boston and Saudi Arabia, One Month Later

Ariana had been very successful in her discussions with Whitelock's partners. Henry Pitt took the lead and began making calls to his investors in Saudi Arabia. They were fascinated and agreed to a Zoom call with Ariana and team, including the Crown Prince.

The call went very well with Michael, Steve and Ariana essentially repeating their presentation to Whitelock. The questions from the Saudis were a bit different in character, more political and less technical in nature.

"You expect Israel to just get up and leave their homeland of 3,000 years?"

"Well, yes, many of them, or die of thirst."

"Good point. But we still don't think it will be so simple. What about Jerusalem? That's their capital."

"Yes," said Ariana, "We have a plan for the City of Jerusalem as well as the Israeli and Palestinian lands around it. We are enlisting the aid of the UN to designate this whole area, including Jerusalem, a World Heritage Site under the auspices of a UN Protectorate. The Protectorate would apply to the Qattara Depression development as well, including the megadam."

"Really? How did you manage that? Of course, we would support it. We have been trying to get a multistate solution to the Palestinian question for decades." The Crown Prince was now fully on board. Unfortunately, the rest of the royal family not so much so.

"It is amazing what can be accomplished when there is a UN State of Emergency and people are dying of thirst."

The Saudi royal family was deeply divided. The Crown Prince and his allies were very progressive and wanted to use the great wealth of the oil revenue to make investments in property throughout the Middle East as a hedge against the rapidly approaching day when oil would not be needed to power the world economy.

Another, more conservative faction, enjoyed the status quo and believed it would continue on long after they and their children were gone. They bought yachts, threw lavish parties, built huge mansions and otherwise spent the oil money like it was nothing. This group had been angry with the Crown Prince and his allies for years. They resented the investments in the future, which limited their own wealth, and dreaded the day when the Crown Prince would become King, even though he was de facto King already. Throughout the long history of civilization, jealousy of the accession to the throne had led to political subterfuge and conspiracy. The House of Saud was no exception.

Saudi Arabia was one of the few fully functional monarchies of modern times. In the ancient tradition, the King would periodically have a "majlis" or royal open house where the people could come and petition the King. In 1975, King Faisal was assassinated by the son of his half-brother Prince Faisal during a majlis. Two bullets struck the King. He was quickly rushed to the hospital and doctors massaged his heart, but to no avail. The King died. It is widely believed the assassination was in response to the secular reforms implemented by King Faisal, including the abolition of slavery in 1962 and bringing television to the country in 1966. It is said that King Faisal had a dream just before his death that his deceased father came for him in a car and asked him to get in. Prescient dreams of assassinations and attempted assassinations are common among the monarchy throughout history.

Shortly after the call with Henry Pitt, the Crown Prince planned a majlis for the people to come with their petitions to the royal family. He wanted to take that opportunity to explain to the people his efforts at modernization and investment in the Middle East and share with them his enthusiasm for the new Qattara Depression Development to relieve the water crisis, especially for the Palestinians.

Unfortunately, the Crown Prince's enemies saw that as an ideal opportunity for an assassination attempt. But the Crown Prince had a dream the night before the majlis. In the dream, he was at the bottom of a well. He kept calling for help but no one heard him. In the morning, he awoke sweating and terrified. The dream, as well as the family history of assassination during the majlis, convinced him to wear a bullet proof vest that day.

As he was at the podium explaining the new Qattara Development Project, two shots rang out and he was knocked to the ground. His bodyguards quickly captured the assassin and as his aids ran to him, he sat up, shook his head and laughed. "So much for assassins," he said. Then he stood up and finished his speech. Many in the audience never forgot how the Crown Prince described a future that could include peace and acceptance. And the attempted assassination only emphasized that Allah was supporting this new idea because the Crown Prince was not injured at all and seemed more vibrant than ever as he continued to share his personal support for the megadam.

Once Henry had the support of the Saudis, he felt it was time for a Water Prize pitch directly to the Israelis. A call was made to Adam Levy and a trip was arranged for Ariana, Michael and Steve to go to Tel Aviv.

"We're going to Tel Aviv to pitch for the Water Prize" said Michael to his father Greg, his voice filled with passion. You and Mom are welcome to come along if you like."

"Yes, I have an old squash buddy who's related to the CEO of the National Water Carrier," said Greg. "I'll give him a call and let him know we're coming."

When Michael's dad was much younger and stationed in Washington, DC, he was a member of the Sport & Health Club on G Street in the city. He was an avid squash player in those days and there was a small group of men, about his age that played squash twice a week at the club.

Michael's dad became very close friends with one of the fellows in his squash group, named Larry Lipman. They often entertained each other's families at dinner parties, or went out to dinner at a local restaurant in North Potomac. Larry's sister and brother-in-law had decided some years ago to accept a job in Israel and they moved their family there, hoping to find happiness and opportunity. Larry's grandmother and grandfather on his mom's side were both Russian Jews who left the country during the time of the great Pogrom of 1903 to 1906. Although Larry had a strong allegiance to Israel, he was happy in the U.S. and had no desire to move.

Larry's brother-in-law, Adam Levy, had done very well in Israel, rising to the level of CEO for the National Water Carrier. His sound knowledge of engineering, educated at Lehigh University, coupled with an uncanny sense for good business propelled him quickly up through the ranks. He was a no-nonsense guy, similar to his brother-in-law, but had a sunny disposition and positive attitude, especially when it came to new technology. Several times a year, Larry and family would journey to Tel-Aviv to see Larry's sister, giving his children a chance to experience Israel and all it has to offer.

The next day, Greg Walters picked up the phone to reconnect with his friend in Israel.

"Is this the Larry Lipman who plays squash?" Michael's dad had a familiar tone in his voice as he called his old friend.

"Yes, and you must be the squash player who I haven't heard from in 10 years." Larry instantly recognized Greg Walters' voice. "What can I do for you?"

"First of all, how are you? How's the family?"

"Everyone's great! The kids are getting big and thinking they know everything. Speaking of kids, Michael should be working on his PhD by this time."

"Well, that's sort of why I called. Michael's working on his PhD in Civil Engineering, and he's discovered something interesting. He thinks he has a solution for the water emergency in Israel. He and his team are going to Tel Aviv to pitch to the National Water Carrier in a week or so."

"Oh, that's great. Congratulations. The situation here is horrible."

Isn't your brother-in-law high up in the National Water Carrier company?"

"Yes, actually he's CEO."

"Maybe you could put in a good word for Michael; he's really excited and from what I hear, he's onto something big."

"Believe it or not, I brought my family here to Tel Aviv to visit Adam for the High Holy Days this year. We are still here. Why don't you come along and I'll arrange a dinner with Adam to give him a heads up before the formal pitch?"

"Larry, sounds like a plan. You're a gem." Greg hung up the phone, excited. It's as the old saying goes, *it's not what you know, it's who you know.*

The first person Michael called was his old Temple of World Faith buddy, Abdul. "Hey Abdul, we're going to Tel Aviv. We finally got approval from Ariana's company to pitch to the Israelis for the Water Prize."

"That's great news. Do you guys really think you can solve it?"

"I'm praying we can if they just give us the chance."

"How can I help?"

"Well, actually that's why I called. While we're there I would like to meet your niece, Bariah in the West Bank area. Do you think you could arrange an introduction? It will be very helpful to get an inside scoop from someone there on the ground."

"Absolutely. Let me know when you will be there and I will set it up. I am sure she would love to meet you two."

"Thanks buddy. You're the best. Ariana and I both think if we can get some first-hand experience of the water problem and how people are dealing with it, we can make a stronger presentation."

"I agree. They really need your help. I'll let you know."

Michael felt much more connected with the situation now that he talked to Abdul. He was looking forward to meeting Bariah face to face.

Chapter 16

Israel, One Week Later

They arrived in Tel Aviv at the end of the week, checked into the hotel downtown and called to let Larry know they had arrived safely. All the years of traveling gave Greg a feeling of home when he checked into the hotel.

"We made some dinner reservations for the nine of us at a great place called the West Side TLV. Best food on the coast and the views of the Mediterranean are amazing," said Larry on the phone.

"Larry, you're the best. I can't wait to see you and meet your sister and brother-in-law," said Greg.

"Well, we have someone watching the kids so it's just us adults. As you can imagine, we're really looking forward to an adult night out." Larry was quite sincere. The long stay with his sister was great for the family but could get a bit tedious with everyone crammed into the one house. The guards stationed conspicuously around the house did little to make everyone feel comfortable.

They all met at the West Side TLV restaurant on a Thursday evening just as the sun was going down over the Mediterranean. The sights and fragrances of spices wafting from the kitchen were intoxicating and the city of Tel Aviv was a modern wonder. The fact that the restaurant had plenty of water while the Palestinians stood in line to get a tiny ration each day was not lost on Greg or Michael.

"Greg, so happy to see you," said Larry and gave his old friend a big bear hug.

"You're looking well," said Greg. "You remember my son, Michael?"

"You've grown up since I saw you last." Michael towered over the 5'7" Larry. They shook hands warmly, then Larry introduced his sister and brother-in-law. "This is my sister Eva and her husband Adam."

"So glad to finally meet you," said Greg.

"I'm the girlfriend," said Ariana.

"Yeah, and I'm the wife," said Michael's mom.

"Me too," said Larry's wife Danielle. "Great to see you again, Sofia."

"And this is the brains of the operation, Steve Williams," said Michael.

The Maître d' showed them to a table at the window and they all sat down. "You weren't kidding about the views," said Greg. "This is magnificent."

"Nothing but the best for our friends," said Larry, smiling.

"Tell us about this lovely young lady, Michael," Larry said. "Have you two been together long?"

"We met just about six months ago. Ariana is an Associate Partner at Whitelock."

"Wow, you don't fool around," said Adam Levy. "They've done some huge projects with the Saudis."

"Michael and I met at a seminar at Harvard about ancient art in Egypt," said Ariana.

"Yes, and I've always had an interest in giant civil engineering projects," said Michael. "Dad took us to see the Hoover Dam when I was in high school and that really got me started." Michael couldn't wait to talk about their project.

"I'm all ears, Michael," said Adam.

Greg was beaming from ear to ear as Michael took over the conversation. Michael explained he was doing his research that suggested the Great Pyramid of Cheops was built using boats and the high level of the Nile during the floods to place the immensely heavy stones. He smiled when he described how one of his professors scoffed at the idea, basically saying that if the ancient Nile were that high, the whole country would practically be under water.

"But when I thought about it, I realized I had no idea whether he was right or not. I decided to follow-up as soon as possible. The good news is that the new satellites have allowed us to make detailed topo maps of the whole country. Here is the thing, when I looked at those maps, it was clear to Ariana and me that there was once a huge inland freshwater lake fed by Nile tributaries that stretched practically to the Libyan border. The lake would have been hundreds of miles long and would have been very deep in the area called the Qattara Depression. In fact, if you look at the locations of the various oases, they are just low spots in the ancient Nile tributary riverbed. They follow the old river exactly."

"Yeah, so there was a lake there 100 million years ago, so what?" said Larry.

"It gets more interesting," said Michael. "The Sahara Desert was not a desert at all as late as 10,000 years ago. That lake could have been there in some form only 5000 to 7000 years ago."

"Again, so what?" This time Adam Levy spoke up.

"The so what is, what if we could refill the lake?" Michael was watching their faces carefully as he said these last words. He cast a sidelong glance at Ariana, and she was holding back a smile.

"Ridiculous!" scoffed Larry. "There's not that much water on the whole continent of Africa."

"Hmmm…," said Adam. "The Nile's a huge artery that gets its water source from Central Africa, not some water that was stored underground 10,000 years ago like in Saudi Arabia."

Michael continued. "Yes, that's right and the water necessary to fill the lake can be collected over 10 or 20 years by taking a small part of the flow from the Nile. Also, global warming is shifting the rainfall away from the Sahara and more toward Central Africa, toward the Blue and White Nile sources, putting pressure on the underground aquifer of stored water, but not the source water from the Nile. As long as people in that region don't divert the Nile water, the amount flowing north into Egypt should increase, not decrease over the next few centuries."

"I'd like to get into the details of how this can be done, but I want my colleagues there for the formal presentation."

"That's what we're here for," said Michael. "Can't wait to show you what we found." Steve was quiet during this exchange, but he would be the main man the next day at the formal pitch.

"This is a social occasion and I think we're boring the ladies," said Larry. Of course, when Michael looked over at Ariana, she was anything but bored, and now her face showed she was slightly annoyed. But she kept her cool and decided she could show her colors tomorrow at the meeting.

"We're all ready for you," said Adam. "We have all the conference facilities if you want to bring PowerPoints or charts, whatever."

"Adam, I want to thank you very much for seeing us tonight before the meeting," said Greg.

"I have a feeling it's I who'll be thanking you," said Adam Levy.

The conversation turned to family and what each of Larry's kids was doing. Adam described his family and how everyone was doing in this time of drought and terrorism. Clearly the violence especially in the Palestinian territories was weighing on everyone's mind. Just to emphasize the point, outside the restaurant was a group of demonstrators protesting the water rationing, carrying signs and shouting at the patrons.

"We had an incident a little while ago where a crowd gathered outside our house and someone threw a firebomb through the front window," said Adam.

"Oh wow. Anybody hurt?" said Sofia.

"Well… not in my family at least. Thankfully, Larry was there. He put out the fire."

"You have armed guards?" asked Michael.

"The violence gets worse every day. No choice." Adam was a bit defensive but firm. "If I could, I would move Eva and the kids out of here."

"So do'ya ever regret moving here to Israel in the first place?" said Greg.

"Good question," said Adam. "For the most part, no. I feel like everyone here is actually family. And after being in the U.S. for several generations, it's a good feeling to be surrounded by people who are, and believe, like me.

"But I must confess, I had no idea how complicated the politics are in this country. Some of it's historical, some religious, but some comes from the time of the diaspora. We all learned different things in our separate countries and cultures. The pogroms, expulsions, and finally the Holocaust give each of us a somewhat different political view." Adam explained that the constant threat of annihilation from countries like Iran didn't help either. "Now the issue top of mind is the drought."

The waiter came and took their order. Adam continued.

"My job's unique in this country since the politics of water is considered a separate issue from the normal day to day problems that our politicians deal with. They expect me to care for these issues and I really don't have the authority or the resources to do it. That situation is the main reason I would have second thoughts about moving here now."

Adam launched into some background about the politics of water in the Middle East. Even as recently as 2000 years ago, at the time of the Roman occupation, there was far more water here in Palestine than there is now.

"But you're making fresh water with desalination, aren't you?" asked Michael.

"Yeah, but nowhere near enough, and it's very expensive and energy intensive, especially for a country with no oil reserves."

"And that, my young friend, is what makes your idea, if indeed it can be done, so intriguing. At our meeting tomorrow, I think you'll be surprised at the comments and suggestions you hear. Also, I have to warn you that not everyone will be receptive to your ideas. We have some who are opposed to anything that is dependent on other Arab countries."

The Palestinian Authority had begun organizing regular protests at the National Water Carrier building in Tel Aviv. Bus transportation was provided and various towns in the West Bank and Gaza areas regularly participated. Aashif and Bariah had come to know each other very well, especially after the incident with the thieves. Aashif was able to buy more food and some medicine for Bariah's mother and also some formula for his sister's baby. His bold action probably saved their lives. Despite keeping quiet about the incident, word spread through the city about what Aashif had done. His courage earned him the respect of many and so, when it came time to gather protestors to go to Tel Aviv, Aashif and Bariah were asked to join. They both believed that the Israelis were holding out on the Palestinian people with regard to the water ration and the black market made everyone angry. It was announced at the Center that there would be a bus on Friday to take demonstrators the 30 miles to Tel Aviv for protest, and they decided to go.

Aashif was thrilled that he would get to spend the morning alongside his friend Bariah with her shy crooked smile and large brown eyes. They boarded the bus in the town square and sat next to each other talking as the bus traveled to Tel Aviv. The conversation rambled on about Bariah's mom, who had been doing better in the last few weeks. Her bouts with Cholera sapped her strength, but the water that Bariah saved for her each day, along with the additional food and medicine from Aashif, helped to clean out her insides and let her immune system do the healing. Aashif was very glad to hear that she was on the mend. He told her that his sister Saabiya struggled each day and that the baby was sickly and weak. He wasn't sure she would make it, and he was furious that the government couldn't even see to it that a newborn baby got the water it needed to survive. He blamed the Israelis and was very glad they were going to protest, not that it would do much good, but he had to do something.

When the bus arrived at the National Water Carrier building, there was already a huge crowd gathered with signs and flags. The rumor was that there were meetings going on inside to try to find a way to resolve the crisis. A man with a bull horn was whipping up the crowd and apparently it was working because the anger and violence were escalating. A man threw a brick through the front window of the building and the crowd surged toward the door. Israeli police in riot gear arrived and began pushing the crowd back. Aashif was carried forward with the crowd, but then hit with a baton and forced back. The peaceful demonstration that Bariah and Aashif had expected came completely unraveled. People eventually began dispersing but not before throwing bricks and bottles at the police. The two young people headed back to the bus.

The ride back to Ramallah was subdued as people considered their predicament and tried to rationalize the injustice. They had no idea of what was happening inside the National Water Carrier building. There were even rumors of a bomb threat. Aashif was so much more receptive to terrorist activity as he learned just how lopsided the justice system was in the Palestinian territories.

Chapter 17

Tel Aviv, Israel

The meeting started promptly at 8am in a conference room near Adam Levy's office.

Outside the building a large crowd was gathered in protest of the water rationing. A man with a bullhorn addressed the protestors saying that rationing was not the solution. The group was boisterous with shouts and signs protesting the drought. As Michael's team entered the building and were scanned by security, Ariana said, "Hope this does not happen every day. Must get old for Adam. No wonder he is having stomach problems." Although Michael's dad was invited, he decided to sleep in, having enjoyed just a few too many "social" drinks the evening before. But despite his struggle, Greg's heart was in the right place. He only wanted to do the best for his family.

Michael and team were surprised at the number of people in attendance at the meeting. There were representatives from the Ministries of Agriculture and Rural Development, Construction and Housing, Economy and Industry, Energy, Interior, and the Prime Minister's office.

Adam Levy opened the meeting by introducing Michael, Steve and Ariana as old friends from America who have some very intriguing ideas on how to address the water crisis. He told them that Ariana was representing Whitelock Partners in Boston who was a lead investor in the project.

"Michael and his team have something to present to us today that, I think, you will find most interesting. Let's just go around the room to let him know each one of you and a bit about your background and responsibilities."

Each attendee introduced themselves and Michael did the same, introducing Ariana and Steve who were sitting next to Michael at the table.

Michael began by explaining how he started looking into this idea and some background about the history of the Western Desert in Egypt. I made a sketch of the area with a dam about 300 meters high." Michael flashed the map on the screen.

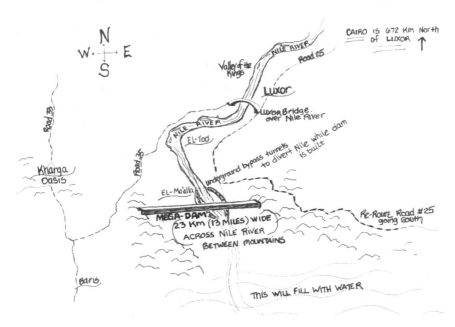

The representative from Agriculture and Rural Development spoke up when Michael put up the map. "I see several issues. Let me start by saying that no one, not even in America, has built a dam that high and that long ever before.

"Second, it will take many years to fill up this region and, in the meantime, the Nile flow will be seriously reduced, downstream.

"Third, the Aswan Dam will be inundated and potentially the oases sites as well.

"Fourth, for this to be financially viable, the upstream countries such as Sudan, South Sudan, Ethiopia, Burundi, Rwanda, the Congo, and Tanzania all must be included in any contractual arrangement and remunerated in order not to divert water from the Nile. This is similar to what happened in the various states in the U.S. with so called 'water rights' when the Hoover Dam was built.

"Fifth, and this is probably the most challenging, have you looked at evaporation rates from such a large body of water at that latitude?"

Michael responded "We have answers for all of your questions except the evaporation question. Let us discuss these one by one." Steve explained the technology of automated dam building being developed in conjunction with Caterpillar, using the In-Situ Calcination patent Michael had just filed. There was general head nodding and it seemed this might be one of the missing pieces in something that had already been considered.

"You've looked at the geology of the area and there is sufficient limestone to allow this to work?" The Minister of the Interior was taking nothing for granted.

"The Nile was once much higher and wider than it is now, so most of the rock is sedimentary limestone." Steve was well prepared for that question.

Michael explained the answers to the rest of the first four questions, including the fact that the Aswan Dam had been built on an active fault line.

"We've known that for years," said the Minister of Economy and Industry with a grimace.

"Lastly, to your concern about evaporation, the answer is no, not really. I haven't calculated the evaporation rates for a lake and river this size. But how much can it really be?"

The group snickered a bit and there was general murmuring.

"Rodney why don't you fill him in," said Adam to the representative from the Interior Ministry.

"Michael, I know we have a non-disclosure agreement in place, but I want to remind you not to divulge what we are about to tell you. And remember, this is not a criticism but rather a teaching opportunity. Please consider it a learning opportunity for you and your team.

Outside the demonstration continued full force. Palestinians, who were getting the worst of the water rationing, burned the Prime Minister of Israel in effigy, set fire to shops and threw rocks and bricks through the windows of government buildings. When there is government rationing, an underground economy springs up and the people with the most money get the most of the rationed item, same as the rationing in WWII. Resentment and violence quickly follow.

Michael and team were shocked and upset by the civil unrest but continued with the meeting. Steve thought, *why is the veneer of civilization so thin? Whenever something goes wrong, even in a place like Israel, people just ignore the law and behave like criminals.*

"At this latitude and with the desert relative humidity being so very low, we calculate the average evaporation rate to be about 50 liters per second per square kilometer. Now then, if we multiply that by the water area shown on your map after the dam is built, we have three quarters of the flow of the Nile lost to evaporation."

Michael's face took on the pallor of a white bedsheet. "That can't be right. How do any of these projects work in that case?"

"Exactly" said Rodney. "And that is the very reason we are going to disclose to you some of our latest technology."

"You may not be aware of this, but in Roman times the Kharga Oasis was the breadbasket of the Roman Empire." Rodney went on to explain that the oasis has dried up somewhat since then, but the secret to this irrigation system around Kharga was a series of underground aqueducts built by the Romans to move ground water around in the aquifer. The irrigation was then done by allowing this water to reach the surface in selected areas. This meant that the water would go to irrigating the fields and not be lost to evaporation.

"Today, we have much better pipeline and pumping technology that can be powered by solar energy, basically for free once the upfront investment is made. So, we would propose to have some areas of the ancient riverbed carry the water supplemented by underground pipelines along with the aquifer to move through higher elevation areas. That way you don't have to build your dam so high. That's one piece of the puzzle. I'm going to let Dr. Cohen take it from here." Avril Cohen was the representative from the Prime Minister's office.

Throughout the meeting the din from the crowd outside was a major distraction. The sound of gunfire caused Michael to give a violent start and the blood drained from Ariana's face as they realized this was a very violent place. More than once, Adam apologized for the disturbance. At one point, Steve leaned over and whispered in Michael's ear "Are you sure we're safe in here?"

Michael just shook his head and shrugged, not wanting to show his concern.

"Ok, not to come across condescending, but what is the purpose of this project?"

"It is to turn worthless desert into arable land for farming, housing, recreation and to solve the water crisis, I think," said Michael.

"Well…," said Cohen. "The purpose of this project, like every other project is also to make money." Ariana just smiled broadly. In her business with Whitelock, that was the "Golden" Rule.

"Well, of course," said Michael. "… that's the result."

"It is, but it is also an attitude about the project, how it is organized, planned and financed. If the goal is to make money, you may do things entirely differently. For example, if the lake you seek to build is 100km in diameter, the vast surface area of water in the middle of the lake generates almost no income and the losses to evaporation are huge. Think instead about a river that has a giant island in the middle of it, or multiple islands and branches. Let's say the rivers are 1 km wide and several hundred km long. The islands can be as big as is practical depending on the topography of the region."

"I have a topo map of the Qattara Depression," said Michael. He put the topo map on the screen.

Dr. Cohen went to the screen and used a marker to draw two huge circles on the Qattara Depression.

"Do you see the areas on your map that are a bit darker near the bottom of the depression, here? And also, on the northwestern face up here? I believe you could create a lake with islands in the middle and just a relatively narrow river surface all around them. These could be maybe 500 to 600 km long. This does two things. First it allows for the maximum lakefront or really riverfront development property. Second, it minimizes the surface area of the water, minimizing evaporation. So, you can see that an island in the middle of a body of water effectively doubles the available waterfront property, doubling the profits.

"By the way, you can't just fill up the lake and let it sit there as stagnant water. It will eventually become salty. So, we must use our underground piping technology to connect the northeast end of the river/lake to the Nile basin and keep some water exchange in the lake.

"And speaking of salt, in ancient times there was a river connecting the Qattara Depression Lake with the Nile in the northeast where you see what seems to be a riverbed. That kept the lake as freshwater. We need to emulate that with our pipeline."

The message was that when the river dried up in the ancient past, the lake became very salty. The dried lakebed today is covered with salt and even pillars of salt. This was not considered a problem but rather an opportunity to harvest and sell this salt all along the new river/lake bed. This salt is free, on the surface, so no mining would be needed, and it can be easily transported to market at Port Said by rail. "The profit from the salt harvesting along the proposed riverbed finances the salt removal, a win-win. By the way, salt is not just for eating and preservative. It is feedstock for chemicals needed to make batteries, a vital commodity nowadays."

Two important companies in Israel were already harvesting not just the sodium chloride from the sea salt in the Dead Sea, but also the rare earth minerals such as Molybdenum and even Gold. These have uses in metallurgy and microelectronics. "In fact, the revenue from harvesting rare earth metals and minerals dwarfs everything else from the salt readily available on the floor of the Qattara Depression," said Dr. Cohen. "There has also been a very important discovery in the Dead Sea salt. We have found recoverable amounts of lithium and we are just now developing methods of refining this metal at reasonable cost. In fact, I dare say that the cost of lithium obtained from the Dead Sea will be substantially less than from any other source."

Adam added, "We suspect that the salts from the Qattara Depression will have similar lithium content. As you know, the most powerful batteries are made of lithium."

Michael was thinking, *they couldn't have dreamed all of this up in the last hour. They must have been considering this as a solution all along and were just waiting on a critical piece of technology, like how to actually build this kind of dam. Massachusetts Institute of Technology to the rescue once again.*

Ariana was eager to contribute to the discussion. "This project is the Holy Grail, so to speak, of energy generation." She explained that if land along the lake/river is developed with private homes, restaurants, marinas, hotels, commercial buildings and so on, every structure could have solar roof tiles on the roof. A power company can finance the solar tiles and then manage the energy, storing some of it, transmitting some to the large cities like Cairo and along the Nile. Storage could be done by allowing the water level to rise and fall through some turbines as is done in pumped storage facilities, worldwide. This would supplement the power generated at the megadam site and would give the power authority a plethora of excess energy to sell to other countries in the region, all of it clean, green energy.

"The amount of money associated with this aspect of the project is enormous, another win-win." Ariana was beaming as she reinforced the minister's approach.

Michael spoke up next. "Aside from the obvious opportunity to build a mega resort that would be an international destination for business conferences and holidays, there could be a treasure trove of precious stones on the ancient lake bed. Keep in mind that the water flowing into the lake in antiquity came from the Sudan or Nubian area, famous for gold and silver, not to mention precious stones and, potentially, rare earth elements. This is similar to what's recently been announced in Liberia and Sierra Leon." These two countries in West Africa had just announced the largest diamond find in the world in the alluvial deposits near the coast.

Next it was Ariana who had a slide from Whitelock on the financial incentives, "Let's suppose there is 500 km on both sides of this lake/river for a total of 1000 km of riverfront land that could be developed. Twenty meters of waterfront property is a very nice developable lot. Just as an estimate then, there would be 50,000 lots of that size per river branch available. They could go for as much as $250,000 or more per lot. That's over 12 billion dollars just for the waterfront lots, on one river branch, not to mention all the development behind the waterfront. I think that 100 billion dollars just for the land is not out of line, then you have the property development, easily another 100 billion dollars. With the suggestion to make several rivers instead of one large lake, this could double or triple for a total of 600 billion dollars."

"This is what we envisioned," said Michael. He flashed a picture of the development of Doha, Qatar as an example of how a desert could be developed as a magnificent waterfront destination.

"That's only for the initial development. Ongoing, there is revenue potential here that is more than the entire national budget of Egypt currently, which is less than $100 billion."

The conversation and brainstorming continued for another hour, surprising Michael, Ariana and Steve.

"I see, I see," said Adam. "There is much more here than just building a dam, filling a lake and solving the water crisis. Thank you very much for your time today, we've learned a lot. One final question. How long do you expect it will take to build this dam? As you can see, there is some urgency." The crowd outside was growing in size and anger.

"Let me answer that," said Steve. "Since we plan to automate everything except the big dozers, we can run the equipment 24/7. We believe it's possible to accomplish this in just twelve months."

"Impressive," said Adam.

Adam Levy paused the meeting "I would like to thank all of you for coming today and for your very learned and creative contributions to the discussion. Michael, we would like some time to confer, make sure we are all on the same page and then get back together to brainstorm on a business and project plan and, most importantly, how to finance and get the buy in we need from Egypt to try to find a way to move this forward."

"Our schedule is open," said Michael. "We can stay here for as long as we need to."

"Alright," said Adam Levy, "Please give us a few minutes to confer before we continue."

Michael, Ariana and Steve left the room somewhat in shock that things were happening so fast and that the meeting participants were so receptive.

Steve said, "There's something up here. It's almost as though the group already had something in mind and were just waiting on the right opportunity to move it forward. I've seen this before. There's much more to this that they haven't told us yet."

"That's ok with me," said Michael. "All I want to do is build the biggest dam in the world."

"Is that all?" said Ariana, laughing.

"But, you know, I can't believe I missed the part about evaporation from Lake Eden. What was I thinking?" said Michael.

They were just sitting there outside the conference room for another hour when the door opened and Adam Levy asked them to come back in.

"Michael, we've been discussing your dam proposal, and I believe we are all in agreement to disclose to you some things we have been working on for the past several years," said Adam.

Adam explained that there is currently an 850-mile diameter plastic refuse area in the Pacific Ocean between Hawaii and California. The ocean currents have somehow swirled around to keep all of this plastic trash in a relatively small area, but there are millions of tons of this stuff just in that Pacific zone alone. Other similar ones exist in the Atlantic, Indian Oceans and the Mediterranean Sea.

The Israelis had designed a special ship that uses large extendable booms to surround the floating plastic refuse and then pull it on board with a conveyor belt. Once on the ship, there are sorting machines that separate the clear plastic from the opaque. The opaque plastic is remelted and formed into structural beams while the clear plastic, bottles mostly, is crushed and heated, just to melting, in order to be sticky enough to form into a sheet of reasonably clear plastic. The combination of the clear sheets and the opaque structural elements are then formed into a sort of geodesic tunnel that is continuously trailed out the stern of the ship. The tunnel is about 50 meters wide and can be many km long continuously. The design is such that the sea water evaporates and condenses on the upper part of the dome, then runs down the side to a catchment trough about a third of the way up the dome. The fresh water is then piped together and into a pumping station where it is piped underwater to the shore and to a major pipeline. The fresh water produced is of order 50 liters per second per square kilometer under the domes.

Adam continued, "Obviously, building ships to harvest the plastic waste that has made its way into the oceans is a win-win, both financially because the material is basically free, finders' keepers, and so is the energy from the sun, but also environmentally since we are cleaning up the oceans. Of course, this technology was developed to supply Israel and the dome tunnels were to be deployed in the Mediterranean near Haifa. But we have discussed this and believe the technology would be well suited to make up evaporative loss from the new Qattara Lake."

The Minister of the Interior spoke up next. "We had quite a debate concerning whether we could convince our population to abandon their homeland of 3000 years and move back to Egypt. The last time we did that, it did not work out so well."

Genesis 37:28

²⁸ Then there passed by Midianites merchantmen; and they drew and lifted up Joseph out of the pit, and sold Joseph to the Ishmaelites for twenty pieces of silver: and they brought Joseph into Egypt.

Genesis 47:13, 27

¹³ There was no food, however, in the whole region because the famine was severe; both Egypt and Canaan wasted away because of the famine.

²⁷ Now the Israelites settled in Egypt in the region of Goshen. They acquired property there and were fruitful and increased greatly in number.

Exodus 1:11

¹¹ Therefore they did set over them taskmasters to afflict them with their burdens. And they built for Pharaoh treasure cities, Pithom and Raamses.

"And of course, the more pressing question is how the financing will be accomplished."

This was a question Ariana was ready for. Ariana said, "Did you ever read the book by Stephen Ambrose <u>Nothing Like It in the World?</u>"

Adam said, "No, what's it about?"

"Well, let me explain, because it could be a way to finance a big project. It is about the building of the transcontinental railroad back in the 1860's after the Civil War in the U.S. It is a great book, but here is the thing." Ariana explained that for such a huge and expensive project, the normal method of investment funding just wasn't going to work because the time required to complete the project was so long and the risk of not completing it was so high, people didn't trust they would get their investment back. By the time the railroad could begin carrying passengers and freight, *if* it ever got done, the investors would all be dead and buried. President Lincoln and the railroad founders, like Leland Stanford, weren't sure what to do to get the capital for the project.

"It turned out that while the U.S. government didn't have lots of cash, they did have lots of land. So, it was decided that the best way to finance the railroad was to cede an amount of land to the railroad companies for each mile of track laid. That way, as the rails were put down, the worthless land on either side of the tracks became more valuable."

"But what did the railroad companies do with the land? They were in the business of running a railroad." Adam was impressed with Ariana's knowledge of the financing.

"They sold it to real estate developers who built towns and housing for the people to service the railroad and for the people carried by the railroad to the new land. Many of the towns became famous, like Cheyenne, Laramie and Dodge City. Of course, the railroad owners and investors got wealthy as well. Overall, it was a very successful way of financing such a large project. I wonder if we could do something similar?"

"You mean cede land around the eventual Qattara development shoreline as the dam is built, based on, say, a percentage completion metric?" said Adam.

"Yes. Whitelock is working with the Saudis to secure financing, but this would be a way to get much more working capital. I've discussed this with our partners and they like the idea. We are planning to have the Saudis approach Egypt to set this up," said Ariana.

The ministers around the table were nodding and clearly impressed with this plan. Not only would this solve the water crisis, it might just make them all rich.

The civil unrest outside underscored the serious urgency.

"OK, if it takes a year to build the megadam, when will the people be able to move in?"

Michael answered, "Yes, it will take a year to build the megadam if all goes well, but we think we can move people almost immediately by tapping the underground aquifer temporarily until the Nile replaces the water."

"This sounds too good to be true, but I support it," said Adam. He leaned over and whispered in Michael's ear. "I want to move my family there as soon as possible for obvious reasons. They are not safe here."

An armed policeman in riot gear knocked on the door and announced there was a bomb threat to the building. "We must evacuate immediately."

"I am so very sorry ladies and gentlemen but we must leave the building." Adam wrapped up the meeting by explaining that he and the ministers were on board, but the proposal had to be discussed with the Israeli Government and that they would get back to Ariana at Whitelock with next steps.

Fortunately, there was a large police presence at the building entrance. Throughout the day, the Israeli police had taken a brutal approach to the demonstration. Michael and team were apprehensive as they walked out the door and to their car. A police line on either side of the walkway kept the crowd at bay, but shouts and insults filled the air and at one point a brick thrown by a protestor whizzed by Steve's head, barely missing him, while demonstrators surrounded the car and banged on the hood and windows. Michael had seen this sort of thing before while with his dad during his years at the State Department, but it was new to Ariana and Steve. What the demonstrators could not know was that, as opposed to their shouting and rioting, these folks just leaving the building could actually do something to improve the water situation for Israel and the Palestinians.

No sooner had they gotten into their car than there was the deafening sound of an explosion with glass, bricks and concrete flying everywhere. The violence and desperation were quite real. Steve slammed the accelerator to the floor and they sped away through the glass and debris.

Chapter 18

New York, the following month

The United Nations had formed a special committee to address the water emergency in the Middle East. Plans were being made for the shipment of water from the Black Sea ports to Haifa to at least prevent a huge loss of life. Henry Pitt used his network at the State Department to arrange a meeting with the U.S. Ambassador's assistant, Elizabeth Hall. Michael, Ariana and Steve traveled to NY City to bring her up to speed on their Water Challenge proposal.

The night before the meeting with Elizabeth, Ariana had a very strange dream. She was with Michael in his apartment when a rattlesnake appeared in the corner of the room. The snake began slithering toward them and she remembered screaming just before she woke up.

Genesis 3:14-15

¹⁴ And the LORD God said unto the serpent, Because thou hast done this, thou art cursed above all cattle, and above every beast of the field; upon thy belly shalt thou go, and dust shalt thou eat all the days of thy life: ¹⁵ And I will put enmity between thee and the woman, and between thy seed and her seed; it shall bruise thy head, and thou shalt bruise his heel.

They were on the way to New York and Ariana recounted the dream to Michael, "I was so scarred, and the snake was hissing and rattling. I never had a dream like that before."

"No, me neither, but it says here that a rattlesnake in a dream means we're facing our deepest fears or unresolved problems. It says it's a journey of self-discovery and that we have to confront our deepest fears." Michael was looking online and found the most common theme for a rattlesnake in a dream. "Well, I guess we're both afraid of what might happen at our meeting today."

This first meeting was nowhere near as upbeat as the one with Adam's team in Israel. Fortunately, there were no protests either. They all met in Elizabeth's office at the UN and Ariana took the lead in the discussion. "The groundwork has been laid and the Saudis, Egyptians, Israelis and Americans are all on board with the proposal with the support of my company, Whitelock Partners. We are keeping the Israeli involvement very quiet since we don't want the Iranians to stir up trouble."

"That's very wise," said Elizabeth. "I must be honest with you; I think this has very little chance of moving forward with UN blessing. And, by the way, why do you need it? Hasn't Whitelock done projects like this before in the Mideast?"

Michael spoke up, "Yes, they have, but this project is unique since the major investors and beneficiaries do not own the land they are developing. And there is the added complication of the Israeli – Palestinian conflict, the 'right of return' and the governance of Jerusalem."

"Talk about a can of worms." Elizabeth's face showed even more skepticism than before.

"When we first proposed this project to Whitelock," said Steve, "they just laughed. They thought just building the dam was impossible, let alone the political issues. But we convinced them that the new technology could do it, and we believe it can."

"$100 million is a lot of money even for a venture capitalist firm. And the billions of dollars in revenue that follow are the real brass ring here," said Ariana. "That is why we are here. People are dying of thirst in the worst humanitarian crisis in recent history, and the UN is the only world organization that can help us resolve the political problems."

"I have an idea," said Elizabeth. "Some years ago, it was suggested that we make Jerusalem a UN Protectorate. If we do that and include the new land, then this area will be a first in world government. The advantage here is that this land has never had a government, so there is no history or political entitlements to contend with." Michael, Steve and Ariana remained silent, preferring to let Elizabeth believe the whole thing was her idea. Ariana knew better than any of them that to actually get something accomplished, there has to be a champion. Most of the time, the strongest champions are ones who believe it was their idea in the first place.

"That is a great idea," said Ariana. "How do we move this forward?"

"Well, we've had the most success in the past by talking to each stakeholder individually. If I can get some level of buy-in before they all come together, we have a shot at it."

The countries of Ethiopia and Sudan were very jealous of the water in the Nile River. It would be a hard sell to convince them to go along with the project. In the end, just like everything else in politics, it came down to the money. When the Ethiopians and Sudanese learned how much money they would make on the project, they happily agreed to participate. In those countries, money flowing to the government was money in their pockets. And the Egyptian government would benefit the most, although they did not agree immediately. Certain details remained to be settled.

The UN vote had two major components; the majority of countries had to agree and vote yes on the proposal, and the countries with veto power had to allow the vote to stand. The first would be a slam dunk since the stakeholder countries all agreed. The second component usually came down to the Americans and Europeans vs. the Russians and Chinese, historically communist bloc countries.

Just a couple of months before the UN vote, the newspapers carried a front-page story of the bombing of the National Water Carrier building in Israel and the spiraling violence. The situation in Israel with the Palestinians seemed to have morphed from "right of return" to "right to have enough water to stay alive." The world watched tensely as the violence escalated and increasing pressure was brought to bear on the UN Security Council to do something.

On the day of the vote, the U.S. Ambassador to the UN, fully briefed by Elizabeth, stood and gave an impassioned plea for UN support of the project. "Ladies and gentlemen, many people in the Mideast are losing their lives due to the ongoing drought. A strong coalition of countries in Africa and the Mideast have put forth a bold plan to develop the world's first UN Protectorate nation state on essentially worthless, barren land in northwestern Egypt. In order to secure this agreement, it has been proposed to add the city of Jerusalem to the Protectorate, making it a World Heritage Site so that all people can visit and enjoy the historical and religious significance of this great city. For the plan to succeed, the UN must agree to be the governing body of this new country, almost as if a new volcanic island arose in the middle of the ocean. American technologists, backed by venture capitalists and the Kingdom of Saudi Arabia strongly believe that the new land, watered by the megadam across the Nile River will save countless lives. I beg of you to approve this resolution and begin a new era in Mideast diplomacy."

Other signatories of the Qattara Development agreement also spoke, and near the end of the day, the vote was taken on the proposal. Everyone waited tensely as the votes came in.

In this case the Russians were more concerned about their precious Aswan Dam than the water crisis, the violence or the money, so although the vote passed, it was vetoed.

Henry Pitt from Whitelock and Ariana had been convinced the vote would pass, it was so much money. They hadn't counted on the optics of Russia's vaunted Aswan Dam being inundated.

Ariana spoke to Elizabeth just after the vote. "I can't believe I missed that," said Elizabeth.

"I have an idea," said Ariana. "When we were researching the megadam, we discovered the Aswan dam was actually built on a major fault line. There have been lots of earthquakes over the years and we believe that the Egyptian government is aware of damage to the dam. The cost of repair and rebuild is just too much, so they are just sitting on the problem, hoping the dam doesn't give way and kill millions. It's basically a cover up."

"OK," said Elizabeth. "I'm listening."

"What if we threaten to go public with this information? This would be extremely embarrassing to Russia since they funded the Aswan Dam, so they could befriend Egypt, and their engineering firms were involved back in the 1950's and 1960's." Ariana knew she was suggesting something very controversial but she felt she had an ally in Elizabeth as the UN Ambassador's assistant.

As the middle east started to crumble under political pressure and climate change demonstrations, the pressure to accept this radical solution was discussed behind closed doors at NATO, at the UN, and special meetings in most major cities brought more pressure to consider the idea of a UN Protectorate State. The momentum built, day by day until those with strong resistance could no longer hold back the tide of innovation.

Michael and Ariana used this time to focus on preparing for their lives to change, with hopes that they would be going to Egypt and continue to lead the project.

A few months later, after intense lobbying and another U.N. vote, the Russians let the vote stand. The announcement was made in the international media.

"NILE RIVER AND WESTERN DESERT REDEVELOPMENT PROJECT ANNOUNCED IN JOINT NEWS CONFERENCE BY EGYPT AND SAUDI ARABIA."

Chapter 19

Cairo, Egypt a few weeks later

Several weeks after the U.N. vote, Morsi contacted the Ministry of Information about holding a news conference. The state-owned broadcast media, Egyptian Radio and Television Union, Channel 1 and Channel 2 as well as the major network news outlets from around the world were there including CTV, the Christian channel in Egypt, Al Jazeera, CNN, Politico, and The New York Times. It was held at the Al-Azhar University and included officials of the Ministry of Antiquities in Egypt.

On the stage, Morsi had tables with a group of skulls and various archeological finds. There was applause as he was introduced by the Chair of the Department of Archeology and Antiquities.

"It is no surprise, I am sure, to any of you that we are experiencing today rapid climate change and the worst drought on record. What you may not fully realize is that the Earth has been going through these climate change cycles for millions of years." Morsi explained that in fact, right there in Egypt they were going through desertification at an alarming rate. And, there was a tendency to believe that the area called the Western Desert was always a desert. "This is not the case. As recently as 5,000 years ago, the climate of Egypt was much wetter with trees, grass lands, lakes and rivers. Please have a look at the slide." Morsi put up a topo map of Egypt.

"With the aid of modern satellite topographical photos, it is clear that the Nile River once was much higher and had more tributaries than it does now. And this was only 5,000 to 10,000 years ago. In the northwestern corner of Egypt, there is a crescent shaped blue area called the Qattara Depression. Blue means this area is actually below sea level. If this region of the Nile was filled with water, the blue area would have been a freshwater lake.

"Today, we are announcing one of the most important finds in the history of archeology," Morsi said with a flourish. "We have discovered a region containing the skeletal remains of five of the most recent hominins in chronological order including, Australopithecus Africanus, Homo Habilis, Homo Erectus, Homo Neanderthalensis, and finally modern human, Cro-Magnon. These have all been unearthed in an area of the Western Desert around the Qattara Depression, where, we believe, there was an ancient freshwater lake, one of the largest, if not the largest, in the world."

Morsi explained that many species of hominins lived on the shores of this lake as it filled during the glacial maximums and shrank during the warming periods when the area became a vast desert. This cycle took place repeatedly over millions of years, every 26,000 years or so according to core samples taken from the area. The wobble of the Earth's axis as well as the atmospheric cycles of the sun combined to create the climate cycles. As the lake shrank, Morsi's team excavated skeletal remains from many species that lived along the shore, and they were accurately dated by means of the core stratigraphy from the sites. In this way, as the lake was shrinking and becoming saltier, the inhabitants would have been forced to find fresh water.

"Many species, once exiled from the site, continued their journeys to the far corners of the earth as shown in the slide behind me." Morsi put up the next slide. The screen behind showed a map of the world with large arrows emanating from an area just west of the Nile River in the Western Desert of Egypt near the Qattara Depression to every part of the world.

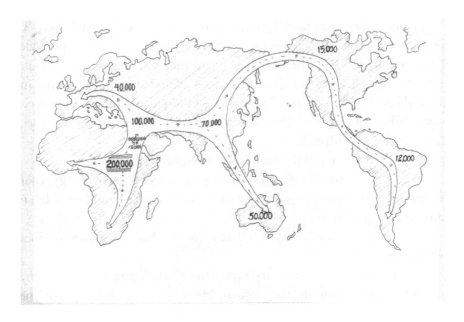

"All of the three faiths, Islam, Christianity and Judaism have scriptures that describe this cradle of humanity as the Garden of Eden. We are announcing today that we believe we have found this Garden of Eden." Morsi waited for the applause and was surprised to hear snickers and some outright laughter instead.

A reporter from CNN asked, "Did you find Adam and Eve too?" More laughter.

"How about Big Foot?" said a cute young reporter in the front row. Things were rapidly coming unglued and even some of Morsi's colleagues were beginning to move away from him on the stage.

"Have you ever heard of Piltdown man?" A reporter from the Guardian referred to the hoax where an Orangutan mandible was altered and put on a modern human skull.

"You may laugh all you want, but you will find that what we have found is the cradle of humanity!" Morsi shouted defensively. The questions continued for another half hour with some reporters ready to announce Morsi's claim about the Garden of Eden, and others who decided it would look too unbelievable to be printed or shown on television. The news about various types of species was reported by all present but the coverage was not what Morsi expected.

The next day, after reading articles on the internet, Michael, Ariana, Sofia and Greg were gathered at the condo in Boston to watch this spectacle as reported by CNN. When Michael heard that Morsi was taking credit for finding the Biblical Garden of Eden, he exploded in anger, "What in the world is this?" he shouted. "That fool is taking credit for our discovery. I can't believe it. How did he know?" Suddenly it dawned on Michael. "Dad...? You told Morsi?"

"Wasn't me," Greg lied. *Yeah, right*, thought Michael.

"So... your friend Morsi after working as an archeologist in Egypt for decades just randomly discovers the true location of the Garden of Eden and starts digging there?"

At that point Greg sheepishly heads for the bar and pours another Jack Daniels.

As it turned out, Morsi called Greg later to apologize, but not for the announcement of finding the Garden. He wanted to tell Greg that the university had made a formal complaint to the Egyptian Department of Antiquities concerning the megadam project and the sensitivity of the sites. "Greg, do you even realize the importance of the sites that will be inundated by this massive project? The Abu Simbel Temples, Kom Ombo and Philae Temple, these are some of the most incredible sites in all of Egypt. This is unacceptable." The depth of Morsi's anger was much more profound than even Greg realized.

"Oh, quit your whining. You and your government are going to make so much money, nobody will even remember those places in the next ten years."

Michael began thinking *This man Morsi is our enemy. We need to watch him closely.*

The response of the reporters at the news conference was one thing, but the scientific response was quite another. It took several months, but soon the refereed journals would be brimming with articles supporting Morsi's claims and confirming that this find was one of the most important in paleo archeological history.

Chapter 20

Afghanistan, this week

Hanbal, from Kharga Oasis, rose through the ranks and fought against the American led coalition in Eastern Syria. This action was a disastrous defeat for the Islamic State and many fighters were killed by air strikes and a combination of Kurdish and Arab soldiers. The relative disorganization of the ISIS fighters left a leadership vacuum that Hanbal was only too happy to fill.

ISIS saw an opportunity in eastern Afghanistan to push the hated Americans out and establish a caliphate. Hanbal joined the fighting there along with his small team of fighters.

There was close fighting in the streets that day in a town in eastern Afghanistan. They hid in doorways, fought from roof tops, and pushed through the narrow streets and alleyways. Most of the resistance they encountered was from the government troops. These were generally poorly trained and poorly equipped, not really committed to the fight and just trying to prevent a radical takeover of their country.

Hanbal and his men were rapidly clearing the town of the government troops.

This type of close quarters fighting was typically done with small numbers of men fanned out and moving door to door down the narrow streets. Hanbal stepped around a corner wall of one of the buildings and instantly heard the pop-pop-pop of the Ak-47 on full auto. A chip of the wall was blasted by one of the bullets and the dust and rock fell on Hanbal's unhelmeted head. He could feel his stomach tighten as he realized it was a close call. *I need to watch more carefully*, he thought. *Luckily, these government fighters are not good shots.* He inched around the corner a bit more to get a view of the two shooters and saw out of the corner of his eye an old man with a long beard. He was just stepping back into a doorway and quickly disappeared into the house. *I'll remember you*, thought Hanbal, *you nearly got me killed. Think you can fight without fighting, do you? We'll see.* The two men had crouched behind a wagon, but Hanbal saw where they were. He signaled his partner, ducked under a fence and went around the back way to flank the enemy fighters. Very quietly he crept around the corner of the building. *Gotcha*, he thought.

Next, he and his partner began to move systematically down the street to the market square, one doorway at a time. Hanbal could see the rest of his group as they approached the square and then, out of nowhere the Americans appeared with an armored personnel carrier topped with a 50-caliber machine gun. The Americans immediately began to lay down fire and several troops could be seen leaving the vehicle. Hanbal and his men fired back but it was no use. The Americans were too heavily armed and well trained. He needed RPG's and armor piercing rounds, but didn't have them. One missile is all that was needed to destroy the Humvee and push the Americans back. He would remember that for future battles.

When they encountered the cursed Americans with their Humvees, sophisticated weapons, close air support and communications, Hanbal's progress was stopped cold. In the space of ten minutes, the tide of the battle turned. Hanbal had to retreat, and as he did, he saw some of the people in the town talking to the American infidels. A deep and simmering anger welled up within Hanbal that these so-called Muslims would even talk to the Americans at all.

As the fighting went on, the horrors of what he saw began to weigh on his mind and forge a malignant hatred of the government as well as the Americans. The bombing strikes were the worst. Hanbal also had a secret loathing of himself, primarily because, when one of his fellow fighters went down, he did not feel sadness or sorrow, he felt glad *because it was him and not me,* thought Hanbal.

The constant horror of war took its toll on Hanbal in other ways. His allegiance to the clerics who preached fundamentalist Islam began to be almost irrational to the point where, when it was time to punish the nonbelievers, he now wanted to be first in line.

Deep down inside, Hanbal felt these acts were justified, since the Americans had pushed back so many Islamic fighters with their air strikes and helicopter launched missiles. The only way to return their land to a rightful government was to establish an Islamic Caliphate. Hanbal was sure of it.

The fact that none of the fighters wore identifying uniforms, and in fact they wore face coverings, was acceptable to Hanbal, just as the American colonists fought in street clothes and used guerilla warfare tactics on the British during the American Revolution.

Darkness finally fell that day and the next morning the Americans were gone. They must have thought they had won and moved on to the next small town. What they didn't realize was that Hanbal and his fighters would be there long after the Americans pulled out, claiming victory but not realizing that neither bullets nor governments could change people's minds.

It was time for the enemies of Islam to pay for their crimes.

The announcement about the new dam across the Nile came one night as Hanbal and his fellow freedom fighters were encamped in Farah Province in western Afghanistan. Only a few of his men were from Egypt, most of the others were from Iraq, Lebanon and Palestine. When Hanbal heard the news about the Qattara Development, he immediately thought *here is another way the Americans and the Jews are stealing our land,* even though there was no mention of America or Israel in the Al Jazeera story.

"Another American and Israeli scheme to steal our lands," Hanbal said. "We must stop this or we will have nothing."

"Why do we care?" said one of his fellow ISIS fighters. "The war is here, now. Let's win at least this one for our cause. The Americans are pulling out anyway. We have a great chance to win here if we don't give up."

"I know it is not your country, my friend," said Hanbal, "but Egypt needs our help too. I'm going home to stop this madness."

"Me too" said one of his Egyptian colleagues. "And me," said several others.

Hanbal began to follow the story of the megadam and the development project of the Egyptian and Saudi governments. Even though there was no mention of the Americans or the Israelis direct involvement with implementing the project, he was sure they were involved. He resolved, when the project got underway, to find a way to stop it, no matter what.

Chapter 21

Cairo, Egypt

The Saudis, Egyptians, Whitelock Partners and the UN scheduled a kickoff meeting in Cairo for the Qattara Development Project and the team from America arrived at Boston Logan for the flight to Egypt, including Michael, Ariana, Steve Williams and Walter Jay.

First stop, when they were settled in their hotel in Cairo, was a meeting with Morsi. The megadam project had gained even more momentum and attention, worldwide, and so had the underground resistance movement among the Muslim Brotherhood that opposed the project.

Michael was worried and wanted to assure Morsi in person, face to face, that the new megadam and Qattara Depression development project would not in any way disturb the new archeological sites that were so important to the Egyptian government's Department of Antiquities, although, just as when the Aswan Dam was built, some of the older sites along the Nile would be inundated. Somehow, he had to convince Morsi that, although they made the proposal to Israel, it was the cooperation of the Saudis and Egyptians that made it happen. The Antiquities Department resistance to the megadam proposal could derail the whole project. Michael also had another agenda. He wanted to find out how Morsi knew where to dig and how he knew about the discovery of the Garden of Eden.

The team arrived at Morsi's office in the late afternoon. Morsi said when they arrived, "I have so much to show and tell you about our discoveries. But it is late, you have been traveling and I bet you are hungry."

"I think we're all starving," said Michael.

Al Khal was one of the best restaurants in Cairo. They have always been famous for their lamb dishes as well as their seafood. Morsi drove them through the winding streets of Cairo to the restaurant a few miles east.

"Is the food here as good as it smells?" asked Ariana.

"Better," said Morsi. The waitress came and as she approached the table, Morsi smiled broadly and said, "I would like to introduce my niece Mesi. She will take good care of us tonight."

"So happy to meet you," said Walt. "Thank you for waiting on us this evening."

"Mesi speaks impeccable English," said Morsi. "And she is very interested in American and international cultures. She is planning on opening a restaurant someday, specializing in international cuisine."

The Americans ordered drinks and some appetizers as the group settled into the luxury and ambiance of the restaurant.

"I now know why you were intent on meeting in person," said Morsi. "I really appreciate it. These are very important archeological discoveries, and your recognitions are the basis of it all."

Michael couldn't contain himself any longer and just blurted out, "There's something else I need to ask you." There was a little disturbance as a server brought out the rokak appetizer, traditional Egyptian dough stuffed with ground beef, onion and spices.

"Michael, you were saying," said Morsi whose curiosity was piqued by this point.

"How did you know about the location of the Garden of Eden and where to dig?"

"I tell you my young friend, I have been thinking about this for years," said Morsi, determined not to reveal his source.

"Not to be too confrontational, but I just don't believe you." Michael was revved up now and ready to have it out with Morsi. "You've been digging in the desert for decades and just now you go to the exact spot on the topo maps that show an ancient lake?"

"Michael, that's enough," said Ariana.

"What? You think you're the only one who can read a map? Anyway, a gentleman never reveals his sources. Tell you what, I will put your name on the papers if it makes you feel better. You can take the credit for the Garden of Eden find. But I'm taking credit for Aqua Man," said Morsi.

At that, Michael calmed down. He was not an archeologist anyway. *Who cares who gets the credit for Aqua Man?* thought Michael. "Ok...," said Michael.

"Tomorrow, I'll show you the topo maps with the proposed dam site, the flooded areas in the western desert and the potential for irrigation, farming and development along the shoreline. There's the possibility for hundreds of billions of dollars, or perhaps even trillions of dollars in revenue from a project like this." Michael was very confident of his engineering estimates. "What we've discovered is that the evaporation from a fully filled Lake Eden is a huge number, so it has been decided to only fill long narrow channels. This gives more waterfront property anyway and the most important part is that your new dig sites won't be disturbed."

"So, this *is* your project," said Morsi. "I still don't see how you got the Saudis involved."

"That was my company, Whitelock, from Boston," said Ariana.

"That's all well and good," said Morsi, "But the train has left the station. We have protests going all over the country. I'm worried. Keep your head down and make sure you have guards at the dam site. Nothing I can do about it." The Muslim Brotherhood was behind all of the protests. And their issues ran much deeper than a few archeological dig sites. The coming months would show just how deep. The leadership of the Muslim Brotherhood went back many years to the time of the Arab Spring. The Qattara development was just another piece of the puzzle.

"Eight AM, my office. I want to hear the rest of this," said Morsi. "And now let's relax and enjoy our meal. This is a social occasion."

"And so, tell me about this beautiful young lady!" said Morsi, looking directly at Ariana.

"Ariana is a venture capitalist and just finished her MBA at Harvard," said Michael. "Art history is her hobby and she does research into the ancient paintings, engravings and sculptures, especially here in Egypt."

"Fascinating," said Morsi.

"Yes, I am very interested in how the ancient Egyptians kept their engineering records. In fact, that is how Michael and I met. We were both attending a lecture about how the paintings and carvings may have been a way to preserve the secrets of construction and engineering for the tombs and monuments, including the pyramids. Michael was working on his PhD so we had a lot in common."

"And did you find any secrets to the pyramids?" Now Morsi was really curious.

"Actually, yes, we did. We found that some of the carvings on the pyramid walls depicted boats, on the Nile I believe, with huge rocks on them and a man sitting atop the stone. Some Egyptologists think this is depicting the journey to the Land of the Dead. But both Michael and I believe it is a description of how the huge stones were moved over the long distance from the quarry to the building site."

"Yes, we've discussed that," said Morsi. He had that annoying habit of always claiming to have thought of something first, although there's never any evidence of that prior to the disclosure. "Seems odd that the journey to the Land of the Dead would involve large quarried stones. And did you use that in your dissertation?"

"Well, yeah," said Michael. "In a way, although my thesis and data had all been completed by the time Ariana and I attended that lecture. But especially the one wall carving showing the stone on a boat, that is part of my thesis. I'm glad I went to that lecture."

There was discussion of politics which was strained and tense.

Michael wanted to change the subject. "It's almost like we have to cram everything back into Pandora's box and just start over. We really want to talk to you about how we are making sure that your archeological digs will be protected."

After all the passionate dialog about politics and history, everyone was relieved when Mesi returned to the table.

"Would anyone like dessert?" said Morsi's niece.

"May we see the dessert menu?" said Morsi. "The desserts here are amazing. I never pass up a chance to enjoy them."

They all ordered the dessert tray with *kunafa, basbousa* and *baklava* and enjoyed coffee while the discussion turned to old times about Morsi and Greg.

At the end of the meal, Morsi drove them back to their hotel. Walt said, "Get a good night's sleep tonight, Michael, big day tomorrow."

"Will do," said Michael.

Michael just couldn't stop thinking about Morsi's niece, Mesi, and how she would make a perfect cook for the construction site team. He was determined to ask Morsi if she would be interested in the job.

"Michael, great to see you," said Morsi the next day as Michael, Ariana, Steve and Walt met at Morsi's office. Michael was very interested in seeing the archeological finds that he and Ariana had predicted could be found by digging near the ancient lake's shoreline.

"We just wanted to assure you again about the megadam project," said Michael, by way of starting the meeting.

"I hear you, but I just don't trust the government when it comes to lucrative development projects, especially when rich countries like Saudi Arabia are involved."

"Ariana's firm believes this is potentially the most lucrative project they ever invested in. Egypt stands to make lots of money and we are very certain the flooded areas will not disturb your new dig sites.

"I understand," said Morsi. "And I'll take your word for it for now, but I am still skeptical. And what about the old sites along the Nile south of Luxor?

Michael confidently replied that plans were in place to protect all archeological discoveries of the past and future as the project unfolded. In fact, Michael suggested that Professor Morsi could be part of any future discoveries, should they occur as the dam was being built. Morsi shrugged and did not want to discuss the dam any further.

"Enough of that," said Morsi. "Let me show you what we have discovered!" Morsi walked Michael and team to his lab where there was a display of the skulls found at several of the Lake Eden sites arranged in the order of lake size and time of occupation.

Morsi explained that the problem anthropologists and paleontologists have is finding skulls in the correct timeline. Finds are made at different sites that are revealed by seismic or erosion activity, but there is no way to see if there were intermediate species that show the timeline of evolution, especially in the last 500,000 years. There are the Neanderthals and Homo Erectus but nothing in between. Then there is the Cro-Magnon, which is clearly different than the Neanderthals, but nothing in between.

"However, at these sites in the Qattara Depression we have clear timelines of occupation, so the skeletal remains are much more gradually changing," said Morsi. "What we have here is the smooth and almost indiscernible evolution of hominins from Homo Erectus to Neanderthal to Cro-Magnon. The brain case got gradually larger and the brow ridges got smaller. Also, the use of fire softened the food so that the jaw got smaller and the protrusion of the mouth and teeth drew inward. Today, we still have an issue of having enough room for the teeth, so many individuals have teeth that are too big for their mouths and need orthodonture."

Genesis 6:4

> **⁴The Nephilim were on the earth in those days, and also afterward, when the sons of God came in to the daughters of man and they bore children to them. These were the mighty men who were of old, the men of renown.**

"We have never had such a complete skeletal record of human evolution. My colleagues and I have concluded that this is indeed the cradle of humanity. Mankind did most of the development right here in the Garden of Eden, just as the scriptures say." Morsi stood proudly beside the display of ancient skulls, bones and drawings.

Michael was awestruck at Morsi's mention of the Garden of Eden as it matched his understanding of the Bible's explanation in the Book of Genesis, "Amazing, I never in my wildest dreams thought this could actually be true. And thank you for agreeing to give us credit," said Michael, and in that moment, he inwardly acknowledged that he may not get the recognition he desperately sought.

Chapter 22

Cairo

The kickoff meeting for the Qattara Depression Development Project with the consortium of participants was scheduled for Thursday of that week in Cairo at the conference room of the Ministry of the Interior.

The meeting was to be hosted by the Prime Minister, but was kept very quiet and away from the news media. Protests were still happening and no one wanted to poke the hornets' nest. The agenda, which ran over two days, was very long and filled with presentations by the various participants in the project, including Michael and his team for the megadam.

Much of what was covered in the presentations was completely new to Michael and team, as was their information to the other participants.

The Prime Minister of Egypt opened the meeting.

"Good morning, everyone and thank you all for coming. Today is the kickoff meeting for what we are jointly calling the Qattara Depression Development Project. For some months now a consortium of technologists, government representatives, investors/venture capitalists, and the UN have been meeting to work out an agreement to build a new future by taking unusable desert and turning it into a paradise for the whole world to enjoy."

The Prime Minister flashed up on the screen the agenda for the two-day meeting. "Here is what we plan to cover over the two days we are together. We will discuss financing and the roles and responsibilities of the project participants which will be presented by the Crown Prince of Saudi Arabia, who we are very glad to have with us after the failed assassination attempt." The Crown Prince nodded and smiled at the assembly.

"Next, we will be schooled in how to build the largest dam ever conceived on the planet Earth by two brilliant American engineers from MIT, Michael Walters and Steve Williams. The resulting water flows and the developments in the Qattara Depression will be explained by our colleague Adam Levy, who is the CEO of the Israeli National Water Carrier.

"I would like to remind our team here that for political reasons, the role of Adam and the Israelis is to be kept very low key. We feel that with the fragile peace here in the Middle East and the uncertainty about the status of Iran's nuclear development, we must not risk a confrontation between Israel and Iran."

As though to emphasize the point, a large group of protesters had formed in front of the ministry building. Apparently, the role of the Israelis, which the Muslim Brotherhood knew about, was purposely leaked and the crowd was angry and growing larger by the minute.

"Finally, and dare I say that this was by far the most challenging aspect of the project, we will hear from the Secretary-General of the UN, without whose capable leadership and vision this project would not be possible."

Michael felt a surge of pride come over him as he realized what had become of a simple idea to build the world's largest dam. And now he was receiving the recognition that his father had been so lax in providing.

"Ladies and gentlemen, the Crown Prince of Saudi Arabia." There was a round of applause as the Crown Prince took the podium.

"Let me say that all of us in Saudi Arabia are very excited about this project. As most of you know, we have been working for some years now to find ways of turning unusable desert land into productive agricultural, industrial and residential property. In this part of the world, the key to achieving that goal is water.

"When Whitelock Partners initially came to us with the megadam proposal, (may I call it that?), we were, of course, skeptical and wondering how in the world something this ambitious could ever be done. The combination of technical vision and brilliant engineering on the part of the Americans and the Israelis has taken what was a stretch goal and made it a realizable project."

"Let me take a few minutes to discuss the major enabling aspects of the project." The Crown Prince explained that some brand-new technologies for dam building, desalination combined with environmental cleanup and conservation, and the willingness to be flexible to achieve the ultimate goal, had led to an agreement between three major collaborators on this project, Egypt, Israel, and Saudi Arabia with the support of the United Nations. The result would be a unique way of solving the water emergency in the Mideast.

A side door to the conference room opened and an aid to the minister whispered something in his ear. "I am afraid there is a protest group outside and they are very rowdy," said the Prime Minister of Egypt. "The police have been called, but there is damage to the building as someone has thrown a brick through the front door. We may need to get out the back way to avoid a confrontation."

The Crown Prince continued, unphased, "To take a high-level view, Egypt has agreed to cede land to the project participants to support the investment in the infrastructure, in a way that is very similar to the financing of the American Transcontinental Railroad during the 19th century. The land is completely worthless when turned over to the consortium, but will become extremely valuable when the project is completed. The trick here is, as was done in the mid 1800's, to cede the land as the project progresses in order to motivate ongoing achievement."

The Crown Prince continued explaining that Saudi Arabia is able to lead the financing of the project, which has an overall budget of approximately five hundred billion dollars. In return, the Saudi government will be ceded a portion of the development lands and in addition will have ownership of most of the stock in the development consortium. The Israelis will also own a portion of the development lands but will be paid for their engineering and construction activity through a combination of cash and stock. "The Americans, in charge of the megadam portion of the project, will be subcontractors to the Israelis and their compensation is determined by that subcontract."

All of that is the easy part. Large international cooperative projects are done every day. However, in this case, the water and land resources are owned by the Government of Egypt as well as some countries upstream of the megadam who may have other ideas for the waters of the Nile. This was the linchpin of the consortium agreement.

"We all struggled with this agreement for many months. Fortunately, our friends at the United Nations came to our rescue. As we are all painfully aware, the city of Jerusalem is regarded by three of the world's major religions as a holy site. The struggle between Palestinians, Israelis and Christians has been going on for many centuries and I dare say we are no further along in the resolution to this crisis than we were 800 years ago. Maybe that is too extreme, but in any case, if we allow the religious leaders to resolve this crisis, it will be, most probably, continuing warfare."

The Crown Prince continued by explaining that there is an opportunity in the case of new lands that are being created from scratch and have no real political history. If all agree to a government appointed by the UN and to establishing a protectorate in this newly created territory, it may be possible to avoid the inevitable religious warfare and entitlements. For this reason, it was agreed by the UN to oversee the protectorate and to writing a constitution that has a strict separation between religion and government.

"The concept of separation of church and state has been a part of the U.S. constitution since the founding. But the vast majority of Americans have come from Europe and are Christian. So, the line between church and state was always somewhat blurred. We are hoping that the new UN protectorate will be more successful than the U.S. in creating a purely sectarian government."

The door opened again and this time the minister's aid was accompanied by a uniformed policeman in riot gear. "I'm sorry ladies and gentlemen, but the crowd outside has swelled to several thousand and the police can no longer guarantee your safety in this building."

The Prime Minister rose and announced, "We will have to leave by the rear entrance. There will be vans waiting outside to take you to your hotels. I am afraid the Nile cruise planned for this evening has to be cancelled. We will contact you with a more discrete location for tomorrow's meeting."

Outside, the protestors were setting fire to automobiles, burning Israeli flags and hanging the American president in effigy. The situation had completely unraveled. A man with a bullhorn shouted, "They have been stealing our land for thousands of years, are we really going to let them take our water too?" The crowd surged forward toward the door. The situation was dire for the meeting attendees.

"We have to go. We have to go now!" said the Prime Minister.

Vans were indeed waiting at the rear of the building, and the attendees hurried out the back door. There were no protestors at the rear of the building, but unfortunately, the Muslim Brotherhood had anticipated this escape route.

A sniper waited at a window across the street. His instructions were very clear. He had a picture of Adam Levy and a high-powered scope on his rifle. As the attendees began coming through the door, he glassed each one until he saw Adam. He aimed carefully, slowly putting more pressure on the trigger. When Adam stepped down off the curb, he stumbled just as the rifle went off. The shot rang out and Adam crumpled to the ground. Fortunately, the bullet missed its mark by a few inches. Security police quickly covered him but the damage was done. Michael, Steve, Walt and Ariana who were nearby dove for cover behind parked cars. Ariana screamed as she saw Adam was hit. He was unconscious, but still breathing when the paramedics arrived. He was quickly loaded into the ambulance and taken to the hospital. Michael rode with him while Ariana, badly shaken by the incident, went back to the hotel room with the other team members.

Michael and team found out later that evening that there had been several injuries at the hands of the riot police as a result of the protests. There was a search for the gunman but nothing found. No surprise there. The Muslim Brotherhood was a powerful underground organization, especially in Cairo. The meeting participants divided into two categories in response to this terrorist attack. One group just wanted to go home and not stir up any more trouble. They weren't sure it was worth the risk just to have a meeting. But the other, including the Americans, wanted to persevere. Michael would remember this incident and have to struggle with his beliefs to have regard for the life of anyone who attacked the megadam project in the future.

Chapter 23

Phones and emails kept everyone busy and on alert that evening as the attendees were briefed on Adam Levy's condition. Michael slept at the hospital while the surgeons worked to extract the bullet and save Adam's life. An informal poll was taken and as the enormity of what had just happened sank in, the majority of attendees wanted to continue the meeting and not let terrorism rule.

The doctors came out of surgery and Michael was there waiting. It was the early morning hour. "Getting the bullet out, which was lodged in his left shoulder, was tricky and dangerous since it was near the heart. But he came through ok and should have no lasting injury. He will need time, maybe six to eight weeks to recover. You need to make arrangements for him to be transported home."

"Thank you," said Michael.

He called Eva from the hospital and gave her an update on Adam's condition. She was relieved but totally rattled by what had happened. "I just want him home," she said.

"I'm working on it," said Michael.

He got an Uber back to his hotel where Ariana was shaken but waiting up for him.

"Is he ok?" she asked.

"He'll be fine, but has to go home. He's going to need weeks to recover. This is going to hit our project hard in the near term."

Ariana said, "I spoke to my boss, Henry, and he understands the situation. He's upset but is determined not to let some cowardly terrorists derail the project. That's just what they want." Despite Whitelock's experience with projects in the region, the company and Henry Pitt were very naïve about the grassroots resistance to the project from the Muslim Brotherhood. This would plague the project for the duration.

The second day of the kickoff meeting was about to begin. A discrete location in the Coptic Christian section of the city was chosen in the basement of St. Mark's Cathedral.

Most of what would be presented today was brand new to Michael and his team, who had been concentrating on the megadam. Michael was especially interested to see how the former arch enemies, Israel and the Arab world, would work out an ownership and government control plan for the dam and the resulting Qattara Depression development.

"Good morning, everyone and welcome to the second day of the Qattara Depression Development Project kickoff meeting." The Prime Minister opened the meeting. "Just a quick update, I am pleased to report that our friend and colleague Adam Levy is out of surgery and doing well. Apparently, the bullet was lodged in his left shoulder near the heart, but the surgeons were able to remove it. He will need time, but we believe he will make a full recovery." The Prime Minister of Egypt had a serious expression on his face and continued. "Also, I would like to apologize for my fellow Egyptians and their behavior yesterday. We have some groups who are against everything that is not traditional, despite how much good it can do for our country.

"The plan for today was to begin with Adam Levy, the CEO of the Israeli National Water Carrier. He would have described for us the detailed plans for the development in the Qattara Depression. Not to be derailed by terrorists, we move on.

"Since there was no time yesterday for the megadam team to present, we have Michael Walters and Steve Williams who will give us an update on the technology of dam building."

Michael and Steve walked to the podium and proceeded to explain how the largest dam ever conceived would be constructed and how long it would take. The presentation lasted for two hours and included details about how the Nile River would be diverted while the dam was under construction. At the end there were many questions, including what risks might be involved.

"Every large project has risks," said Steve. "But especially with respect to earthquakes and volcanic eruptions, the rock filled earthen dam with in-situ calcination will withstand any seismic activity this area may experience." Some heads nodded.

"We believe the risks are more political than physical," said Michael.

The Prime Minister added, "I believe our friend Michael is correct. But we are determined to make a success of this project. As a segue to that, next, we are very pleased and honored to have with us the Secretary General of the United Nations, Dr. Adia Abebe. She will discuss the governance agreements that have been achieved for our project, Dr. Abebe."

The Secretary General was a tall, slender Ethiopian black woman with short hair and piercing eyes. Her movements were very fluid and filled with confidence as she rose to take the podium. "Hello everyone and thank you for inviting me to join you today. Over the last several months, I have been thrilled to be a part of this visionary and world changing project.

"The Palestinian people have, since the creation of Israel, clung to their 'right of return' and to the eventual liberation of Jerusalem, while the Israelis have long believed that God gave them the 'Promised Land' extending from the great river of Egypt to the River Euphrates."

Michael, who was sitting next to Steve Williams in the meeting leaned over and whispered to Steve, "You know the African Americans have a 'right of return' too. We were not only plucked from our ancestral homeland; we were enslaved into the bargain."

"I know," whispered Steve, "but every time we talk about the 1800's when some freed slaves were sent back to Liberia, the African Americans get defensive, and quite rightly in my opinion."

Michael was ready with a response, "That's because they didn't want to be *sent* back. But the right of return is really an opportunity to *choose* to go back, totally different question." Michael believed that greening the North African Sahara Desert could possibly be the most important worldwide economic opportunity in history. And the African Americans from the U.S. along with the rest of the North and South American countries are by far the best positioned to do it. Michael and Steve had discussed this many times while at MIT.

"Maybe that's next, Steve," said Michael.

Dr. Abebe continued, explaining that a project of this magnitude with so many countries and diverse interests needs a government that is not embroiled in local politics, but can oversee the rights of all who live there.

"It has been agreed by the Arabs, including Egypt, the Israelis, the Saudis and the African nations along the Nile watershed to create a United Nations Protectorate called Qattara. This new land will be created from desert land and watered by the Nile River as a result of the megadam. The Protectorate will also include the City of Jerusalem and will be accessible to all and defended by an international peacekeeping force under UN control. Each of the stakeholders in this agreement has given something and gained something. It is in the true spirit of peace that I make this announcement today.

"It has been agreed that all people will be allowed to purchase land in this Protectorate and to live and worship as they please. There will be a strict separation of 'church and state' similar to the American Constitution and in fact, much as the founding of the U.S. was based on colonists seeking religious freedom, the Protectorate will be a place of refuge for all people seeking to practice their beliefs and way of life, culture without the threat of prejudice, racism or discrimination of any sort." At this statement the entire room erupted into spontaneous applause and the Secretary was given a standing ovation, shouts of 'Bravo' and there was a loud buzz in the room as everyone was hugging and shaking hands.

"Thank you very much for your attention today. I am sure there are many questions and concerns and these will be, I hope, ironed out in the coming months. I am happy to discuss with you in smaller groups and in one on ones."

Again, a standing ovation and shouts of 'Bravo' from the audience as Dr. Abebe walked from the podium.

"That concludes our very exciting meeting for today," said the Egyptian Prime Minister. "We are pleased to host the team at the Presidential Palace of Al-Ittihadiya this evening at 7:00pm. Dress is formal."

When Adam began recovering from the bullet wound back home in Tel Aviv, he had two immediate things on his mind. Now that the kickoff meeting was done, he wanted to begin working on the Qattara development with temporary deep wells until the dam got completed. Adam's plan was to move his family there as quickly as possible.

The second item that needed his immediate attention was the initiation of contracts to build the first plastic salvage ship for the freshwater geodesic domes. If these ships could be built and operated in the next twelve months, the deep wells for fresh water in the Qattara development could be supplemented with evaporative distillation from the Mediterranean Sea and more people could begin moving there soon.

Chapter 24

Luxor, Egypt

Michael, Ariana and the rest of the megadam team were planning on staying in Luxor until the heavy equipment began arriving. The aqueducts and underground tunnels to divert the Nile River had been started, using the same technology used with other dams, including the Aswan Dam that was 194 km south of Luxor. The 75' wide underground tunnels allowed the Nile to flow as usual and the area above the tunnels would be dry to accommodate the dam construction. Steve continued doing the surveys necessary to lay out the dam foundation and the team used Range Rovers to become familiar with the mountainous areas on both sides of the Nile. Soon the construction trailers, which were large single story prefab buildings on train wheels, would be trucked to the site and set up while the dam base rail lines were laid.

On their first night in Luxor, Michael booked reservations at the Al-Sahaby Lane Roof Terrace restaurant so the team could socialize and formally begin the project that would be the focus of the next several years. The view of the Nile and the city of Luxor was magnificent and the food was internationally recognized. The Roof Terrace had an exotic décor and boasted a full bar for foreign tourists.

Michael wanted to level set his engineering team and to kick off the megadam construction project with a flourish. The security and administrative teams were also beginning to gather in Luxor and Michael coordinated with them on a daily basis. This evening was just for Michael's small group. When dinner was ended, he began his leadership role with confidence.

"I just want to say a few words about the project and to thank all of you for being here. You know the idea is the easiest part of any project. Now we're in the doing stage. You know the 7 phases of a project?"

1. Wild enthusiasm - That's the phase we're in tonight!
2. Disillusionment – Maybe inevitable but I hope not!
3. Confusion – I'll do my best to avoid that.
4. Panic – In my limited experience there is always a little bit of that.
5. Search for the guilty – We're a team. I promise you that will not happen on my watch.
6. Punishment of the innocent – Same with this.
7. Promotion of the non-participants – We are a High-Performance Work Team and so there are no promotions, demotions or terminations for the duration of this project.

"As you all know, I have zero experience with large projects like this one. For that reason, I am appointing Walt Jay as the Project Manager. Steve and I will function as the Chief Technical Officers, but all construction activity will report to Walt. Before joining Caterpillar, Walt was a Project Manager at Bechtel.

"The plan for the next several weeks, while we wait for the first of the equipment to arrive and be assembled, is to do daily visits to the site where each of us'll prepare for our respective jobs and get the site ready to rock and roll. We have normal size construction equipment which should be on the way here by truck for tomorrow. This'll be used by Steve, while he is surveying, to level and clear the site in preparation for the tracks to be laid. The tracks are standard railway size and our construction site buildings and living quarters will move on the tracks as the dam is built."

Everyone was listening as Michael continued, "We won't have site security from the UN 'til the construction trailers arrive, hopefully in two to three weeks. But on the other hand, there won't be much out there, so we don't expect any trouble. Please keep me posted during the day as you prep. Walt, I'd like twice weekly updates to the team as to the status of the big equipment. We've hired some local laborers here in Luxor to help with the preliminary construction and site prep.

"Each morning we'll have a short huddle meeting to coordinate for the day. We'll have a weekly review on Friday afternoon with Walt before happy hour to go over the accomplishments for the week. We expect to be working most Saturdays, and occasionally we'll have a long weekend so you can visit Cairo or just relax in Luxor. Walter has EMT training and there'll be first aid kits at the site, so if anyone has a medical issue, please see Walter. In case there's a medical emergency, we can have a helicopter here and fly you to Luxor in minutes and Cairo in under an hour. I've made arrangements for temporary tents to be set up, similar to what is used at the archeological sites up north.

"Are there any questions?" asked Michael at the conclusion.

"What if we stumble into some ancient artifacts or archeological finds?" asked Steve.

"It's possible, but I'm not expecting anything like that. We're far from Luxor and this site is a long, mostly flat plain 'til you get to the mountains on either end. It is very important that we give serious attention to any possible findings, such as pieces of pottery or stones that could have been part of a building. Let me know right away if you come across anything like that. The Egyptian government has appointed an acquaintance of ours, Professor Morsi, who is an archeologist in Cairo at Al-Azhar University, to be our first point of contact should we discover anything. I'm sure he'd be most interested if we do. Oh, and I almost forgot, Professor Morsi's niece, Mesi, will be joining us in a few days. She's agreed to cook our meals and keep the place shipshape for the duration of the project. Anything else?"

Walt stood up to say "I'd just like to say how happy I am to be working with such a capable group. This is one of the most exciting things I have ever done. It will change the world. And the huge equipment that will arrive soon will make our job feasible."

He continued, "You know, I'm by far the oldest of all of you, and I agree 100% with Michael about the seven phases of a project. But I would just like to add that in my experience, it's the people and their attitudes that can make or break this project or any project. Some people… it's as though they *want* the project to fail or be stopped, not 'cause it's not a good idea, but because it's not *their* idea. I've watched this happen on nearly every project throughout my whole career. It makes me sad and angry, but also makes me ready. I'd like to suggest that all of us on the team stay ready… for anything."

"Thanks very much for those words of wisdom, Walt. Obviously, I second that sentiment," said Michael. And he concluded the meeting by saying, "Ok, enjoy your evening everyone. See you in the morning in front of the hotel at 7:00am sharp"

The team arrived at the dam site the next morning after the half hour drive from Luxor. Trucks with the bulldozers and front-end loaders were already there and being unloaded. Michael talked to the labor foreman and asked that the tents be set up, the equipment unloaded and the site cleared in preparation for the surveying to be done by Steve.

The dam site had an enormous amount of loose rock and stones covering the bedrock on either side of the fertile areas watered by the Nile. Those first few weeks at the site would be spent clearing this so a good survey could be accomplished. Eventually, military style temporary bridges would be used so both sides of the river could be accessed.

The initial plan was to drive the short distance back to Luxor each night and to stay in town. But starting on that first day, as the tents got set up, Michael said to Steve, "Ya know Steve, I told everyone they could stay in nice digs in town. But I feel like I'd like to soak up the atmosphere and stay closer to the project. I think I'm staying right here. I can get a bunk set up with a makeshift shower and then be here when the workmen arrive in the morning."

"I'm with you Buddy," said Steve.

"Yeah, now I just need to convince Ariana." Michael went to find Ariana who was busy talking to Henry on the satellite phone and giving a status update.

"I'm in," said Ariana. In fact, she was thinking she would be much safer here with Michael rather than in town.

That evening as the sun set over the desert, stars came out more brightly than Michael had ever seen before.

"C'mon, let's go for a walk," he said to Ariana. "I wanna see what the desert looks like at night." They walked through the tent door into the night and looked up. Without the usual light pollution of civilization, the stars and planets were so bright and so numerous that the two of them were in awe. The dry scent of the desert air and the bright starlight were intoxicating. As they held each other tight that first night in the desert, a shooting star passed overhead and made a dip near the horizon when the meteor disintegrated in a bright fireball.

"Finally," said Michael. "Our dream is coming true. Thank you for believing in me. I couldn't do this without you!"

"We are a good team and you are the most interesting man I ever met," Ariana responded. "I am just so glad we are together." Ariana was doing her best to work closely with Michael and keep their relationship professional and personal at the same time. She did not want to push Michael for any type of commitment for the future because this project was consuming her full attention. At this moment, she just wanted to enjoy the feeling of being in love and knowing that the feeling was mutual. The rest would take care of itself in the future.

Michael had his guitar and the two of them sat on the bed while he played for her the old song from the 1960's by Marvin Gaye and Tammi Terrell.

Oh, if I could build my whole world around you, darling
First, I'd put heaven by your side
Pretty flowers would grow wherever you walk, honey
And over your head would be the bluest sky
Then I'd take every drop of rain
And wash all your troubles away
I'd have the whole world wrapped up in you darling
And that would be all right, oh yes it would

Morsi's niece Mesi arrived a few days later and quickly became a favored member of the team. Her cooking was amazing and she always seemed to be around when needed.

Over the next few weeks as the heavy equipment began to clear and smooth the site, Michael, Ariana and the rest of the team started to feel a sense of home and belonging out there in the desert. There was a regular buzz of team conversation among them as each person moved their part of the project along.

When a substantial amount of the overburden had been cleared from the dam site, Steve went to work on refining the survey. It didn't take long before he realized that the initial plan of going straight across the desert to the hills on either side was not going to be anywhere near that simple.

"Michael, this's not really what I was expecting," said Steve. "The satellite topo maps were just not detailed enough to pick up the kind of terrain we're going to have to build on here. I'm getting mounds 40 feet high and craters almost as deep, some really large in size. Sorry but we're going to have to snake around these obstacles just like they did with the Transcontinental Railroad." Steve had calculated everything and continued, "I'm trying to figure out if we can actually make these tight bends or if we're going to have to dig out the hills and fill the valleys in. We should have done an on-site ground survey much sooner."

"Time to talk to Walt," said Michael. "let's go out there and see what we can see." The three of them, Steve, Michael and Walter, walked out to the area being surveyed and immediately saw why Steve was concerned. The land was pock marked with craters and hills.

"Well, we didn't design the tracks and large equipment to make hairpin turns," said Walter. "What about a compromise? Steve, d'ya think you could limit the inclines to less than about a degree so we can drive the equipment up? And maybe try to get around the worst of the hills and valleys without too tight of a curve. I'll see what can be done with the tracks and trolleys and how much of a bend we can tolerate. We may have to do some major surgery."

"I'll keep you posted as I do the survey and dam route," said Steve. "We might wanna blast some things away independent of the blast pit trolley. We'll probably need another crew to do more comprehensive site prep."

Michael said, "Your words were very prophetic, Walt. This is where the rubber meets the road, as they say."

"I'll try to find a reasonable way through this," said Steve.

Michael responded, "In the words of the Yoda, 'Do. Or do not. There is no try.'"

"Got it," said Steve.

As if that wasn't enough, the survey kept running across small caverns that the tracks would have to avoid. These areas were like sink holes. The whole site, rather than being a simple flat riverbed was a veritable mine field of obstacles to the dam construction.

The next few weeks were spent with Steve heroically blazing a trail around the obstacles and Walter redoing his calculations and talking to the engineers at Caterpillar to see if the equipment could be modified to deal with this unexpected issue.

"I've got the best man for the job with Bill Wong," said Walter. "If he can't figure out how to work this, no one can."

It was early one morning after they had been working at the dam site for several weeks that the foreman, a man named Tarek, came running into the tent to see Michael.

"Hey Michael," he said. "You better come have a look at this."

Michael and Steve followed him to a place where one of the big dozers was tipped over and in a hole. There on the ground in front of the blade there was a hole with a smaller opening at the top. "What do you make of that?" Tarek asked.

"Can you back the dozer out of there?" asked Steve. After much forward and backward maneuvering, the dozer finally backed out of the hole.

Steve stuck his head into the hole and could see in the dim light something at the bottom.

"Can we dig out the top?" said Michael. "I wanna see what's in there." This was done in short order, carefully and with shovels, and the things at the bottom of the hole turned out to be bones, big ones.

"This might be important," said Michael. "I think this's a good one for Professor Morsi. And it's part of our agreement with the Egyptian government. I'll send him pictures by email today. At least this hole is in an out of the way location, we may have to stop work around it. I hope not, but Morsi will decide."

Morsi arrived the next day early in the morning and began examining the holes and bones. Plaster of Paris was poured into a hole, similar to what had been done in Pompei and Herculaneum to recover the bodies that had been buried in the ash from the Mount Vesuvius eruption. It turned out they were a very large hominin, about the size of an American Sasquatch, but without the hairy body.

Michael was forever fascinated by the tales of the 'squatch.

Morsi of course stayed with them in the construction tents that night and for the next few nights as the excavations continued.

Later that evening at dinner in the 'club' tent, Morsi said, "You know, the Native Americans and the Eastern Asians have no facial hair, or chest hair for some groups. But yet, the Scotts in northern Europe not only have facial and chest hair, they actually have back hair!" He couldn't help laughing. "Could this be the ancestor of the Sasquatch, if they do exist? I have always wondered if there were some Neanderthals that actually crossed into North America on the land bridge even before the last ice age, during a previous ice age. They would have had time to develop very hairy bodies during the several inter-glacial maximums."

In the following days they found earthenware jars with some primitive form of writing on them in the vicinity of the giants. Morsi said, "These creatures had fire and developed a form of writing. This is the earliest writing we have yet found, and it's not even our own species. Imagine that!"

Genesis 6:4

> **⁴The Nephilim were on the earth in those days, and also afterward, when the sons of God came in to the daughters of man and they bore children to them. These were the mighty men who were of old, the men of renown.**

The bones were sent off for DNA evaluation and several weeks later Morsi said, "We know they are not a pure Neanderthal, but we do see some genetic similarities. I think we are dealing with an entirely new species."

Numbers 13

> **³³And there we saw the giants, the sons of Anak, which come of the giants: and we were in our own sight as grasshoppers, and so we were in their sight.**

"So, my friends, since you discovered it, you get to name it," said Morsi.

"Really?" said Michael. "Ariana, I think this is all you."

Ariana thought for a moment then got a smile on her face. "How about Nephilopethicus, after the Nephilim in Book of Genesis?"

"And so it is," said Morsi.

Chapter 25

Dam Construction Site

The next several months passed while the very large machines got delivered. Delivery for such huge machine parts was a challenge. Fortunately, there are good railroads from Port Said to Luxor. From there, double ganged tractor trailers were used to haul the parts to the site, closing all the main roads. Assembly was done much as skyscrapers are constructed, using cranes that ratchet up floor by floor to build the highest rock conveyors.

Despite the care and experience of Bill Wong and Walter Jay, one death occurred due to a toppling crane. The crane was positioned about midway up the gantry structure when a high wind from a sandstorm caught the boom and tipped it over. The storm came up suddenly as sometimes happens in the desert and caught the construction crew off guard. Michael and Ariana watched in horror as the cab fell nearly 500 feet killing the operator instantly. *I can't believe I let the construction continue in the middle of a sandstorm,* thought Michael. *Next time I shut it down until the storm passes. I'll be lucky if I don't get sued. Even with people dying of thirst in Palestine, we still have the temporary wells at Qattara and it's not worth a man's life just to hurry.* Michael knew he was not an experienced project leader, and that was the reason for appointing Walt as Project Manager. They had made the decision to continue through the storm together, mostly because of the time pressure.

The big dozers were able to clear the site of the dam based on Steve's surveys and the tracks were laid for the blast machines and conveyors. Bill Wong and Walter Jay worked out the changes needed in the conveyors, trolleys and associated machinery, including the control software so that the tracks could make bends as tight as 100-meter radius of curvature and one-degree upward grade. Steve threaded the route through the pock-marked desert and held to these specs. Soon the tracks were in place on both sides of the megadam wall on the east side of the Nile River.

It was agreed that the construction would start from the West and proceed eastward toward the mountains. At last, the day came to try out the new machines. "I think we're ready, Michael," said Walter one morning. "Let's kick the tires and light the fires!"

"Really? D'ya have to be so dramatic?" Michael and Steve were laughing as they walked out to the mega machines. The scene was like something out of a Jules Verne novel. The size of the drilling rigs, conveyors, crushers, sorters and kilns dwarfed the men standing next to them. Treads on the big dozers were over 20 feet high. A small elevator type lift was needed to get up to the operator's cab. The rock conveyors were over 1000 feet tall and nearly 100 feet wide. Standing at the bottom looking up gave Michael chills as he realized what Walt had accomplished. On the north or downstream side of the dam site, a 100-acre array of solar panels had been installed. These, along with a 25 MW-hour battery storage system would allow the machinery to run totally self-sufficient, 24/7.

"Ok, guys, here we go." Walter walked into the operator's cab and moved the drilling rigs for the blast pit into position. He flipped the switch and 42 huge drills began drilling deep into the limestone bedrock. It took only about an hour to drill deep enough to be ready to set the 42 charges of dynamite. The drills were withdrawn and the tubes containing the charges dropped into the holes. The charges were fired in groups by automated digital signal from the main controller in the cab. As the blast pit trolley and main conveyor trolley moved forward on the tracks, a huge pile of rocks and boulders was revealed where the blast had just taken place. The mega dozers began shoveling the rocks onto the blast pit conveyor which in turn fed the crushers.

Now there was the din of the crushers starting up as the rotary lime kiln got its first taste of the gravel from the fine crusher. The solar panels on the downstream side of the dam powered the lime kiln. Soon the crushed calcined stone was being fed onto the dam wall conveyor along with large and medium sized rock from the blast pit. The rock tumbled down onto the ground on the upstream side of the dam and the team stared in amazement.

"Ladies and gentlemen, we are building a dam," said Walt over the PA. There were whoops, shouts, clapping and horns blowing from all the big dozers. The project was under way. Walt just sat there and smiled as the LIDAR system automatically moved the trolleys and conveyors to build the dam wall at the exact right slope and height. From this point on, the only human intervention were the operators of the mega dozers feeding the rock and gravel from the blast pit onto the conveyors.

"Drinks and dinner on me tonight," said Michael as he watched in admiration. "This's truly a historic accomplishment."

By that time, it was late afternoon and the team drove the half hour back to Luxor for a much-needed celebration.

"I propose a toast," said Michael when they had all gathered at the Al-Sahaby Lane Roof Terrace restaurant. "To the largest dam ever built in the world."

"Here, here," they shouted.

"And to you, Michael, our fearless leader," said Ariana smiling.

Chapter 26

Kharga Oasis, a few months later

The Muslim Brotherhood was a worldwide movement that sought to establish an Islamic caliphate first in the Mideast, but eventually the whole world. The Brotherhood was responsible for the formation of the more militant Jihadist groups such as ISIS and Al-Qaeda. When Hanbal returned to Egypt, a clandestine meeting was set with the Brotherhood leader and Hanbal in Cairo.

"We have to cut the head off the snake," said the leader. "I need you to put a plan together to attack the dam."

"OK, I get it. We're with you on this. What have we got to lose?"

One night some of Hanbal's men, who had come with him from the fighting in Afghanistan, came to his house in Kharga. They met in the front room while Lapis made herself useful in the kitchen. She couldn't help overhearing their shouts and planning.

"The dam site is poorly guarded," said Hanbal. "I believe they have only a few government troops and no heavy armor or weapons. I think we should attack at night."

One of his men spoke up and said, "Why not just blow up the equipment?"

"That won't help," said Hanbal. "They'll just repair it and keep going."

"You know," said another. "We could kidnap the woman and make the ransom a complete abandonment of the project. We tell them that if they restart the project, someone else will be kidnapped and this time no ransom demand. That way they will be afraid to start back up again."

"Ok, very clever," said Hanbal. "Let's plan on mounting a frontal attack on the compound where they are staying and take the woman hostage. We can bring her back here to Kharga to negotiate with the Egyptian Government. They will never find her out here."

"Are we agreed?" asked Hanbal.

"Yes," said each of his fighters.

"Two weeks from tomorrow," said Hanbal. "Meantime I will nose around the dam site and see what things look like."

What Hanbal didn't realize was that his wife, Lapis, could hear them when she was in the kitchen. It was as though she was just invisible to him. She froze with fear and she dropped the dinner plate. Her heart rate increased and she thought, *what should I do now? If I tell anyone he may kill me. But if I don't ...*

Lapis had no one to confide in except her friend from the neighborhood. But her friend did have a cell phone. She resolved to talk with her friend when Hanbal had left the next day and notify the authorities.

Chapter 27

Dam Construction Site

When Michael and the team returned to the construction trailers the next day, they were surprised to find several thousand demonstrators picketing the entrance to the dam site, complete with news reporters, cameras and protest leaders with bull horns. What they didn't know was that the Muslim Brotherhood had been hard at work organizing the protest, hoping to derail the project. Many were carrying signs that read "Stop the Dam" and "No Resettlement, No Dam." Michael was surprised since he believed the land grants to those living in the new lake region were very generous and most of those people would become independently wealthy as a result. But having a home where families had been living for over 5000 years was much more important to some than just money. Also, Michael and the team were very naïve when it came to the politics in Egypt. The Arab Spring, the fundamentalist Islamic movement, the vice-like grip the military leaders had on the government all combined to make a very complex society. The demonstrators were very angry, and not just at the megadam, but a host of other issues as well. As the vehicles drove up, the picketers began to circle the car and shout insults in Arabic. The protest was getting ugly and super dangerous.

Michael was very hung over from the previous evening's libations. He rarely had more than one drink at a social occasion and was in no mood for this. He sat in the car steaming as these unreasonable people surrounded his car. As one of the men started banging on the hood of the car, Michael's anger boiled over. He slammed the car in gear and tramped the accelerator to the floor. The Humvee lurched forward and nearly ran over several demonstrators, who, seeing the massive car blasting forward, dove out of the way just in time. The thousand or so demonstrators, when they saw that they'd been beat and that the caravan was entering the dam site, got even more rowdy. The lesson for Michael and the team was that this is a hostile environment, even though the people would become very wealthy.

As their car moved forward, people pushed in closer to prevent them from going forward. There were so many people in and around the dam site that people began to climb up onto the huge crushers that fed the conveyor belts. All this was being filmed by the news media.

When Walt and Steve were designing the dam building machinery, they determined that the only way to build the megadam in any reasonable amount of time was to automate everything as much as possible. Then the machines could run 24/7 with no operator in the control room, just a simple computer screen. All the data for the amount of rock deposited at the wall, LIDAR information as to the shape and size of the wall as well as location of the machinery on the rails was recorded automatically with no operator intervention. The dam was being built the whole time the team was in Luxor. The only humans on the site were the guards posted in the shacks at either end of the moving machinery and the dozer operators.

As some of the demonstrators began to climb up onto the machinery, it was running at full speed. Every hour or so, the drilling rigs blasted more rock from the damsite base and the huge dozers scooped it up onto the crusher conveyors. When the blasts from the drilling rigs went off, the ground shook all over the site. Unfortunately, one of the demonstrators was too close to the edge when a drilling rig blast went off. He tumbled backward onto the main conveyor and landed on the gravel being lifted to the dam wall. The fall was only six feet or so and he landed on his back. But the conveyor was moving very quickly and by the time the man got up he was already a third of the way up the conveyor, way too far up to jump to the ground. Seeing his situation, he began to try to run back down the belt over rocks and gravel, but the conveyor belt was moving too fast carrying him further upward toward the top. He began to scream and wave his arms while the news cameras rolled, live. Millions watched as he was carried a thousand feet up in the air.

Walt could see this and knew no one in the crowd could stop the belt without the password. There was a kill switch but it was hidden beneath the control panel. Having someone fall onto the giant belt was just never expected by Walt, Bill Wong or Steve. "Get me over there, now," shouted Walt. Michael sped up and demonstrators parted as the car approached the control room. Walt jumped out of the car, climbed the ladder to the control room and headed for the kill switch. As millions watched on nationwide TV, the poor demonstrator, scrambling to get down the belt, lost his race and was carried over the edge to be forever buried in the body of the megadam, just like workers at the Hoover Dam a hundred years earlier.

Of course, the news media had a field day. Michael and team were now officially at war with the protestors, inspired by the Muslim Brotherhood, and the press. This was the first loss of life over the megadam.

"Yeah, and then they started picketing the car," said Michael to Adam Levy on the phone later. "I just couldn't believe it when that guy climbed up on the crusher. We'll never hear the end of it. We need more protection down here."

"Let me see what I can do," said Adam. The upshot of the incident was an addition of more guards from the Egyptian Ministry of Defense to help keep the peace at the construction site. The site would be woefully understaffed, even with this addition.

It was agreed that the machinery building the dam would run 24 hours a day, 7 days a week until the dam wall was constructed. Periodic outages of a few hours would be required to check and maintain the machines, but it was 'balls out' until they were done.

"Don't you think you could come up with a better expression than 'balls out?'" said Ariana.

"You have a dirty mind," said Michael. "It actually comes from the old steam engines with the so called "flyball governor." In the old steam engines, the engine turned a shaft or a wheel. To regulate the speed of the train the main steam valve had a mechanism that was turned by the shaft and had two steel balls, one on either side. These were hooked to a slider that moved the valve open and closed. If the engine moved the shaft too fast, the balls would spin further out and pull the steam valve closed. If it was going too slow, the balls moved in and opened the valve, keeping the shaft speed constant regardless of load."

"I liked my idea better," said Ariana and laughed.

And so, it began in earnest. Blast pit explosions followed by the mega dozers loading the rocks onto the blast pit conveyor followed by the crushers and solar powered lime kiln with storage batteries for night time operation, followed by the dam wall conveyor chugging along and putting the rocks in place to build the dam wall, back and forth, all day and all night.

The construction trailers were really just doublewide mobile homes on tracks like a pullman car on steroids. There were 'sleeper' cars with small bedrooms, a large dining car and a rec room area. The offices were in the lead car and there was an open floor plan where all the team members could see each other as well as the dam wall and machinery. Michael had taken the precaution of having perimeter cameras set up and wired to monitors in the office. A laser fence around the perimeter was designed to alarm if anyone entered the area. A handful of government troops patrolled the site perimeter at night but fencing the area with chain link was just not practical.

At the same time he was envisioning a plan to demolish the dam, Hanbal applied for a job running a big dozer at the construction site. He used the internet to learn how to operate the machine and, with fake credentials, easily got the job. Since he had been issued a pass, he could come and go as he pleased and not set off an alarm.

Chapter 28

Construction Dam Site

A guard shack consisted of a small rail car which was in front of the construction trailer cars and the main trolley. Inside there were monitors for the perimeter cameras as well as radio communications with the perimeter guards and the construction office. The entire arrangement, including the guard shack car, optical perimeter fencing and camera setup could move with the conveyor trolley as the dam was being built.

The large area array of solar panels and storage batteries powered the trolley and conveyor motors, lime kiln, and control systems as well as the AC and power for offices. The entire complex was self-sufficient except for food and water.

Michael and Walter both enjoyed hunting and shooting back in the U.S. Prior to the trip to Egypt, Michael had purchased AR-10 rifles from Daniel Defense, one of the highest quality and most expensive of the assault rifles. He also decided to buy night vision scopes for the rifles and ten additional 20 round magazines each. What Michael liked about the AR-10 compared to the much more popular AR-15 was that it fired a Winchester .308 round, a thirty-caliber, supersonic, high powered rifle bullet rather than the 5.56mm NATO round of the AR-15. The thirty-caliber round could stop an elephant at 200 yards or twenty elephants in 10 seconds, as he liked to remind his dad, and was a preferred weapon of snipers worldwide. He had the team sight-in the rifles and become proficient in the off chance that they had to defend the dam. *I hope I never have to use this thing, he prayed.*

It was just shortly after two in the morning when Hanbal and his band of terrorists approached the guard shack car from the west.

The plan was simple. Hanbal would cut the power to the construction complex. They were all equipped with night vision goggles. A small group would then take out the perimeter guards who were left in the dark and move toward the trolley conveyors. An IED would destroy the main conveyor creating a diversion, while Hanbal entered the construction cars and took the woman, Ariana, prisoner. They would drive her west to Kharga and hold her at Hanbal's house there. A ransom call would be made to the Egyptian Government demanding that the megadam project be stopped and dismantled. They would have 24 hours to comply.

It was the night of the new moon so the desert was very dark as the truck approached the construction site. Hanbal stopped the truck while still several hundred yards away and they covered the rest of the distance on foot. When they were still about 200 yards away, Hanbal set up a makeshift rest for his rifle and with one single shot took out the guard in the guard shack car. The men moved quickly to the shack and shut off the main breaker to the complex. The whole site was plunged into darkness. They then moved toward the construction trailer cars and the main trolley.

Michael was lying awake when the night light and lights on the complex went out. *It could be an equipment failure that tripped the breaker,* thought Michael. It was then he heard the pop-pop-pop of the assault rifles. Michael quickly grabbed his rifle, woke the others and said, "We'll see what's going on. Ariana, Walt, Steve, get your guns and come with me."

"What's up?" said Steve.

"Looks like we're under some kind of attack. Come on."

The others quickly pulled on clothes, grabbed their rifles and followed Michael out the construction trailer door. A sweep of his night vision scope told Michael what was happening. The dozer operators were both dead, along with the perimeter guards and a small group was standing near the main conveyor trolley setting what looked like charges on the conveyor. The four of them took cover behind the smaller dozers, invisible to Hanbal who approached the construction trailer from the other side.

This was it; this was exactly what Michael was afraid of. Michael could feel the emotion of anger and aggression rising in his head, the blood pounding in his temples and his hands beginning to shake with the flow of adrenaline. Without hesitation he threw up the rifle, trained the night vision scope on the terrorist setting what looked like an IED and fired. The man crumpled and fell to the ground. There was a total of 15 terrorists in the group. Some returned fire, with bullets hitting the trailer wall behind them, but by that time Ariana, who was an excellent shot, returned fire hesitantly.

Michael continued to fire but heard a shout as Walt was hit and went down. Steve managed to get off several shots before turning to look at Walt. They were badly exposed behind the smaller dozers, but Michael didn't really care. He was seething with anger and kept on firing. Ariana was crouched down by that time using the dozer tread as a rifle rest, and continuing to lay down fire as best she could.

The terrorists had night vision goggles but not IR scopes for their rifles. They were at a distinct disadvantage and apparently didn't expect such strong resistance. The fire fight continued for several minutes, but when the terrorists saw that they were losing, one by one they broke and ran. The night vision scopes were not good at rapid movement in low light, so Michael's angry, rapid-fire shots missed as they ran and the rest of the men, only three of them, got away with one being half carried, apparently hit in the leg. Michael could have gone after them, but was concerned about Walt.

Meanwhile, Hanbal was in the main construction trailer car and looking in the bedrooms for Ariana. He had seen her, he thought the only woman on the complex, and was determined to find her and take her back as a hostage.

When Mesi heard the trailer door open, she hid in the closet, not being one to have or even shoot firearms. In fact, Mesi was totally against guns and desperately wished that she hadn't taken this job.

Hanbal looked in all the bedrooms and finding them empty, he began to look in the closets. Soon he came to the closet where Mesi was hiding. When he yanked open the door, Mesi just closed her eyes and said, "Don't shoot."

Hanbal grabbed her by the arm as the fire fight raged in front of the trailer and took her to the truck, dragging her across the desert so that she fell multiple times. When they got to the truck, the only three men left alive were already inside. "Where are the others?" said Hanbal.

"Dead."

"Ok, let's get out of here before they come after us."

"Michael, Walt's hit," said Steve.

"How bad?"

"He's gonna need an ambulance," said Steve. "It's 'is left leg. He's unconscious, but still breathing. We gotta stop the bleeding. Come on, let's get him inside." They carried Walt inside the trailer while Ariana called for an ambulance.

"The bullet hit so high in his leg I can't really get the torniquet on properly," said Steve.

"How long for the ambulance?" said Michael.

"They said twenty minutes," said Ariana. "Hang on, Walt."

Michael did the mental calculation between taking Walt in a chopper or waiting for the ambulance that had EMTs and equipment. He quickly decided on the ambulance. Steve continued with direct pressure on the wound.

"Nice shooting there, Rambo," said Steve as he looked up at Michael. "You and Ariana drove them off."

"Yeah, and who knew Ariana was such a good shot?" said Michael.

"Rifle team at Harvard," admitted Ariana.

Michael was breathing heavy and the artery in his neck was pulsing wildly. He had the expression of a wild man.

"You better calm down, Buddy," said Steve. "I don't want you to have a stroke."

"I'm ok. I just get so angry I want to strangle the terrorists."

"Looks like you and Ariana did the next best thing. C'mon, let's call the Luxor police. They won't be back tonight."

"Ok, ok."

Michael began to look for Mesi who had stayed inside.

"Mesi?" called Michael. "You ok?" No response. "Mesi, where are you?"

"Guys, look around for her. Maybe she's hiding somewhere and afraid to come out."

Ariana went to call the authorities in Luxor and began a room-to-room search while Michael looked everywhere for her.

"She's just not here," said Michael. And then it dawned on him. "They must've taken her. Very clever, the one group causes a diversion while the other whisks her off. I have to assume she's either kidnapped or dead."

"But if she were dead, why would they take the body?" said Steve. "No, it must be some kind of ransom thing."

"I don't get it," said Michael. "Why take a servant girl?"

"Yeah, unless... maybe they thought she was Ariana and they are holding her hostage."

"The police and ambulance are on their way," said Ariana.

Chapter 29

Kharga Oasis, the next day

Hanbal and what was left of his group sped off. The pontoon bridges had not yet been constructed, and since the dam site was about mid-way between the two available bridges over the Nile, one at Edfu in the south and the other on Route 60 to the north, they had to drive the roughly twenty miles south to the closest bridge. Then there was the drive back north along the river to the Luxor-Kharga Road, another 50 miles. Finally, there was a three-hour drive to get to Kharga. Mesi was gagged and blindfolded for the entire trip so when they got to Hanbal's father's house in Kharga, she had no idea where she was.

"Tie her to the chair," said Hanbal. "Lapis, take care of our friend here."

Hanbal had no idea that the young lady they took was not Ariana at all but Mesi, Morsi's niece. For her part, Mesi had no idea why she was kidnapped. She kept her thoughts to herself, petrified.

"Hanbal, what are you doing?" said Lapis. "You're not being reasonable."

"Quiet woman," said Hanbal. Lapis hurried off to the kitchen, terrified.

Hanbal's father was just heading off to the market stall. It was early morning. Now he was afraid of Hanbal as well, but his sentiments were with the Islamic State fighters. He left the house without saying a word.

Mesi looked around in terror as Lapis came into the room.

"Would you like some water?" asked Lapis. "You must be very frightened."

Mesi said "Yes, thank you."

160

"You two stay outside the house and keep your eyes open. They won't attempt a rescue, I don't think, since they don't know where she is. But, just in case," said Hanbal.

His men sat outside the house with their rifles and played the ancient Egyptian game of Backgammon.

Later that same day, Lapis went to the market stall as usual. She knew she needed to find a way of telling the authorities that a woman was being held captive in her house. She desperately hoped she would see her neighbor friend in the marketplace that day. But it would be another day before the woman appeared. When her friend stopped by the market stall, Lapis said, "I need to use your phone. My husband is doing something reckless. It's a matter of life or death."

"Yes, dear. What's going on?" said her friend.

"Please don't tell anyone," said Lapis, "A woman is being held hostage in my house and I am afraid of what my husband will do."

Lapis' friend could see the look in her eyes. "Here's my phone," she said.

The authorities in Kharga were aware of the kidnapping at the megadam, but had no idea she was being held right under their noses.

The police in Luxor had decided not to release any information on the identity of the kidnapped woman.

Police in Kharga relayed the message to the authorities in Luxor who, in turn, told Michael and his team. *Well, at least we know where they're holding her,* thought Michael.

At the dam site, they were shut down while the police conducted their investigation. Michael was waiting for a ransom call and the police had set up tracers and recording on Michael's cell phone.

The call from the terrorist kidnappers came in just after noon on the third day. Hanbal's voice was disguised and his cell phone had been set up to bounce off towers in multiple locations so it could not be traced. Of course, Hanbal didn't know that Michael already knew where Mesi was being held.

"Stop the dam project and the woman will be released. If you agree and then start back up again, another will be kidnapped," was all Hanbal said and then hung up.

It was only a matter of minutes before the entire Qattara Development Project team knew what was going on. What they couldn't understand, at first, was how the ransom could be enforced. They could always agree, get Mesi back and then start up again. *Looks like the kidnappers are not that naïve,* thought Michael.

"Michael, it's Adam Levy. I want you to know how sorry we all are for this kidnapping. What's going on now?"

"They've demanded ransom; they want us to stop working on the dam. They think they have Ariana. They threatened that if we lie about stopping the project to get her back, they will capture someone else," said Michael. "I'm not sure how to stop them, or how to negotiate. We can't protect everyone on the project team all the time."

"Of course, you know that we don't negotiate with terrorists, anyway," said Adam. "But the most difficult part of these scenarios is finding the location where the subject is being held. In this case we already have that, so we have a suggestion."

"Ok," said Michael, a bit skeptical but willing to listen to anything that could get Mesi back.

"This case is special in the sense that there is usually a ransom that is traded for the hostage, done deal. But now they are threatening to continue the kidnappings if the 'ransom' is not continued, the megadam construction is restarted. So, like 'Ender's Game', the sci-fi novel about an epic battle between two worlds, we need to win this exchange and all the future ones as well. Only way to do that, like Ender, is to eliminate them all." Adam had little scruples when it came to kidnappers and terrorists.

"I remember that book," said Michael. "But how?"

"We have some newly developed technology for these situations, which, unfortunately we have to deal with all the time. I'm going to explain it to you but only if you swear to absolute secrecy."

"Done," said Michael.

"Our military has developed some very small drones that are heavily armed but nearly undetectable even with radar since they fly at 5,000 meters. The trick was figuring out how to keep them aloft for days since, as you know, these things used by UPS and so on are usually only able to fly for 40 minutes or so because of limited battery charge.

"Our scientists have found a way to convert chemical to electrical energy at very high efficiency and use this to recharge the batteries while aloft. The drones we now have can stay aloft for over five days and fly over 20,000km. They have guns, cameras and navigation systems to allow us to cruise at 5,000 meters, or higher, out of sight of enemy radar. When the coordinates have been identified, the drone can drop down and hover only a few meters from the enemy and eliminate them, then go back up to 5,000 meters and disappear.

"We think we can bring these drones to the house where Mesi is being kept, drop down and deal with the guards, then our car can come in and get her out of there. If we can get a cell phone to the woman who is our contact, we can be sure the coast is clear inside the house before the raid."

"Sounds like a plan," said Michael. "Let's do it." It had already been three days since the kidnapping and nearly 20 hours since the ransom call. There was no time to lose.

It was after evening prayers that Hanbal finally decided to get some sleep. He left the two guards in front and one inside the house. "Keep a sharp eye on her. If they somehow find out where we are keeping her, I want to move her right away," said Hanbal.

"Don't worry, they won't find us," said the terrorist inside the house.

Mesi heard them and was even more terrified than before.

"I just don't know how long he'll be asleep and there's one of them inside the house now," said Lapis quietly. She still had her friend's cell phone and was in touch with the Kharga police who relayed information to her about the rescue plan.

"We're right around the corner," said Michael, "tell her to go to her room and stay there and this will be over before she knows it. We'll take her with us."

Michael and team were in constant communication with the several elite Israeli commandos in the pickup van experienced in this type of operation. They had helmet cams similar to the operation to take out bin Laden.

"It's always their Achilles heel in this part of the world," said Michael. "Technology."

"Don't worry," said the Israeli driving the truck. "Technology is *not* our Achilles heel." They had to move fast since they didn't know how long Hanbal would be asleep.

Lapis had plans of her own. She had been beaten and verbally abused, as well as held prisoner by Hanbal since the day they were married. She thought Hanbal was behaving like a wild man, but regardless, she had had enough. A long-bladed kitchen knife was under her dress as she crept into their bedroom where Hanbal was sleeping.

As the truck turned the corner onto Lapis' street, the two drones that were less than half a meter in size and were cruising at 3000 meters quickly dropped down in front of the house, took aim and eliminated both guards before either of them knew anything was amiss.

The commandos got out of the truck and headed for the house. The guard inside heard the commotion and stood with a pistol to Mesi's head. "Come any closer and she dies," he shouted. Unfortunately for this particular terrorist, the room had a window and the drones, which were controlled by an operator in the truck, both moved to the side of the house so the terrorist holding Mesi was visible using IR through the curtained window. Both drones locked onto the terrorist. Game over.

The two commandos burst into the room, "Are you ok?" they asked.

"Yes, but I feel like I have to throw up," said Mesi, which she did as soon as she was untied.

"It's ok," one said. "It's all over now." *She looks terrible* thought Michael as he watched her on the helmet cams. *I guess I would too.*

The two Israelis quickly searched the house, room to room to be sure there were no other terrorists in the building. "Clear," they shouted as each room was searched. "Hello, we're your friends," said one commando as he found Lapis standing in the corner of the bedroom. "you're safe now. We've come to get you out of here."

"Thank you, thank you," said Lapis. She was white as a ghost and her hands were shaking uncontrollably. They brought her downstairs and she and Mesi had a hug.

"Thank you," said Mesi. When Mesi asked about Hanbal, she said, "Allahu Akbar. He deserved it."

The trip back to Luxor was very quiet and subdued. When they got there, Michael, Steve and Ariana were waiting for them. Walt was at the Luxor Hospital. His injury was much more serious than at first thought. By the time he got to the hospital he had lapsed into a coma and was now on a respirator. There was some question as to whether there was permanent brain damage and he continued in a coma.

"Thank you for saving their lives," said Steve to the two commandos.

"That's what we're here for," one said in answer. "I think we cut the head off the snake. The others, if there are any, are long gone by now."

"Looks like technology is the answer, at least around here," said Michael.

"We have to be getting back," said the Israelis. "Take care of yourselves."

"Thanks again," said Michael. The megadam team decided to stay in Luxor that night and get some sleep. They had a quick bite of room service and went to bed.

With so much adrenaline coursing through his body, Michael was wide awake after the excitement and danger of the day. He was also very glad to have Ariana there with him. If she hadn't participated in the fighting, it could have been her that got kidnapped. As they walked back to the hotel, the moon was full over the desert. Ariana looked absolutely radiant in the moonlight. They stopped and Michael looked at her almost in a new way, for the first time. "I love you very much, Ariana," he said.

"I love you too, Michael," said Ariana.

Michael held her face in both his hands and kissed her full on the lips. It was the kind of kiss that was much more than sexual. It was a kiss that connected them on the level of one infinite soul to another in an endless universe. A soft, warm glow infused both of them as they experienced something magical and transcendent. No matter what happened in the future, these two soul mates would be joined forever in a way that made verbal communication unnecessary. That night, Michael resolved not to let his thoughts stray to any other woman again.

Part III

Return to the Garden

I see skies of blue
And clouds of white
The bright blessed day
The dark sacred night
And I think to myself

What a wonderful world – Louis Armstrong

Chapter 30

Construction Site, 18 months later

The Prime Minister of Egypt formally thanked the Israeli government for their help with the terrorists. Lapis stayed with her friend in Kharga, and Michael kept a low profile at the dam site.

The megadam team resumed work and the dam wall began to take shape on the eastern side of the Nile River. There would be four more months of work on the east side before work could be started on the west side of the Nile. The bypass tunnels were nearing completion so the river portion of the megadam could be started when the east and west sides were finished.

Meanwhile, the Israelis were busy building the underground aqueducts through the Old Euphrates ancient aquifer. Construction began on the developments, wells and waterways in the Qattara Depression and the first of the new residential homes were built in what would become a waterfront development in Kharga.

The residential and business developments in the Qattara Depression, aka Lake Eden, would take fully five years to complete. Meanwhile, ongoing development would begin in other parts of the waterways.

* * *

Almost on schedule, three years after the dam construction first started, it was time to allow the water from the Nile to back up against the dam. The great hydroelectric turbines had been placed in their tunnels at the center of the dam structure and wired into the electric grid. The solar panels from the construction were left in place to provide additional power to the local developments on either side downstream of the dam. Michael and his team were on hand to begin filling the great dam by closing the bypass channels on both sides of the Nile.

The protestors, who had been so much of a problem at the beginning of the project, were quieted by the enormous amount of money they received to relocate. In the end, it was the money that talked. The Muslim Brotherhood was persuasive but not rich, and although they still harbored resentment, there were no more attacks on the megadam.

A ribbon cutting ceremony was arranged with all of the original Qattara Development team members, including the Prime Minister of Egypt. Michael and his team were beaming from ear to ear. Adam Levy was fully recovered and there for the ceremony as well. Unfortunately, Walt was still in rehab, but was no longer in a coma and improving daily.

The Egyptian Prime Minister had some remarks. "In the spirit of international cooperation, we come together today to mark the first step in a project that will transform many thousands of square miles of empty, barren desert into a lush tropical paradise for all the world to enjoy. I would like to thank the members of the Qattara Development team for all of their sacrifice, dedication and vision in taking this, the first of our Sahara water projects, to completion.

"I would also like to give a special thanks to Michael Walters and his team for their selfless dedication to the project goals at great personal risk. I know all of you share my gratitude for Michael and his team for their perseverance in the face of many adversities including terrorist attacks, kidnapping, protest demonstrations, technical difficulties and financial hardship.

"It gives me great pleasure to announce here today that Michael and his megadam team have been awarded the International Medal of Freedom for their work on this project." The Prime Minister opened a box and placed the medal around each of the necks of the megadam team members.

Michael was astonished since he didn't even know such a medal existed let alone that his team was nominated for one. "Thank you so much Mr. Prime Minister," said Michael. "My team and I are very honored."

"And with that," said the Prime Minister, "I'll turn this over to Michael Walters."

Michael stepped up to the control panel and moved the levers that partially closed the huge bypass valves, beginning the process of filling the great megadam lake. There was handshaking all around and it was broadcast live with drone cameras capturing the magnificent scene of water slowly reaching the dam as the diversion tunnels were closed.

So, although the megadam was now officially operational, there were many challenges yet to face. It would take months before the water level began to creep up the dam face, and even more months before the great turbines could be started, since only a fraction of the Nile River water was diverted.

Chapter 31

Iran, Next Year

Unfortunately, the incident with the ISIS terrorists had much greater long-term consequences than anyone on the megadam team could ever have expected. Somehow, the fact that the Israelis were involved in the rescue leaked out and the Iranians found out about Israel's large role in the project. For years, the Ayatollah was furious and made it clear that he thought the megadam project plan was to steal more land from the Islamic countries and expand Israel's territory to include much of Egypt. Finally, with the Muslim Brotherhood's support, the Iranian president put their nuclear forces on high alert, alarming the rest of the world who had no idea they even had a nuclear capability. Of course, the Israelis responded in kind by going on high alert as well. It appeared that the first worldwide nuclear confrontation since the 1960's Cuban missile crisis was under way. True to form, the UN was afraid to do anything. This was the first real test of the new Protectorate.

Revelation 12: 1-2

> [1] **And there appeared a great wonder in heaven; a woman clothed with the sun, and the moon under her feet, and upon her head a crown of twelve stars:**
> [2] **And she being with child cried, travailing in birth, and pained to be delivered.**

³ And there appeared another wonder in heaven; and behold a great red dragon, having seven heads and ten horns, and seven crowns upon his heads.

⁴ And his tail drew the third part of the stars of heaven, and did cast them to the earth: and the dragon stood before the woman which was ready to be delivered, for to devour her child as soon as it was born.

Ariana was thoughtful and said to Michael one day in the midst of this, "Remember the 'third woe' in the Book of Revelation? I am wondering if the 'Great Red Dragon' represents the nuclear capability and the seven heads of the dragon are the G7 economic powers with their seven crowns of wealth. The ten horns mentioned in Revelation are a mystery to me, but anyway, I wonder if the current situation with Israel and Iran is this confrontation? The dragon's tail is supposed to draw the third part of the stars from heaven and cast them to earth."

Michael thought a moment then said, "Ok, ok it's possible, but it's just like any other prediction, Nostradamus, Jean Dixon, who predicted the Kennedy assassination, you can make almost anything fit if the prediction is allegorical and suitably vague."

"Yes, I get that, but what if this is real? The passage mentions a woman with a crown of twelve stars. What if the child she is pained to deliver is really our megadam project, our crystal world city? The dragon is supposed to devour her child as soon as it is delivered. So, the question becomes, can the outcome of this passage be changed by the collective faith of humanity? Or will the nuclear war destroy our project and perhaps much of the world with it?"

"I feel like the megadam is in some ways our child too," said Michael. "But I never in a million years dreamed that it'd be the cause of a nuclear war."

After a few minutes of silence, Ariana turned to Michael and reached for his hand.

"I think maybe I could be that woman," said Ariana. "I could be a bridge for peace. I have been thinking and I have ideas. There are still a few things about me you do not know."

Michael was stunned by that thought. Ariana and Michael had been following the news reports closely as the megadam project continued. It seemed that each day the rhetoric and threats by both Israel and Iran escalated. The world waited with bated breath and struggled to find ways of diffusing the situation.

"Somehow, I don't see you clothed with the sun and the moon under your feet," laughed Michael. "And what about the crown of twelve stars?"

"I do not know and I do not care," said Ariana. Michael let the matter drop hoping that Ariana would think twice about it.

That night, Ariana had a dream. In it, the woman clothed with the sun and a crown of twelve stars flew on the wings of a great eagle, not to the wilderness to hide from the dragon, but to Iran, to her home. In her dream, an angel appeared and told her she must fly to Iran and meet with the Ayatollah. She must go alone. The angel said that the Ayatollah would see her and she would convince him to join the coalition. He would sign a peace agreement in exchange for prime land along Lake Eden where a new caliphate would be established for all the Islamic faithful to live and practice their faith in peace. The angel told her to meet with the leaders of the Qattara Development team and convince them to offer the peace agreement and land to Iran, that she would be God's messenger of peace.

Revelation 12:13-14

¹³ And when the dragon saw that he was cast unto the earth, he persecuted the woman which brought forth the man child.
¹⁴ And to the woman were given two wings of a great eagle, that she might fly into the wilderness, into her place, where she is nourished for a time, and times, and half a time, from the face of the serpent.

"I have to go and try," said Ariana to Michael as they lay in bed the next morning.

"How? asked Michael. "You have no influence there."

"Well… that is not exactly true. I never wanted to talk about my dad so I just told you he worked in the government. Did you notice how I didn't talk about his job? I never told you that my father is the Minister of Foreign Affairs in Iran. I just didn't feel safe if too many people found out."

"What? Are you serious?" said Michael. "You've been holding out on us. I knew he worked for the government, but I had no idea he was in such a position. I can't even believe this. Do you think he would listen to you?"

"Oh, Michael, I have so much to tell you." Ariana sat down and covered her face with her hands. "Now that I told you this much, I have to tell you who I really am. You are the only person in the world I can talk to. I know that your secret is that you have all this pent-up anger inside and that you keep thinking you're going to lose control of your anger. Well, I have a secret too. Back when we first met, I told you I read the Bible.

"It gets more complicated. All the Bible stories that I know so well were actually taught to me by my mother when I was growing up in Iran. She is one of the Muslim Background Believers, a group of mostly women who are rejecting traditional Islam in favor of Christianity. We kept her Christian conversion and baptism a secret from the men, even in our own family, but she is actually a Christian women's leader in Iran. If the government ever found out, my father could be imprisoned or executed. So, we say nothing. But I believe if I talk to her, we might be able to convince my father to speak to the Ayatollah to back off and agree to talks with the Israelis."

"I think the probability of you being held hostage or taken prisoner is high," said Michael. "Please don't do anything so reckless, especially now. You're scaring me." Michael's love for Ariana was consuming him at that moment and he was terrified that she would be imprisoned or killed by these radicals if she went there. The incident with Mesi's kidnapping was still fresh in his mind.

"I had a dream. I'm supposed to meet with the development team and try to offer the Iranians something. I need to offer them land in exchange for a peace agreement.

"And anyway, I think they are bluffing. I do not think they have any nukes, and I am going to prove it." Ariana knew from her time growing up in Iran that much of the saber rattling done by the president and his ministers was a hollow threat. Of course, they could have made tremendous progress over the last few years, but that seemed unlikely without the support of other nuclear powers such as Russia or China. The supposed collaboration with North Korea was also mostly talk. "I think that if I can find some evidence that the nuclear program is stalled, then the rest of the world can relax and let our project go forward. They would not dare attack Israel without a credible nuclear threat."

"You're going to spy on your own father? And maybe get him imprisoned, or imprisoned yourself? It's not worth it. Let them attack Israel if they really don't have any nukes and see what happens."

"They might just do the unimaginable, thinking that Israel is not going to be the one to fire off the nukes first. And Iran's army is huge compared to Israel's."

Michael's demeanor changed from one of concern for the project to a horrifying recognition that the love of his life might just go over there, that he might never see her again.

"Ariana, please don't do this," said Michael.

"I have to. I'm going." The time that the two of them had been together made Michael aware of Ariana's stubborn determination. He knew when she made a decision it would be nearly impossible to change her mind.

Ariana spoke to her mother that day and told her she was coming for a visit. Her mom was delighted, but worried with the world situation and Ariana's involvement with the megadam.

Michael made the contacts with the Qattara Development team and was relieved to hear that they were all for a peace agreement with Iran in exchange for the land. A strawman proposal was hastily drawn up and sent to Michael and Ariana with the authority to offer it to the Iranians.

Ariana booked a ticket to Tehran and was surprised to see the price of the ticket was $666.

Revelation 13

> [18]**Here is wisdom. Let him that hath understanding count the number of the beast: for it is the number of a man; and his number is Six hundred threescore and six.**

Michael drove Ariana to the Cairo Airport. The scene there, with the kiss goodbye, the sad wave as she went to the gate area and the long, fervent prayer that he might see her again was one that Michael would never forget. His heart sank as she walked through the gate and out of sight.

The flight on Qatar Airways from Cairo International to Tehran Imam Khomeini Airport took about six and a half hours with one stop in Doha, Qatar. As the plane flew to the airport in Tehran, Ariana thought about her dream and her mission. *Anything radical is evil*, she concluded as she considered the political situation in the Middle East. *It all seems to start with people trying to be alpha, mostly men*, she thought. *Just like what Michael's dad always says 'everything in moderation.' Of course, he does not live by that rule at all! Oh well, nobody is perfect.* But in the end, she had come to believe that everyone deserved a chance to live the way they wanted, without being discriminated against or ostracized.

Arriving home, she spent time with her mother and sisters whom she hadn't seen for several years. They visited the Tajrish Bazaar with many people shopping and talking. Men and women mingled freely, but the women wore the traditional headscarf. The fruits, vegetables, flowers and grains in the market were plentiful, and the smells of the marketplace took Ariana back to her youth. Toys, jewelry and games lined the shelves of the market stalls. Men wore mostly blue jeans and sneakers. It was quite a bit cooler than Egypt so many had light jackets and hats. The Bazaar was a happening place, filled with bustling shoppers and vendors in open-air market stalls. The music, smells of the open markets and fresh cooked food enveloped them as they strolled around. Tehran is a beautiful city with little crime and friendly, welcoming people.

Ariana's mom, Sara, began to tell her about the recent events with the Muslim Background Believers. "Women are more outspoken in the last few years since you went away," she said. "There have been many incidents of women being imprisoned and tortured, but we will not back down."

"How can you fight the government?" asked Ariana. They can take you prisoner and you are never heard from again. Doesn't that scare you?"

"Of course it does. But nothing ever happens without courageous acts. We must fight on. Your father knows about us, but he is keeping quiet about it. He is in great danger if they find out I am involved with the movement. Ariana, I am committed to making life better for women here in Iran. I don't care what it costs."

"What about Dad, is he on board with that?" Ariana's concern was rising with each sentence.

"We have agreed to disagree. The men are not going to give up their control without a fight. The Imams are tyrants. They would take our country back a thousand years if we let them."

The recent political turmoil took quite a toll on all of Ariana's family, including her father. But she was glad to be home in her beautiful Tehran neighborhood.

After several days of catching up with family, Ariana became impatient about the confrontation and resolved to set about her mission. She knew her father had been working from home recently. Late one night, while everyone was sleeping, she quietly stole downstairs to her father's office, and went through his mail. Sure enough, there was a report on the nuclear enrichment project noting the difficulties and costs associated with getting enough material for a nuclear weapon. But the report also said that there was a capability, that the weapons had been tested and that the threat was real. So, her hunch about the bluff was wrong. She took pictures with her cell phone of each page and quietly left.

"We have to stop this madness," said Ariana to her mother the next day. "This could start World War III and destroy our civilization. How can we let this happen without at least trying to stop it?"

"That's why we've been demonstrating," said her mom. "The Christian women in my group feel the same way, even though we know we're taking a great risk of being discovered. But we have no power to influence anything. And if we speak up openly, your dad could be imprisoned. I just can't do that."

"What if we sit down with him and I explain that I am here on a mission from Allah. I have agreement from the Israeli, the Saudi and the Egyptian governments to propose a peace treaty that includes ceding prime land in the Qattara Development to Iran in exchange for a promise not to attack Israel or destroy the megadam project."

"I can't say how successful you'll be," said Ariana's mom. "You know your father. But at least there's a possible resolution to avoid war.

"There's something else that I want to talk to you about," said Ariana's mother. I know this may not be the right time, but your father and I agreed to wait until your education was complete before telling you. It's been more than a few years, and it's long overdue, so let me begin."

Ariana sat down close to her mother on the couch, wondering what her mom would say.

"We've talked many times about Abraham and how his twelve sons created the twelve tribes of ancient times, about 4,000 years ago. The descendants of his son Ismael founded Islam, and the descendants of his son Isaac were the foundation of Judaism and later the Christian faith. And you know only a part of the story about the other ten lost tribes of Israel. Those people were a sort of pre-diaspora and went to different parts of the world, including Africa, India, Iraq and some here to Iran. Well, our family, on my mother's side, passed down the story that we were a part of that diaspora who emigrated to Iran after the Babylonian captivity and were actually from one of the ten lost tribes of Israel, the tribe of Naphtali." Ariana's mother showed a sketch of the Children of Abraham, in the shape of a tree, that illustrated how the religions of the various peoples changed over time. A part of this sketch was the ten lost tribes of Israel.

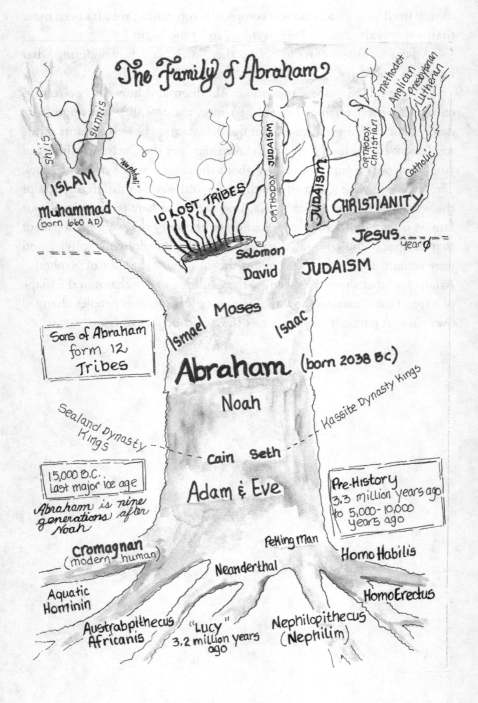

The Family of Abraham

shiis · sunnis

methodist · Anglican · presbyterian · Lutheran

ISLAM
Muhammad
(born 660 AD)

"Nephtali"

10 LOST TRIBES

ORTHODOX JUDAISM

JUDAISM

ORTHODOX Christian · Catholic

CHRISTIANITY

Jesus
year Ø

Solomon

David   JUDAISM

Moses

Ismael   Isaac

Sons of Abraham
form 12
Tribes

Abraham (born 2038 BC)

Noah

Sealand Dynasty Kings

Kassite Dynasty Kings

Cain   Seth

15,000 B.C.
Last major Ice age

Adam & Eve

Pre-History
3.3 million years ago
to 5,000-10,000
years ago

Abraham is nine
generations after
Noah

Peking man

Cromagnan
(modern human)

Homo Habilis

Neanderthal

Aquatic
Hominin

Homo Erectus

Austrabpithecus
Africanis

"Lucy"
3.2 million years
ago

Nephilopithecus
(Nephilim)

In fact, the woman clothed with the sun and the moon beneath her feet with a crown of twelve stars from the Book of Revelation is thought to be from one of the ten lost tribes of Israel. "The twelve stars are the original twelve tribes, the children of Abraham. Two tribes remain until present day and the ten lost tribes dispersed and integrated into the various religions or were considered 'lost.' We are part of the lost tribes, but we have never really been lost. The history has been passed from mother to daughter for almost 3,000 years."

Ariana looked at the chart for the next half hour, asking her mother detailed questions about how this information was passed down from mother to daughter. And how old was this map, this drawing of the family of man? She took a pencil and lightly added the Nephilim "Nephilopithecus" in the lower right corner, explaining the recent archeological finding from the dam construction site.

Later that day, Ariana was more convinced than ever that her destiny was to intercede just as the prophecy of St. John had foretold. *Could the ten lost tribes be the ten horns of the great red dragon?* She thought.

Ariana's father, just like Michael's father was very experienced in foreign service and, as such, had a pragmatic philosophy about how to deal with highly charged international issues. He was a good man and only wanted the best for his family and his country. Although Ariana's mom had tried to keep her Christianity a secret from him, her dad was well aware of his wife's involvement with the antiwar protests, as well as the feminine push back against Sharia law. Ariana's father believed that it would only be a matter of time until the Christian movement in Iran became powerful enough to bring down the Islamic government. Already over 40% of the Iranian women had secretly converted and joined the demonstrations against the threat of war with Israel. Their voting reflected a move toward a secular government and the few powerful women in the Iranian parliament were gaining traction. Women had been attending university in Iran since 1937 and the general movement to the left and away from fundamentalism was similar to what was happening in other countries, including the U.S.

Ariana's mom spoke to her husband about having a family discussion, that Ariana had something she wanted to talk about with her dad and that's why she came home. The sisters were invited and everyone came together in the small courtyard of their home in Tehran for a family meeting.

"I am sorry I put you in this position Papa," said Ariana when they had all arrived and were seated. "We never intended to stir up so much controversy. The megadam is really Michael's project and the involvement of the Israelis was just a way of getting help with the Qattara Development. My company, Whitelock is there for the financing and, in fact, the profit. I really do not know how much the Israelis even recognize this, but the discovery that the real Garden of Eden is in Egypt, not Iraq, and that the Euphrates River in the Bible creation story is actually a tributary of the Nile, not the one in the Fertile Crescent, changes everything about the Jewish claims of a 'Promised Land.'

"The rabbis have always believed that, because the Euphrates River is in Mesopotamia, all the land east of the Nile all the way to Baghdad was promised to them by their God. Now it is clear that if there ever was such a promise, it is only the narrow strip of land west of the Nile to Old Euphrates River, essentially the location of the four oases." Ariana told her dad she was hoping that the struggle for land in the Palestinian area would end with this new development and Jerusalem under a UN Protectorate. The Palestinians would achieve their long sought 'right of return' and the constant fighting over the West Bank and Gaza would stop. "The Qattara Development will be a place where people from all over the world can live together and practice whatever beliefs they want without fear of oppression. The whole world, collectively through the UN, will govern the area."

Ariana's dad just threw his head back and laughed. "You're a dreamer," he said. "The people in this region have been fighting each other and the Europeans for centuries. It will never stop."

"I think you are wrong," said Ariana. "And I think the reason is because, for the first time in history, women will have a strong voice in government. We are the linchpin for world peace."

Ariana's dad sat in silence for a very long time. Then he said, "Ok, what do you have in mind?"

"I have been authorized by our project team and the participating governments to offer Iran prime land on the water in the Qattara Development in exchange for signing a peace treaty with Israel."

Ariana's dad thought about it, then he said, "I will take this offer with all sincerity to our president. No guarantees, but it does look attractive. Hopefully they will agree."

Ariana considered herself very fortunate that the authorities didn't notice her presence in the country. Her father was in a difficult political position since she was officially an enemy of the state due to her involvement with the megadam.

"As I said when you first arrived, I want you to stay in the house and keep hidden," said her father at the end of the meeting. "If they find you here you may be arrested, and me too for that matter. Don't call your friends and don't let anyone know you are here. I will do my best with this situation, but promise me you will be quiet. If you are discovered, I can't help you. Once the authorities find out you are in the country, they will alert the airport security personnel and you may not be allowed to leave."

"Papa, I understand."

It was early the next morning when the military police knocked on the door of Ariana's house. Her father, who was working from his home office, answered.

"We have an order to arrest your daughter sir," said the officer. "Is she here?"

"You have no authority to do this," said Ariana's father. "What is the charge?"

"She is being charged with treason. If you try to interfere, we have been told to arrest you too. Please step aside." The guards roughly pushed the Minister of Foreign Affairs aside and stepped into the house.

Ariana and her mother heard the commotion and came into the room. "What is going on Papa?" asked Ariana.

"These soldiers have come to arrest you," said her dad, his face full of pain and regret.

"Do something," shouted her mother. "They can't do this. She has done nothing wrong." Unfortunately, and Ariana's mother knew this, women have few rights in Iran.

"There is nothing I can do," said her dad and turned his face away in anger and shame.

Ariana just looked her father directly in the eye and said, "I understand. I knew the risk when I came home and I am ready to face whatever happens." *So glad I was able to have the family meeting and present the proposal before all of this*, thought Ariana.

She went quietly with the police while her mother wept and her father brooded in anger. She was thrown into jail, awaiting trial on the charge of high treason, for which the penalty is death. The cell was dark, cold and damp with no windows. As the cell door closed, Ariana was gripped by a deep consuming fear. She looked around, felt faint and threw up in the sink. Then she sat down, said a prayer and waited.

The "interrogations" started the next day. Two men in masks came to her cell. "We have some questions for you, young lady. Come with us," said one of them. They opened the cell door and roughly led her to a concrete block room that smelled of pee and vomit. The walls were bare and, in the center, there was a table with a chair on either side. A ring in the middle of the table served as a binding for handcuffs which were put on her wrists. A man with a camera on a tripod was positioned just a few feet from the table so as to take a video of her "confession."

"We can do this the easy way or the hard way," said the second man. "We know that you have been conspiring with the Israelis to steal Arab land, which is a treasonous act. If you confess your actions and renounce this evil, you will live. It is that simple.

"Do you admit that you have done this in violation of the laws of Allah?"

"I do," said Ariana. "But this is not against the law of Allah. I come here in peace to make peace according to the will of Allah. Please let me speak to the Ayatollah."

"And do you now confess that this was wrong and that the attempt to steal Arab lands was a grave sin against Islam?"

The word "No" from Ariana and the cloth going over her head were nearly simultaneous. The chair was tipped back and the interrogation continued. The question was repeated. "Do you confess this was wrong and renounce these treasonous acts?"

"No, I am here on a mission to see the Ayatollah. You must let me talk with him." And so it went for many hours until Ariana was exhausted and the interrogators were frustrated. The handcuffs were removed and she was led to the wall where there was another ring. Again, the cuffs were placed on her wrists and through the ring. The interrogation continued. When she responded with "No, please let me see the Ayatollah," the interrogation continued, this time more forcefully. She awoke back in her cell in excruciating pain. The pain and terror kept her awake all night. All she knew how to do was pray. She thought of her father and the danger she had put him in. She thought of her mother and the good times they had together growing up. It was like her whole life was a movie in fast forward. The sadness that gripped her as she contemplated losing her life with Michael brought racking sobs.

The next day was the same. And so it went for many days, so many that Ariana lost track of how long she'd been there. Her family had no idea what was happening to her. But each night she prayed for the strength to face the next day and not to break.

The Ayatollah, Supreme Leader of Iran, was determined to stop this latest plot by the Israelis to take more Arab land. He knew in his heart that he was right and that the Jihad against the infidels was justified. His view, and that of his colleagues in the Islamic government, was that the Jewish people had led the world in lust and greed. The true believers should never tolerate this kind of culture. This man was a man of Allah, a true believer and strong in character to follow what he thought was Allah's Holy will.

Revelation 12

> **7 And there was war in heaven: Michael and his angels fought against the dragon; and the dragon fought and his angels,**
> **8 And prevailed not; neither was their place found any more in heaven.**
> **9 And the great dragon was cast out, that old serpent, called the Devil, and Satan, which deceiveth the whole world: he was cast out into the earth, and his angels were cast out with him.**

It was on a night a few days after Ariana was first imprisoned that the Ayatollah had his first dream. In the dream he saw a great battle with terrible nuclear explosions, people screaming, young children crying and the collective work of centuries of men's effort destroyed in an instant.

> **¹⁰ And I heard a loud voice saying in heaven, Now is come salvation, and strength, and the kingdom of our God, and the power of his Christ: for the accuser of our brethren is cast down, which accused them before our God day and night.**

In the midst of the dream with all the destruction and terror, the Ayatollah had a vision of Moses, Jesus of Nazareth, Muhammed, and a young woman, clothed with the sun and the moon under her feet and with a crown of 12 stars on her head.

> **¹² Therefore rejoice, ye heavens, and ye that dwell in them. Woe to the inhabiters of the earth and of the sea! for the devil is come down unto you, having great wrath, because he knoweth that he hath but a short time.**
> **¹³ And when the dragon saw that he was cast unto the earth, he persecuted the woman which brought forth the man child.**

A loud voice in the midst of his dream said "Why do you persecute my messenger, Ariana? All that was foretold will surely come to pass and woe to the whole earth if these prophecies remain."

The Ayatollah heard himself saying in the dream, "How can I alter this course of events?"

The voice responded, "If the current course of human events remains unaltered, the prophecies will remain."

This continued for several nights. At last, when the Supreme Leader awoke from his dream again covered with sweat and shaking, he finally sent for Ariana's father.

"I've had a terrible nightmare that made me believe that the end of the world is at hand…, by my hand. Tell me about your daughter."

"My daughter has come in peace to heal a great rift in our world. It took tremendous courage for her to come here, even though she grew up here and feels that this is her home.

"She has come with a message and proposal from Egypt, Israel and Saudi Arabia. She has been authorized to propose a peace treaty with Iran in exchange for prime land along the new Qattara Development. She has come to ask that Iran become part of the project. All will be governed by the United Nations to maintain peace and security for everyone living there, regardless of their beliefs or place of birth. The land represents a huge sum of wealth that will help Iran join its rightful place in the world order. In return, there will be guarantees that no attacks will take place on either Israel or the megadam project.

"Everyone in the world is afraid that this may be the beginning of World War III, that the death and destruction will spell an end to our civilization. Some Christians believe that this end has been foretold to them by St. John the Divine in his famous Book of Revelation. Somehow, this great cataclysmic event must be avoided. That is what Ariana is here to do."

The Supreme Leader was silent for some minutes. Ariana's father felt that the tension could be cut with a knife. His head was pounding and his pulse raced.

"You have been one of my closest allies for many years," said the Ayatollah. I trust you and would like to explore your daughter's proposal for the benefit of everyone in the world. None of us can afford the death and destruction of a nuclear conflict. And my dream last night brought a message from Muhammed, just as the Pharoah's dream brought a message from Allah in saving Egypt from the great famine in the time of Joseph.

Genesis 41:14-16

[14] Then Pharaoh sent and called Joseph, and they brought him hastily out of the dungeon: and he shaved himself, and changed his raiment, and came in unto Pharaoh.

¹⁵ And Pharaoh said unto Joseph, I have dreamed a dream, and there is none that can interpret it: and I have heard say of thee, that thou canst understand a dream to interpret it.

¹⁶ And Joseph answered Pharaoh, saying, It is not in me: God shall give Pharaoh an answer of peace.

I will speak with your daughter. Please bring her to me."

"As you wish. Thank you."

The meeting with Ariana lasted less than an hour and the Ayatollah was convinced that the proposed peace agreement was in fact sincere. She was instructed to carry a message to the Qattara Development Consortium countries that Iran was willing to sign the agreement.

The news that an agreement had been reached with Iran spread like wildfire in the Muslim world. When the Muslim Brotherhood heard, they were infuriated and just couldn't believe it.

Many of the Muslim Brotherhood then began to have the dream. In it, the four appeared including Moses, Jesus of Nazareth, Muhammed, and the woman clothed with the sun and the moon under her feet and with a crown of 12 stars on her head. The woman told them in the dream that this was the time to form a caliphate, that the new land of the Qattara Depression would be filled with Allah's children who wanted only to live in peace and serve Allah. She also told them it was their duty to lead the formation of the caliphate, that they should talk to the Imams in Egypt and use the bond of the Muslim Brotherhood to work toward this goal, abandoning any violence and working toward a true peace in the new land.

When they shared these dreams with each other it became clear that this was the will of Allah. They resolved to build a sort of virtual Muslim caliphate for all the believers in the new Qattara Development and live as they had hoped for many decades. Although the animosity toward Israel remained, at least for a few decades, when they found that their Palestinian brothers would have all the land and water they wanted and could stop struggling with the Israelis, the aggressive feelings toward the Israelis eventually subsided.

In the same time frame, the Israelis began to have dreams as well. It started with the rabbis but then spread from Orthodox to Reformed. In these dreams as well, the four appeared including Moses, Jesus of Nazareth, Muhammed, and the woman clothed with the sun and the moon under her feet and with a crown of 12 stars on her head. She explained that this time when the children of Israel migrated to Egypt, it would be to the Promised Land that God gave to Abraham. There would be no more slavery as in the time of Joseph, no more pogroms, expulsions or Holocaust and all people would live as God's children, without hunger or thirst or warfare. Many in Israel thought that they were the only ones having the dream, but later in the Synagogue the word spread and there was a general buzz about migrating to the new homeland. The dreams would be written in a new book, the Book of Promise. It would be the first book added to the Torah in nearly 5000 years. The Jewish people were finally going home.

•

Chapter 32

Cairo, Egypt

Ariana flew from Tehran to the Cairo airport and Michael was there to meet her. She walked through the gate toward the baggage claim area and saw Michael eagerly waiting for her, waving. As she got closer, he saw that she had lost a lot of weight and her face was pale, dark circles under her eyes, with the sunken cheeks of daily pain. She ran up to him and they hugged long and hard. What Michael didn't know was that the hug must have been just excruciating. Fortunately, Michael couldn't see the expression of pain on her face. Ariana was afraid that if she told the whole story of her captivity and treatment at the hands of the Guardian Council, Michael's anger might make a sudden appearance. Now that her sacrifice was over and the peace agreement was signed, she really' didn't have the strength to calm Michael if he became angry. All the way home on the plane, she could only thank God/Allah that she was given the strength to carry out her mission and not collapse under the fear and pain she endured.

In some ways the deep emotion Ariana felt as God's messenger was felt just as much by Michael. The reunion was one of the happiest moments in both their lives. The six-hour drive back to the dam site flew by as Ariana shared most of her experience with her family and the Ayatollah. But Michael was not so gullible as to believe that the pale and gaunt look Ariana had was from stress alone.

"Did they eventually arrest you?" he asked.

"Well…yes. But everything turned out ok in the end."

"What happened after you were arrested? Couldn't your father help you?"

"Ok, I might as well tell you. But I want you to promise me that this will remain our secret. And no, my father would have been arrested himself if he tried to step in."

"I promise." But Michael was praying, *please help me to forgive.*

When they arrived back at the dam site, Ariana showed Michael her back and cried softly as he stared in horror.

It took several weeks for Ariana's back to heal. Each evening Michael put salve on the open sores, carefully smoothing it on, as lightly as possible, while Ariana closed her eyes and endured the pain. She was sad and embarrassed that Michael had to see her this way.

Their days together during that time were filled with relaxation and visits to Cairo for shopping and dinners. When the color returned to Ariana's face and her back had healed, Michael took her to Luxor for a celebration dinner at their favorite place, the Al-Sahaby Lane Roof Terrace restaurant.

"I was afraid you wouldn't want me," said Ariana as they got ready for bed that night after dinner. "The scars are horrible."

"A wise person once told me, 'Scars give you character,'" said Michael.

The celebration that night was glorious with both Michael and Ariana feeling very fortunate that they had each other in the midst of the mad world. Next day, Michael, who occasionally sang acapella, was in a mood to sing. He looked at Ariana and began to sing the old Crosby, Stills and Nash song "Lady of the Island."

Holding you close, undisturbed before a fire
The pressure in my chest when you breathe in my ear
We both knew this would happen when you first appeared
My Lady of the Island
The brownness of your body in the fire glow
… …

Ariana just smiled and seemed very happy. Their love had grown from a curious infatuation to the deep, abiding, committed friendship that is the basis of true happiness. They had endured so much in the past few years and nothing could separate them now. Michael began thinking about the events of the past few weeks. He remembered Jesus' teaching about forgiveness and decided that regardless of how unjust Ariana's treatment was at the hands of the Ayatollah, he should be forgiven. Michael resolved to do that in spite of his anger. That resolution was the beginning of healing for Michael and he was thankful to God.

Chapter 33

Dam Construction Site, a few months later

The dam continued to fill over the next several months with only a fraction of the water of the Nile closed off to raise the water level. The valves to the Old Euphrates River aqueduct remained closed while the water level came to the design height behind the dam. One thing that the team had not fully considered was the weight of the water, backed up by the megadam, on the slip planes at the Afar Triangle or triple junction where the three tectonic plates come together. The probability that some sort of seismic activity would happen as a result was high, as it turned out, but Michael hadn't really thought about it. This entire area is an active seismic zone and has been earthquake prone for millions of years. Michael, Steve and team knew that during the design process, but were relying on the massive rock dam to be earthquake proof due to its size and construction.

Revelation 11:13

> ¹³ **And the same hour was there a great earthquake, and the tenth part of the city fell, and in the earthquake were slain of men seven thousand: and the remnant were affrighted, and gave glory to the God of heaven.**

Revelation 12:15

¹⁵And the serpent cast out of his mouth water as a flood after the woman, that he might cause her to be carried away of the flood.

Michael and Ariana had just finished lunch in the construction cars when they felt a sudden rumbling and heard a loud banging.

"What was that?" said Ariana.

Michael thought, *oh no, it can't be. An earthquake here, now? Those are hundred-year events!* "I think it was an earthquake, a small one," said Michael. No sooner had he spoken those words than a substantial shock began pushing them back and forth, uncontrollably across the floor. Fortunately, the construction offices were really just doublewide trailers with a unibody type of construction, so there was little danger of them coming apart. But everything was flying around inside and coming off the shelves. "Get under a desk!" shouted Michael.

Ariana and Michael both dove under desks while the world shook around them. The shaking continued off and on for 30 full minutes and much of the megadam construction equipment was destroyed. When it finally stopped, Michael was cautious as he peaked out from his hiding place. "You ok?" he shouted to Ariana.

"I got a bump on the head, but nothing serious," she said. "I will live."

"I'm gonna check on the dam," said Michael. "It was made to withstand an earthquake but this was a big one, more like a five-hundred-year event, not one hundred." Michael got up and looked around at the devastation inside the construction trailer. It was totally trashed. He went to the door but the frame of the trailer had been twisted by the shocks. He had to put his shoulder against the door to get it open.

Michael walked outside and the air was thick with dust. He looked up at the megadam structure, a wall of Empire State Buildings as far as the eye could see. From what he could see, it seemed intact, at least there at that location. Afraid to take the elevator to the control station at the top of the dam, he decided to climb the stairs, all 1200 of them, to take a look at the area upstream. When he got to the top, the upstream lake looked fine, but then he noticed that the bypass tunnels were not flowing and the water level of the Nile downstream of the dam was dropping rapidly. He went to the control room and the operators there were busy staring at the water level indicators and trying to open the bypass valves. A red flashing warning light with an annunciator showed that the bypass tunnels and valves had been damaged. *So much for the earthquake proof dam,* thought Michael. *The dam itself is earthquake proof, but not the bypass channels or the underground aqueduct leading to the Old Euphrates. Oh no,* he thought, *the water level is going to rise and spill over into the old river channel. The oases are going to flood. I've got to warn them.*

Michael called the local authorities in each of the four oases along the Old Euphrates. "The bypass valves on the megadam are jammed and the water is backing up behind the dam," he said. "You've got to evacuate the area and tell people to get to high ground. They have about six hours before the water floods the town."

His phone began ringing with calls from all over Egypt, including the Prime Minister's office. "What are you doing to us?" he said. "Get those tunnels back open or we will blow the dam."

"It's not that simple sir," said Michael. "If we blow the dam structure, the water will pour through and flood the Nile valley. Many thousands will be drowned unless they can be evacuated to higher ground."

"How long to clear the bypass tunnels?"

"Well, it took six months to build them. If the tunnels have collapsed, months. If the tunnels're ok and just the valves are jammed, it could take only a day or two. But either way, a lot of people are gonna have to be evacuated in the meantime."

"Six months!!?? You said the dam was earthquake proof! That's why we agreed to build it in the first place. This is your responsibility Michael Walters and you better think of a solution. We've got major damage in Luxor from the earthquake and we're trying to free thousands from collapsed buildings there. This was a 7.8 on the Richter Scale, the worst we have experienced in a thousand years."

Michael immediately called Steve Williams. "Steve, it's Michael. We have a major problem here."

"So I've heard," said Steve.

"Do you have any suggestions?"

"Well, the first thing to do is to get some people in there and inspect the bypass tunnels. If they're ok, we should be able to rig some charges to blow open the valves. You should also check out the Old Euphrates aqueducts and valves. If we could open them, we could bleed off the water underground. Otherwise, I think we're in a lot of trouble."

"Thanks a lot," Michael said sarcastically, "we'll check the tunnels." Michael was thinking, *if there is no water in the tunnels, if it's just the valves that are blocked, I should be able to go in there and check it out, at least see if the tunnels themselves have collapsed.*

"Are you out of your mind? If there is another aftershock, the whole thing could open up and wash you away." Ariana was much more pragmatic than Michael when it came to problem solving.

"Well, I can't very well send someone else in there to risk their life, now, can I? Remember when you said 'I have to try?' That's the way I feel now. And anyway, what else are we gonna do?"

"I can see I am not going to talk you out of it." said Ariana. No sooner had she said that than the first aftershock occurred. It was a minor shaking but Ariana said "You feel that? We just had an aftershock. And no, I do not know what else to do but there has to be another way. And if you are going, I am going with you."

"Maybe, but it will take weeks to set something up. I'm going. And no, you're not going with me. I seem to remember a girl who said, 'I have to go alone'? Well, that's how I feel now." And with that, Michael walked out the door heading toward the bypass tunnel. He called the operator in the control station above and said, "Tarek, get down here, I need your help. And bring some ropes and life preservers from the station. Don't take the elevator; I don't trust it."

"I'm on my way," replied Tarek.

The Nile bypass tunnels consisted of three ninety-foot diameter pipes on each side of the river that connected the Nile River upstream of the megadam to the downstream side. In each tunnel there was a plenum wall with a series of ten-foot diameter butterfly valves to control the flow of water around the dam. When the valves were open, the full flow of the Nile River was allowed to bypass the dam and flow as though the dam was not there. The valves could be partially closed to allow some of the Nile water to back up behind the dam, or to cause it to flow into the

Old Euphrates underground aqueduct and on to Lake Eden. Each bypass tunnel opens onto the river and there is a small catwalk at the bottom of the tunnel with a series of ladder rungs up the riverbank to the ground level on either side of the river. A small observation area with a railing and parking lot had been built on both sides of the river to allow workmen to inspect the bypass tunnels.

Michael parked the Explorer and he and Tarek walked to the access ladder on the west side of the river. His heart was beating fast and hard as he said a little prayer and climbed down the ladder toward the catwalk. If there was a serious aftershock now, a 90-foot-high wall of water could wash away everything from here to Cairo, including Michael Walters. He walked along the catwalk to the first tunnel, climbed over the guard rail and got down onto the bottom of the bypass pipe. A trickle of water was making its way along the bottom of the pipe to the river. As he walked back up the pipe toward the valve plenum, it became obvious what had happened. The shaking had torn the pipe and surrounding rock apart leaving the upstream and downstream portions of the pipe offset. All Michael could see as he shown his searchlight at the end of the bypass pipe was a solid wall of rock. Desperately hoping there would be no more aftershocks, especially now, he walked back to the catwalk, entered the other two pipes and found the same thing.

Michael knew it would have been very wise to have worn a life jacket. But despite his concern about aftershocks, his mind was elsewhere. As he was climbing the ladder back up to the parking area, an aftershock hit. Fortunately, he was only a few rungs up the ladder but the shaking threw him tumbling into the river. He was stunned but able to get his head above water and began swimming toward shore.

Tarek was quick thinking and ran to the riverbank, downstream. He threw the life preserver with the line attached out to Michael, who grabbed it, and Tarek pulled Michael in to shore. There were no docks or ladders at that point and the bank was very steep, but holding on to the line, Tarek was able to help him up to the top of the riverbank, coughing and spitting, but very thankful that the megadam itself held. *No sense inspecting the other side, the tunnels are completely blocked,* thought Michael.

"I think we're out of luck," Michael said to Ariana when he got back to the construction trailer. The only hope we have is to somehow see if the

Old Euphrates aqueduct is still open and try to unblock the valves so we can bleed this water off. I'm gonna call and see if we can get some divers down here in the next few hours. I just hope that's soon enough. The water level is rising very fast and I'm just afraid the oases are gonna flood."

"You are all wet!" said Ariana. "What happened?"

"There was an aftershock when I was on the ladder. I got thrown in the river."

"Oh my! Are you alright?"

"Yeah, I was lucky." Michael was smiling as he explained to Ariana what happened. "I'm gonna get changed and call the office in Cairo. I think the folks in Luxor have their hands full."

It took a little over an hour for the helicopter to arrive at the dam site with a couple of scuba divers and their equipment. Michael and Ariana scrambled aboard and they flew the 200 miles south to the Old Euphrates aqueduct intake.

The opening to the underground aqueduct and the control valve system was situated south of the megadam and consisted of a 250-foot diameter concrete opening with a series of metal plates across it, each with a dozen 12-foot diameter butterfly valves. These valves were about 30 feet below the surface and could be opened or closed from the main control station or locally to control the flow of Nile River water into the underground aqueduct. The development plan called for the valves to be opened as the water level behind the megadam increased so as to gradually fill Lake Eden 600 miles to the north. With the passage blocked, the water level would rise and flow into the Old Euphrates riverbed, flooding the Kharga Oasis. Michael's concern was that he no longer had any control over where the water would go and what damage could be done.

His phone was ringing as they stepped out of the helicopter at the aqueduct intake.

"What's the situation and where are you now?" asked the Interior Minister. "We've got a lot of worried people here wondering what's going on."

"The divers are just heading to the intake. We should know in a few minutes whether we can open the valves."

"Please let me know right away."

"Yessir, will do," said Michael.

The divers were worried about aftershocks as well. If the valves somehow opened while the two were in there, they could be swept into the aqueduct tunnel and seriously injured or killed. Everyone was tense as the divers stepped into the water and approached the intake.

Both divers had acoustic communication gear and could talk to one another as well as Michael at the surface.

"It's really murky down here. But we're seeing a large crack in the intake tunnel," said one of the divers as he shone his light on the interior wall. "Something happened here. Oh yeah, now I see it. The valve plenum has been twisted by the quake. No wonder the valves don't work, they're jammed into the seats by the twisted plenum plate."

Michael was concerned but not panicked just yet, "Can you see if the aqueduct itself is damaged?"

"Well, we do see a big crack in the intake concrete, but no, I can't tell if the tunnel is open downstream of the valve plate."

"Ok, come back up. We're gonna have to dynamite the valves and hope that the tunnel is open. Only way to prevent a flood in Kharga," said Michael.

The divers emerged and prepared to go back down with plastic explosives to be placed on each of the valves. The detonators would be acoustically operated so that all the charges would explode at the same time. The hope was that an explosion on one valve would not jam a neighbor and prevent full flow into the aqueduct tunnel. The whole plan was iffy in the sense that even if the valves could be opened, there was no guarantee that the tunnel beyond was not collapsed. The last thing they wanted to do was to damage the aqueduct tunnel with the explosions.

When the explosives had been placed, Michael, Ariana and the divers retreated a safe distance from the water. "Everybody ready?" asked Michael.

"Go for it," said Ariana. And with that, Michael pushed the detonator and the water was roiled as the explosions shook the lake in the area of the aqueduct intake. Everyone waited, hoping to see the water level drop as the aqueduct filled and drained away the water.

"What do you think? Is it going down?" asked Michael.

"I hate to say this, but it looks like it's getting deeper," said one of the divers.

"Let's wait for a while and see. There's a lot of water here," said Michael, praying that the plan would work. They waited and waited, until, 45 minutes later, the outcome was clear. The water was definitely getting deeper.

"Sir, the plan didn't work," said Michael on the phone. "You'll have to evacuate Kharga at least."

"What? This is completely unacceptable," said the Interior Minister.

"I'm doing the best I can," said Michael with resignation and by way of apology.

The evacuation of Kharga was begun that afternoon as the water level rose in the Old Euphrates River basin. The combination of the earthquake, the aftershocks and the threat of a major flood had the people of Kharga terrified. Families had been living at that oasis for thousands of years, since the desiccation of Lake Eden, with no serious threats, other than the Roman soldiers, until today when there were two major threats at once.

Revelation 12:16

16 And the earth helped the woman, and the earth opened her mouth, and swallowed up the flood which the dragon cast out of his mouth.

"I want to see what's goin' on," said Michael. "Let's get in the chopper and have a look." They all piled into the helicopter and rose to inspect the Old Euphrates riverbed. As they flew northwest, along the river, they could see the water had gradually filled up the low areas and was flowing along toward the Kharga Oasis. As the helo approached the town of Kharga, they could see a mountainous region to the west. Rather than meandering on toward the oasis town, the water was cascading down into the abyss as a huge waterfall, effectively "swallowing up" the flood.

"I can't believe it," said Michael. "We actually have a reprieve. Looks like the water is flowing into the underground aquifer. Maybe we can duct it into the aqueduct piping near Kharga while we repair the intake valves." He called the Minister's office and explained the situation. Then he talked to the development office in Cairo.

"Get a crew out to the area just west of Kharga and see if we can start to work on a fix to get the water going into the aqueduct. I think if we do that, the city won't flood while we repair the valves and aqueduct piping at the Old Euphrates intake."

Fortunately, the canyon swallowing up the water did connect to the underground aquifer, allowing construction crews to quickly blast a tunnel to the aqueduct. The megadam team was very lucky, and Michael knew it.

Michael and Ariana were fortunate enough to not only have this project team bond but also the lifelong bond of a strong, committed relationship that would carry them through the good times and bad. Michael said a prayer, thanking God for helping them avoid a major catastrophe.

Chapter 34

Lake Eden and Ramallah in the future

The completion of the Qattara Development project meant that the areas in and around Palestine and Israel were abandoned by all who could afford to make the move. This took the pressure off the water supplies in the region and allowed a return to life somewhat like it was before the water crisis. Aashif and Bariah, whose relationship had been forged in the struggle for life, became even more committed to one another and Aashif, with the help of Michael and Ariana, was able to establish a market stall in town selling fruits and vegetables imported from the Qattara Development. Aashif asked Bariah to marry him and they finally achieved their dream of being together and having a family of their own.

They stayed in Ramallah as their ancestors had for thousands of years determined to make a good home for their family. They prospered and eventually Aashif was able to afford to buy an olive grove on the outskirts of town. The Palestinian Authority built more desalination stations and supplemented the water supplies in the region with the geodesic tunnels similar to the ones used for the Qattara Development. Eventually, fruits, vegetables and pasture land was established in the area with Aashif taking a lead role in the initiative.

Aashif and Bariah's love would grow stronger and deeper as they raised their children, sent them abroad for their education and made a happy, peaceful community in the once war-torn area.

Qur'an 56:25-26 assures the believers,

"Therein they will hear no abusive speech, nor any talk of sin, only the saying, "Peace, peace."

Aya, who had graduated and taken over for Professor Morsi at the university, came to visit Michael and Ariana. "We have made a discovery even more important, I think, than the hominins around the Qattara Lake. Most of our digs were further back from the deepest areas on the shorelines where the lake was still fresh water. I suggested we see if there is anything along the shores of the saltwater lake. When we began excavation, we came across what looked like a large stone sarcophagus which we at first thought was a tomb." She explained that the contents were not a mummy at all; rather, this was a sort of ancient seed bank. Biologists examined the seeds and found they were a species of wheat that had never been seen before. DNA analysis confirmed that this type of wheat is very similar to the marsh grass that grows in the backwater regions near the Mediterranean Sea. It is highly salt tolerant. "We have tried it and, even using salty water from the Dead Sea, it grows like anything, producing huge grains with good flour that can be made into bread or beer. This is the first major food grain ever found that can grow in saltwater marshes.

Aashif and Bariah heard news, from Michael and Ariana, of Aya's discovery of the salt tolerant wheat in the Qattara basin and decided to take the risk of investment in a company to develop this resource. They contacted Aya and suggested that a company be formed and that they would be angel investors. Michael was happy to invest as well, and Ariana's contacts at Whitelock provided a generous supply of venture capital.

The first harvests of this Qattara wheat were in the area of the Dead Sea, just about twenty miles from their home in Ramallah. The new wheat was so successful, Ariana contacted Whitelock who made a bid of $250 million for the fledgling company. Aashif and Bariah became very wealthy and many hungry people in the area were fed, not just from the wheat products but also from the animals that could graze on the salt tolerant wheat grasses. As usual, there was environmental controversy because of the development of the wetlands. But people have to eat.

In the decades ahead, as global warming inundated the shores of most continents, this new wheat would become a staple and prevent mass starvation as the freshwater resources in much of the world dried up. The Everglades National Park in Florida would be transformed into salt marshes as the rising sea covered most of the state. Using the salt tolerant wheat, the Everglades would become a vast agricultural region supplementing the Midwest as the breadbasket of the U.S. The areas around the Black Sea, the Caspian Sea and Great Salt Lake would similarly become highly productive agricultural areas.

Chapter 35

Lake Eden in the future

Michael and Ariana won the $100 million Water Prize, got married and were ceded a beautiful home on the shore of Lake Eden. It had 80 feet of waterfront with a large boat dock and a trim 60-foot yawl at their back door. A sandy beach with palm trees and a cabana completed the ideal place to relax and enjoy the view of the lake. Their bedroom on the second floor of the estate was all glass facing the lake. They could lie in bed and gaze out onto the water with sailboats, cruisers, diving platforms and pontoon party boats. The clear blue sky and high puffy white clouds completed this idyllic picture. It had been quite a journey for the two of them and their love was stronger than ever. Michael leaned on his elbow in bed one morning and said to Ariana, "Did you ever think it would end with us rich and living in a place like this?"

Ariana just said, "I was so in love with you, I didn't really care. Wherever you and I are together, it's a mansion."

"I feel that way too, but you know it's like my dad always said, 'No matter how rich or poor you are, it's always nice to have money.'" Michael chuckled. "But... having said that, I think we have to do something good with this money. Aashif and Bariah are clearly on their way, thanks to you and Whitelock."

"Let me think about it," said Ariana.

"By the way, I heard from Steve yesterday. Can you believe he's in Liberia of all places? He says they just announced the largest diamond find in the world in the alluvial deposits of Liberia and Sierra Leon. Hey, look at this." Michael opened his bedside table drawer and pulled out one of the largest diamonds either of them had ever seen.

"To be honest, it came from Steve. He gave it to us as a belated wedding present." Michael just smiled broadly and put the ring on Ariana's finger.

"You know I cannot wear this in public," she said.

"Then you can just wear it inside!" Michael laughed and held her face in both his hands as they kissed.

Ariana just shook her head and said, "I love you very much, Michael Walters."

On the north shore of the main part of Lake Eden a new capital, Eden City, had been built to rival and even outshine the New City capital of Egypt that had been built east of Cairo. Eden City was to have a population of over 25 million people when completed.

Revelation 21:23-26

> **23 And the city had no need of the sun, neither of the moon, to shine in it: for the glory of God did lighten it, and the Lamb is the light thereof.**
>
> **24 And the nations of them which are saved shall walk in the light of it: and the kings of the earth do bring their glory and honour into it.**
>
> **25 And the gates of it shall not be shut at all by day: for there shall be no night there.**
>
> **26 And they shall bring the glory and honour of the nations into it.**

On the roofs of all of the buildings were high efficiency solar panel shingles and in the basements were three-day battery packs that could store enough electrical energy to carry the city and surrounding developments through the nights. The solar panels were networked together and to a central electrical authority control room, but the only generation of electricity was from the solar shingles on each roof and the huge turbines of the megadam. All energy was completely clean and renewable for not only the Lake Eden community, but also much of the rest of Egypt and the surrounding countries. The power authority only managed the flow of electricity, not the generation. Once the investment in solar infrastructure had been completed and paid for, the energy was nearly free and plentiful. Of course, the fact that the area was a desert meant that most days were clear and brightly sunny, a perfect place for solar generation.

Revelation 22:5

⁵**And there shall be no night there; and they need no candle, neither light of the sun; for the Lord God giveth them light: and they shall reign for ever and ever.**

At the center, a giant obelisk building, the tallest by far in the world, was built to be a beacon of the shining new world "Crystal City." The obelisk building, named Pyramid Tower would be over 3,200 meters high, nearly 2 miles, and 461.2 meters on a side at the base, exactly twice the width of the base of the Great Pyramid of Giza. And, of course, the Pyramid Tower was oriented exactly true north and south just like the Great Pyramid, but without the error from the 26,000 year wobble of the earth's axis about the north star. Humanity and science had made some progress since then. Pyramid Tower when lit at night would be visible from the International Space Station, a great leap forward for mankind.

The top floors were so high they had supplemental oxygen in the HVAC system. Not since the Great Pyramid of Cheops had mankind constructed anything so massive and majestic. It would house nearly 2 million workers and residents, and the view from the top observation deck stretched 200km, all the way to the Mediterranean shore and the city of Cairo. As far as the eye could see there were vast areas of fruit orchards, vineyards, grain fields and vegetable gardens, enough to feed the entire Middle East. The top floor housed the Temple of World Faith sanctuary, a mosque, a synagogue, a Catholic church, a Protestant church, a Buddhist temple, a Hindu temple, a sweat lodge, and many other religious buildings from all the religions of the world.

On the outskirts of Eden City, a fully enclosed air-conditioned stadium was built to host world soccer games and Olympic events. The stadium had been equipped with cameras from every angle and boasted a state-of-the-art surface, real grass on an underlay of soil. The stadium was designed for a capacity of 500,000 people.

The city of Jerusalem, then under the auspices of the United Nations Protectorate, became a destination for many of the world's religious pilgrims, not limited to Judaism, Islam and Christianity, but a World Heritage Site for anyone interested in the deep historical past of three of the world's great religions.

It had taken years to build the megadam and the new developments around Lake Eden. With each passing month, Michael and Ariana grew closer and more comfortable with each other. Their love morphed from a steaming romance to a warm glowing respect and friendship. Theirs was one of those special relationships that progressed from the bright dancing flame of burning paper to the soft warm glow of a steady coal burning stove.

One evening as they walked through the streets of the crystal city in the cooling desert air, Michael said to Ariana, "Do you ever think about what we're doing here as a major shift in our civilization, I mean both religious and cultural? Everyone speaks their own language, but most know English now as a sort of world language, so everyone can communicate once again. It's sort of like the end of the period of the tower of Babel."

Genesis 11:8-9

> **8 So the LORD scattered them abroad from thence upon the face of all the earth: and they left off to build the city.**
> **9 Therefore is the name of it called Babel; because the LORD did there confound the language of all the earth: and from thence did the LORD scatter them abroad upon the face of all the earth.**

"Yes," said Ariana, "it seems like your dream of being the architect of the Crystal City has actually come true."

The parcels of land ceded to each of the countries working on the Qattara Depression project are shuffled so that cliques don't form and just like in America, the people will get to know folks that used to live 12,000 miles away as their next-door neighbor. As in the Book of Revelation, people are finally living together with one language again.

Ariana had thought about this too. "It is like Dr. Abebe said at the project kickoff, 'Tolerance is the soul of enlightenment.'"

They decided to take the hyper elevator to the top floor of Pyramid Tower and stand at the observation deck looking out over the crystal city before the Temple of World Faith meeting. Michael's old friend Abdul from his student days at MIT rose to a leadership position in the Temple of World Faith, moved to the Crystal City and now kept care of the TWF sanctuary at the top of Pyramid Tower. The building was nearly two miles high, so the elevator operation was a challenge to get people to the top and back down in a reasonable period of time. The designers knew that and created a large elevator car that could quickly accelerate to over 120 miles/hour, reaching the top in under a minute. Riding that elevator was an exhilarating experience and one that had to be done sitting down, like a spacecraft launch. One side of the car was all glass so people could see the city shrink beneath them as they rose higher and higher.

When they arrived at the observation deck, Ariana said to Michael, "You know, when I was learning the Bible stories from my mother as a child, I learned that the Book of Revelation was written by St. John the Divine when he was dreaming on the Isle of Patmos." She was really thinking out loud and told Michael she kept thinking about his mother's dreams of the Garden of Eden. So much of what they had found in this project, the archeological digs of Morsi and what was found at the megadam site seemed to support what she saw in her dreams. She wondered if maybe the same thing was true for St. John the Divine. "Maybe there was a lot of Christianity mixed in and since he was an early Christian apostle, he saw things through that lens, so, much of what is in the Book of Revelation is about his fears and his daily experience. But some of what he saw, like the crystal river with the tree of life on either side, may just have been a prescient dream of the Qattara Development project."

The ancient Garden of Eden had actually been re-established, so many people from all over the world could live in peace and harmony without fighting over resources. The whole world owned the new Lake Eden development, Eden City, and the surrounding farms, orchards and vineyards. The new Garden of Eden is governed by the whole world, the United Nations.

Revelation 22:1-3

> [1] And he shewed me a pure river of water of life, clear as crystal, proceeding out of the throne of God and of the Lamb.
>
> [2] In the midst of the street of it, and on either side of the river, was there the tree of life, which bare twelve manner of fruits, and yielded her fruit every month: and the leaves of the tree were for the healing of the nations.
>
> [3] And there shall be no more curse: but the throne of God and of the Lamb shall be in it; and his servants shall serve him:

Michael said, "I'm so sorry that you had to endure the wrath of Iranian government politics."

"There is nothing good without sacrifice. I know that now and I have the physical scars to prove it," said Ariana.

"Yeah, and I have the psychological scars."

"Do you think the megadam would have been accomplished without your anger backed determination?"

"Well…maybe not, but it wasn't fun and still isn't. I just want to be like everyone else."

"I think if you were like everyone else, the Western Desert would still be a desert." Ariana wasn't having any of this self-deprecation.

They gazed out over the lush farms, orchards and gardens of the area surrounding Eden City with that warm, happy feeling of accomplishment that comes when a dream is fully realized.

"When we first started talking about this," said Michael, "I was in awe of what we discovered. I couldn't believe that after all these years, the Jewish people thought that the 'Promised Land' was in the Fertile Crescent. But all it took was a realization that the great River Euphrates was really a tributary of the Nile to realize that the Promised Land was right here in Egypt, west of the Nile.

Genesis 15:17-18

> ¹⁷ **And it came to pass, that, when the sun went down, and it was dark, behold a smoking furnace, and a burning lamp that passed between those pieces.**
> ¹⁸ **In the same day the LORD made a covenant with Abram, saying, Unto thy seed have I given this land, from the river of Egypt unto the great river, the river Euphrates:**

"And it seems, you know, from the Jewish point of view, God has kept his promise to the people of Israel. There's enough land in the Lake Eden development to accommodate all of the population of Israel and any other Jews in the world who want to move here. So, they can all now live in the Promised Land. And in a way, it's not just the Jewish people to whom God promised the land, but all the people of the world. So, all people could live together in peace and harmony regardless of their race, color, creed, ethnicity, history, or beliefs. Maybe it's also a fulfillment of the ancient prophecy of Isaiah."

Isaiah 2:4

> ⁴ **And He shall judge among the nations, and shall rebuke many people; and they shall beat their swords into plowshares, and their spears into pruning hooks; nation shall not lift up sword against nation, neither shall they learn war anymore.**

"I have to admit," said Michael, "I was wondering whether the Jewish people would ever agree to leave their homeland around Jerusalem. But I heard from Adam's wife that many in Israel began having dreams shortly after the megadam was finished. The dreams were about moving to the Promised Land. It worked! Our prayers were answered."

Ariana added, "This is a first step in the 'healing of the nations' from Revelation and all people can live in this Protectorate, together, practicing whatever beliefs they want to follow."

"So, in many ways, although allegorical and filled with things that humans added over the millennia, we have the basic word of God. I feel like this project is one of the fulfillments of the ancient prophecies."

Chapter 36

Lake Eden

It was two years later. Michael and Ariana were married and their first child was just turning one year old. They were now living in the beautiful waterfront villa on Lake Eden. A large dock with a sixty-foot sailboat stood ready for carefree days of sailing, swimming and partying to their hearts' content. The channels that had been created for the Qattara Development actually connected with the Nile in what was once called the river Hiddekel, allowing boats on Lake Eden to sail into the Mediterranean Sea.

The past ten years had been very challenging, but as with all things worthwhile, no pain, no gain. Both Michael and Ariana felt completely fulfilled and happy with their accomplishment. Ariana's family lived just up the street in a huge waterfront property. Michael's mom and dad were about a mile away in the Pyramid Tower on the nine hundredth floor. The view from their condo was like nothing any of them had ever dreamed of having. You could see all the way to the Mediterranean Sea, with fruit, nut, and date trees nearly the whole way. To the south was the Crystal City with houses, marinas, canals, restaurants and shopping. Michael's dad had quit drinking, joined AA and found much better health, happiness and relationships as a result.

It was an international playground where movies were made, startup businesses were founded and families lived and worked together. No need to move away in search of a better life. This was the life.

After winning the Water Prize of $100 million, Michael and Ariana donated $50 million to MIT for a new innovation center, to be named the

Michael and Ariana Walters Innovation Center. Michael was awarded an honorary degree of Doctor of Letters by MIT. So, in the end, he could be called Dr. Walters anyway.

Michael and Ariana were awake early after an evening at home. Michael was on his computer and said to Ariana, "Hey, look, I just got an email from Steve Williams. He says he's still in Liberia and wants to come talk to us about an idea he's working on. Do we have anything going on this week?"

"Tell him we would love to have him come visit," said Ariana. "I cannot wait to see him."

Michael responded that any day was good for them. It was a four-hour flight from Roberts International in Liberia to Cairo and then a one-hour bullet train ride west to Eden City.

"Me too! You know that guy is always full of ideas. Wonder what he's doin' in Liberia?"

"You did see the announcement that Liberia and Sierra Leon found huge deposits of rare earth minerals in the alluvial sands not far from the coast?" Ariana was excited to think about a new project.

"Yeah, I saw that," said Michael. "I also saw that they found large deposits of Lithium and Titanium deep underground. Maybe the American Colonization Society had a premonition." Michael laughed.

"Why don't you tell him to come Wednesday and we'll make a long weekend of it. We can take him on the boat and go for dinner like we used to in Luxor."

"Ok, will do. Oh, and he also said our additional patents for the In-Situ Calcination had finally issued. He just filed another one for an automated robotic mole that goes underground to form aqueducts in the aquifer so that huge volumes of water can be moved, subsurface."

"That is a mouthful," laughed Ariana. "We sure could have used that for the megadam project."

"You know, I've been thinking," said Michael. "How do you feel about investing the rest of the $100 million water prize in Steve's new venture? He helped us so much and now it's our turn to help him. I think $50 million is enough weekly random acts of kindness to last a lifetime!"

"I am in," said Ariana. "It will be fun!"

One of the benefits of Eden City with the large lake, along with the greening and agriculture in the Qattara Depression was that the climate had actually changed. Today was one of those rainy days in the desert. A deep soaking rain that returned some of the evaporated water from the lake and canals of the Qattara Development was now a regular occurrence in Eden City.

"So, what d'ya want to do today? asked Michael.

"I think I would just like to stand outside in the rain!" said Ariana.

The End

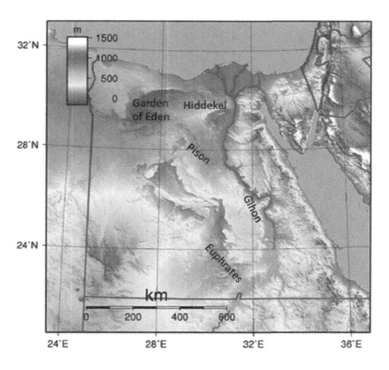

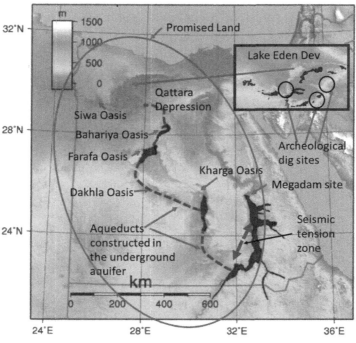

Epilogue

Genesis 2:4-14

⁴ These are the generations of the heavens and of the earth when they were created, in the day that the LORD God made the earth and the heavens,

⁵ And every plant of the field before it was in the earth, and every herb of the field before it grew: for the LORD God had not caused it to rain upon the earth, and there was not a man to till the ground.

⁶ But there went up a mist from the earth, and watered the whole face of the ground.

⁸ And the LORD God planted a garden eastward in Eden; and there he put the man whom he had formed.

¹⁰ And a river went out of Eden to water the garden; and from thence it was parted, and became into four heads.

¹¹ The name of the first is Pison: that is it which compasseth the whole land of Havilah, where there is gold;

¹² And the gold of that land is good: there is bdellium and the onyx stone.

¹³ And the name of the second river is Gihon: the same is it that compasseth the whole land of Ethiopia.

¹⁴ And the name of the third river is Hiddekel: that is it which goeth toward the east of Assyria. And the fourth river is Euphrates.

Resources

Secrets of the Great Pyramid by Peter Tomkins

Floating Stones: Great Pyramid Built with Water Power by Samuel Sampson and Michael Read

The Aquatic Ape Hypothesis by Elaine Morgan

Startup Nation by Dan Senor and Saul Singer

Personal Faith by Walter Jay with Elizabeth Simpson

The God Delusion by Richard Dawkins

Nothing Like It in the World by Stephen Ambrose

Guns, Germs and Steel by Jarod Diamond

Sasquatch by Jeff Meldrum

Roots by Alex Haley

Before the Dawn by Nicholas Wade

Sapiens: A Brief History of Humankind by Yuval Harari

Burn by Herman Pontzer

The Hadza: Hunter Gatherers of Tanzania by Frank Marlowe

https://bigthink.com/the-past/eurasia-migration-ancient-humans/

https://www.youtube.com/watch?v=RAEQXUVqoyg

https://microbiomejournal.biomedcentral.com/track/pdf/10.1186/s40168-021-01106-w.pdf

https://www.youtube.com/watch?v=QXQrvT23rPw

https://history.state.gov/historicaldocuments/frus1958-60v13/d251

https://www.youtube.com/watch?v=CYoa9hI3CXg

https://www.newsweek.com/irans-christian-boom-opinion-1603388

https://www.youtube.com/watch?v=E-SH9XVU4s8

https://youtu.be/ZZDxQPDBe30

https://www.youtube.com/watch?v=oH_OK6OGr80

https://www.youtube.com/watch?v=QoZUTJHZyr8

https://www.youtube.com/watch?v=j3J196bLP5E
https://www.science.org/content/article/lush-wetlands-arabia-lured-waves-early-humans-out-africa
https://www.npr.org/2021/08/27/1031659020/four-legged-whale-legs-discovered-43-million-years
https://youtu.be/D6Kz_OcOgvE
https://www.youtube.com/watch?v=2VWS_F_UeQI
https://www.historicmysteries.com/where-was-the-garden-of-eden/
https://www.youtube.com/watch?v=DRUt8hy6zyU
https://answersingenesis.org/genesis/garden-of-eden/where-was-the-garden-of-eden-located/
https://www.peopleofar.com/2013/12/02/armenia-the-forgotten-paradise/#:~:text=The%20Bible%20mentions%20a%20spring,garden%20of%20Eden%20in%20Armenia.
https://www.youtube.com/watch?v=r3Vl1l-aeYQ
https://www.youtube.com/watch?v=AQVIo4ZDF9Q
https://www.youtube.com/watch?v=5o8qpTVFk00 2.6 million views
https://youtu.be/tQmFVcD-Mbo 4.1 million views
https://www.miningweekly.com/article/over-40-minerals-and-metals-contained-in-seawater-their-extraction-likely-to-increase-in-the-future-2016-04-01
https://mail.google.com/mail/u/0/#inbox/FMfcgzGrbbrwLkbWbfqXSCwpQsnPzXNr?compose=new&projector=1
https://www.youtube.com/watch?v=kd3mawWMpBc 1.3 million views
https://www.youtube.com/watch?v=BoBapnk6TB8 1.2 million views

About the Authors

A Biblical scholar, PhD scientist and inventor who loves to tell stories, Jeff Shakespeare is passionate about finding ways to better society and encourage strong personal faith. His 13th great grandfather was William Shakespeare's grandfather!

Barbara Bouse is a watercolor artist from South Carolina.

Please visit us at www.ReturntoGardenofEden.com to learn more about our latest research and podcasts! Or send us an email at Contact@ReturntoGardenofEden.com

Printed in the United States
by Baker & Taylor Publisher Services